Some 7
but way   still plen~7
Spice!
of kissing though!

Bookshop
Soundtrack

THE
PLAYLIST
↓

Nicholas Lyon

4/22/26

Bookshop Soundtrack

Cover Art by *Tina Lynn Stout*

The Wild Rose Press, Inc.
PO Box 708
Adams Basin, NY 14410-0708
Visit us at www.thewildrosepress.com

Publishing History
First Edition, 2026
Trade Paperback Print ISBN 978-1-5092-6537-4
Digital ISBN 978-1-5092-6538-1

Published in the United States of America

Dedication

To Ashley who reminds me every day of
Love's second chances.

Chapter 1

The smell of a new book is both comforting and exciting at the same time. When someone pulls one from the shelf and cracks the pages for the first time, the smell punches their senses. It promises everything they love about books but keeps secret everything they'll love about *this* book.

Jane scoops another stack from the box that arrived that morning. She loves the smell of them, each one with their individual story but with the same smell. There's something poetic about it.

She shakes her head, not allowing herself to get lost in these silly thoughts. Of course, working in a bookshop, one tends to do exactly that: get lost in books. It's part of what attracted her to the job in the first place.

She places another book on the shelf, certain it will be coming off again soon. It's one that has been popular lately with the younger girls in town. She asked one what attracted them to those particular books, and she wished she hadn't. The girl had told Jane that she read them for the story, yes, but also she liked it when they got steamy. The girl's cheeks had reddened, but not as much as Jane's would have when she was the girl's age.

The bell over the door rings, and Jane looks up to see a customer come through. It's an old man, a regular, whom she doesn't know very well. She's not fantastic at remembering names, and so she normally makes up names for the customers in her head. This man she thinks of as Everything, but not because she has a crush on him. Certainly not. Instead, it's because he comes in frequently and only buys an Everything Bagel. It isn't the best nickname, but she has nothing more to go on. She doesn't want to think of him as Bagel. She eats them too often for that to not feel weird.

"Hello, hello," the man says, his wide mustache covering the fact that he has a mouth on that face.

"Good morning." Jane rushes to set aside the books. "Here for your bagel?"

"Yes, indeed." He places his wallet on the counter while he waits for her. He hums to himself, but she can't make out what song it is.

She gets the bagel bagged up—he never wants it toasted—and rings up the total. He always pays in cash but never has the correct amount of change. What does he do with all the coins from his daily bagel? Without asking, she passes them over to him.

"Have a good day," she says.

He nods and walks out, brown-bagged bagel in hand.

Most of the customers who come in throughout the day have nicknames she's given them, like Fanny, the high school girl who pops into the shop on her way to school to get a morning coffee. She's not sure why, but for spirit week, the girl dressed as a tennis player, and to Jane, she looked like a Fanny. There's Bowl Cut, the middle-aged man who fancies himself a writer and sits in the corner with his laptop, attempting to soak up the relics of the past. Those are his words, not Jane's. He doesn't even have a bowl cut, but he looks like the kind of guy who would have had one as a child.

She putters around the store, putting the new books where they go and moving the misplaced books to their proper places. The door dings again. Jane takes one look at the frail old lady coming in through the door, and a smile breaks out on her face. "Good morning, Ms. Johnson." Jane makes her way over to the customer, leaving her last couple of books behind on the floor. Bowl Cut looks up from his computer, then goes back to typing.

"Hello, deary," the old lady says. Her last name really is Johnson, though Jane doesn't know her first name or if she's married. She seems like the type of old-fashioned woman who would be married to the same man for sixty years. Jane sometimes wishes she could have been married to the same man for sixty years. Hell, she would have taken twenty-five, but then that would have been seven more years of misery.

"Anything you're looking for today?" Jane asks. "I just got that new Erin O'Rourke book you've been wanting."

Ms. Johnson's eyes light up. "Oh, is it out? I had hoped it would be here."

Jane smiles. "I'll grab it for you. Anything else?"

"I just wanted to see a friendly face." Ms. Johnson's mouth turns down, and her blue eyes show a hint of sadness. "I'm afraid I'm going to have to sell my house and move in with my daughter up in Topeka."

"Oh no." Jane pauses on her way to find the novel. "All the way in Topeka?"

Ms. Johnson nods. "I'm not sure who would want to live in Kansas, but I guess when it comes down to it, there's not a lot of difference between Oklahoma and Kansas. Still, Crescent has been my home for as long as

I care to remember."

Jane finds the book and brings it to the counter. She's genuinely sad at the prospect of losing one of her favorite customers, even if she doesn't know the elderly lady's first name. There is so much more to knowing someone aside from their name, like knowing their favorite author.

Ms. Johnson stays and chats for a bit longer before purchasing her book, the last purchase she'll make at Paper Pages, and then leaves the store behind. The bell above the door has a melancholy sound when it rings, and instead of jumping back into work, Jane stays behind the counter and considers the store for a moment.

It's not a big store, but the owner, Sylvia, has made it feel expansive and yet cozy. There are comfy chairs in the front, like the one currently occupied by Bowl Cut, and there are books everywhere. Occasionally, unexplainable things happen in the store, usually only when Sylvia is around. Still, she's certain that once a bookshelf was actually much bigger than it appeared, and she could store all of the books on it without any problems. When that happened, she realized that there wasn't any stock in the back room, ever, just always enough room on the shelves that seemed like they wouldn't be able to hold it all. Another time, she watched a customer walk out with her favorite pen. A local woodturner had made it. Jane was distraught, but ten minutes later, Sylvia found the pen on a shelf near the front. At the time, Jane had been so happy to have the pen back that she hadn't given it much thought. Since then, though, she's thought about that off and on and wonders if Sylvia had anything to do with it.

When Jane interviewed for the job, Sylvia asked her

why she wanted to work in a bookshop. Jane answered, "It's the closest I'll ever come to being in a storybook." Her eyes, Sylvia said later, glistened when she said it, like a child's might have while looking at a plate of cookies.

Often Jane imagines what her life would be like as a movie and what song might play during certain moments or in certain places. In the bookshop, when she's just cleaning or straightening, it would be something light and jazzy, maybe something from the 1950s.

Thinking of music has a positive effect on her mood because when the door opens next, the bell over the door sounds bright and cheerful. Her eyes slide to the man entering the shop. As she meets his cool gray eyes, she suddenly finds breathing less important. Maybe, she thinks, I actually am in my own storybook story.

Chapter 2

When Jane was just a girl living in Arizona, her father had worn a wide-brimmed hat. Not quite the brim equivalent of a cowboy hat's, but nearly the same feel. He called it a Durango and wore it nearly every day of his life. The only time he would not wear it was on the rare occasion that he would drag the family to church. But still, she had a difficult time picturing her father, who had died twenty years earlier, without that hat on.

The man enters the bookshop wearing a hat similar to the one her father wore, though this one would probably be classified as a fedora or something. For a moment, the memories of her father being the mightiest man in the entire world stir inside her. Then the man removes the hat from his head and sweeps back his fine silver hair. The gray eyes meet hers—whatever color hers may be; she can't currently remember—and a smile breaks from the mouth below.

"Is this it?" he asks, that smile infecting Jane's own face. "Have I reached Eden at last?"

She giggles—she actually giggles—and says, "It's as close to paradise as I've found."

He's focused on the small space, but when she speaks, his eyes land on her, and his smile is replaced with a look only described as awe. "Well, hello."

"Hello. Welcome to the bookshop."

Over in the corner of the store, she sees Bowl Cut

look up and shake his head. She ignores him, though her cheeks burn just the same. Am I really flirting with a complete stranger? She doesn't let the thought stop her from putting her left hand on top of the counter so that the stranger can clearly see that she doesn't have a wedding ring on her finger. She learned that when she reached a certain age, this was important information.

He takes his gaze away from her and moves around the room. "There's just something about a bookshop." He glances at her. She is, of course, waiting for him to say more. He steps over to one of the nonfiction sections that houses the military books. He picks a book up, seemingly at random, to flip through. She allows her eyes to linger on him while he shops, but finally, she gets back to work.

She's distracted as she tries to put the last couple of books on their shelf. She wants the stranger to speak to her again. Even more, she needs Bowl Cut to quit cutting glances her way.

"We have coffee," she says as she steps onto the aisle adjacent to the one he's currently occupying. She just blurts it out, unable to keep herself from speaking. By this point, he's moved to the insubstantial poetry section.

He smiles deeply, revealing the dimples in each of his cheeks. "Oh, do you? I could go for a cup."

"Sure, bring your book over to the counter, and I'll pour some."

He follows her but goes to the left when she turns to the right to step around the pastry case. There are four stools next to the restroom. Sylvia always jokes about the five stools at the back of the shop, counting the one in the bathroom. Jane almost says it in her haste to make the stranger smile again, but fortunately, she's able to stop herself. She may not be above flirting with a stranger, but she is above toilet humor.

She grabs the pot, pours a cup into a white mug, and places it in front of him. "Would you like cream or sugar?"

He holds her gaze and takes a sip, the white steam rising up around his nose. "I don't think it needs it."

She smiles at him; it seems she's done a lot of that since he came in. It's making her cheeks hurt. "What book did you find?"

He holds it up. It's not anything she's read or paid attention to before. "It's poetry." He clearly sees her confusion. "Robert Browning, to be specific."

"Ah," she responds, "'That's my last duchess there.' I always liked that poem."

"My, you do have a dark side if that's the first of Browning's poems you thought of."

She allows her smile to drop off and tilts her head slightly. "Maybe I do."

The ridiculous action earns her another full-throated chuckle from the stranger. He shakes his head. "I'm William." He holds out his hand to her, and she takes it. Is he naturally this warm, or is this from the coffee?

"I'm Jane." She knows there's a tremble in her hand, but she manages to at least keep it from her voice. It occurs to her that this is the first customer she's introduced herself to and probably the first that she knows by name.

"Sweet Jane."

"Excuse me?"

"Oh, I didn't mean to offend; it's just a Velvet Underground song."

"I wasn't offended. I just wondered why you didn't sing it." She then proceeds, in spite of her inner voice shouting out against it, to sing the chorus louder than is necessary in such a small store. William's smile couldn't possibly get any bigger, but then it does. He joins in singing with her. A sound of pure harmony rings through the small store, and the soundtrack in the bookshop goes from jazzy to the early stages of punk rock.

Movement from the front corner of the room catches her attention, but it's just Bowl Cut packing up his computer. Their voices joined together in song don't earn them any fans. She doesn't care, focusing only on William. *When was the last time I sang out loud in front of someone*? She's not quite sure, but the bell jingling, itself singing of Bowl Cut leaving, is a reminder of a different part of her life, something she's not sure she's ready to experience.

Chapter 3

In Jane's experience, the word "alone" usually has a negative connotation. People like to be around other people, especially those they like. Being alone can lead to loneliness and depression. But being alone *with* someone can have a whole new exciting and terrifying connotation. Jane feels this way as soon as Bowl Cut is gone. It's a weird feeling to have, considering she just met William, but it's there nonetheless.

She's been so focused on his eyes, his smile, and those dimples that keep appearing that she's forgotten to look at the third finger on his left hand. Finally, she does. And it's as naked as she'd like for him to be. The thought causes her to suck in her breath like she's just been hit with cold water.

Unfortunately, he notices. "What's happened?" he asks.

She puts a hand over her face to hide her shame. "Oh, nothing."

He chuckles like he knows. She turns her back on him to collect herself. "You can tell me," he says.

"It's just that I noticed you didn't have any, uh, rings on your fingers." All of this she says while facing toward the pastry case, and the whole thing makes her start laughing. It's the kind of laugh that tickles deep down and brings no sound with it, just rushes of air.

"Well, no, I don't have any rings. I used to wear one

or two, but I don't anymore."

He's talking behind her, and she tries desperately to get control of herself. There's no reason to laugh. In fact, she's embarrassed, has tears in her eyes, and suddenly feels the overwhelming need to pee. Unbidden is the image of her running to the toilet that he's sitting two feet from. He would probably be able to hear her pee before she even learns his last name. That makes her laugh even more.

"Jane, are you all right?" His voice is now full of concern, and then she feels his warm hand on her shoulder. She can't take it anymore. She's going to wet her pants if she doesn't go, and naturally, that makes her laugh even harder.

"I'm fine," she manages to get out between gasps of air. "Excuse me." She turns back to him so she can slide over the top of the counter to get to the bathroom. She has to move quickly and carefully; each step will likely release the Niagara Falls in the middle of the bookshop.

She can't stop giggling but just manages to get inside the small bathroom and shut the door. She gets her pants down with only a second to spare. The relief is palpable, and finally, she can get control of herself. She wipes at her eyes, smiling still, but also starting to feel the horror of what William might think of her. She would probably be better off if, when she came out of the bathroom, he was gone.

She washes her hands, dabs at her face with a paper towel, and comes out of the bathroom. He's gone. Her heart breaks, but then she sees him off to the left, poking around in the horror section. The relief of seeing him is better than making it to the toilet on time. Still, she hesitates to approach him. Unfortunately, as she takes a few quiet steps toward him, the bathroom door closes behind her. It has one of those automatic closers on it that is far too powerful for such a small door. It snaps back into its frame loud enough to be mistaken for a gunshot at close range, or so she imagines. It's been quite some time since she's heard a gunshot.

William's head whips around to face her. Again, Jane's embarrassment tries to take over, which causes her to snort. Her hand flies to her face to once more cover it from view. If ever she escapes this situation, she'll have a story to tell for sure. And if there is any love to come, well, she's not ready to think of that yet.

"Are you okay?" William asks. He's holding another book. The man seems to take almost as much pleasure holding the books as she does.

"I think so," Jane answers. "Though it was touch and go there for a moment." She wants to kick herself for saying that but decides that would just make her look stupider.

Luckily, William throws back his head and laughs. "Sweet Jane." He shakes his head and returns the book; she makes sure to remember which book.

She rubs her cheeks, trying to ease some of the pain in them from smiling so much since William entered. "I'm not so sure about the 'sweet' part."

"I think I am." He walks toward her; a look comes into his eyes that she hasn't seen in years. It is straight desire, and she feels every nerve in her body erupt at the expectation of him kissing her. He steps up to her, and she's ready. She can't remember the last time she kissed a man, but she's sure that Creed was still cool when it happened.

Her heart is racing, and suddenly, he's there in front

of her, his gray eyes locked on her own. There is no hint of humor in his smile, only desire. "Jane," he says, his voice barely more than a whisper.

"Yes."

"I'd like to kiss you. Would that be okay?"

"Oh yes."

Jane is certain that this will play out perfectly, with this being the beginning of a beautiful relationship that poets might dedicate poems to, which young lovers would then come to this bookshop to buy in the hopes that some of this magic might rub off on them. He puts his hands gingerly on her hips, tugging her into him. The warmth of his body wakes her, and her skin tingles in a way that it hasn't for so long.

Another part of her mind reminds her that this whole venture is crazy; this man just walked into her bookshop, and here she is, ready to allow him to kiss her. She shuts that part of her mind down and tries instead to think of the perfect love song to play right now. Maybe that Elvis song would be perfect for such a moment as this.

He leans over, and, right as their lips are about to touch, the bell over the door jingles, and Jane hears the voice of her boss reverberate through the small store.

Chapter 4

Panic always has a way of encouraging people to make strange decisions. A near car accident may find the driver calling someone from high school to apologize for some imagined indiscretion. Or being a witness to a crime might leave the person quitting their job and moving to Jamaica. When Jane hears her boss coming into the store, panic shoots through her, and she physically jumps back away from William lest she be caught nearly kissing a customer while on duty.

Sure, the action is not really akin to moving to Jamaica, but when Jane sees the look of absolute hurt on William's face, she thinks it may be even more extreme. Actually, a house in Jamaica might not be so bad if she could transport herself there instantly and not have to deal with the fallout of this situation.

"It's my boss," Jane whispers to William in the hopes that some of the pitiful hurt will slip from his face. It works, slightly. Thankfully Sylvia is on the phone; otherwise, she might have caught Jane either making out with a customer or performing lifesaving measures on a man standing in the bookshop.

Jane returns back behind the counter and moves things around to make it look like she's been working. William steps over to the Oklahoma authors section and browses the titles there.

Sylvia comes behind the counter, ends her call, and

smiles at Jane. "Slow morning?"

Jane shrugs. "Not too bad. I've managed to get a lot of the new stock put away."

Sylvia nods at the two books not shelved yet. "I can put those away. I need you to contact the book clubs about their choice of books for next month. Swords & Scones, the fantasy group that eats all our pastries, is looking for something in the comedy fantasy category. Though I do think they're tired of Pratchett." She grabs a pen and writes on her notepad on a sheet already nearly covered in ink. "Then there's the Christian-fiction group. What are they called?"

"Crosses & Cross Stitch," Jane supplies. Out of the corner of her eye, she watches William pretending to peruse the stacks. Every now and then he steals a glance her way, and she tries not to smile.

"… a book club wanting to incorporate cross-stitching, but whatever." Jane jumps back into what her boss is saying, trying to stay focused. Sylvia writes another note on her pad. "I think there's something new that could interest them, but you just reach out to April. She always seems to know what she wants. You know how lawyers are." She shakes her head, her eyes focused on the paper. Then she drops the pen. "I guess I shouldn't say things like that. My uncle was a lawyer, I think. But you never know who you might be offending. That man there could be a lawyer."

Jane's heart nearly stops as Sylvia points at William. He could be a lawyer. But a lawyer wouldn't be reading poetry, would they?

Sylvia's hand lands on Jane's arm. "I'm sorry, dear, I don't remember. Did I tell you about the book clubs?"

"Yes." She thinks about all the times she's had

Sylvia tell her these things. After working in the bookshop for almost nine years, she knows all of this, maybe as well as Sylvia. But still, it does her boss good to talk, and honestly, Jane likes her and enjoys it when she carries on like this. Usually.

Today there is the distraction in the way of a handsome stranger who—*oh, my God, did he try to kiss me?*—seems to also have a healthy interest in the written word. The chaotic energy of a folk punk band with too many instruments thrums through her. A need to slam dance comes over her, but she has to listen to her boss. That is until she notices William look at his watch and frown. Her heart sinks; he clearly has somewhere else to be, but she doesn't want him to go.

He turns and begins the methodical walk, not toward her, but toward the register. She makes a move like she's going to manage the register, but Sylvia blocks her and says, "I'll handle this, dear; won't you go into the office and make some of those phone calls?"

Jane splutters, trying to come up with a response that will keep her here. "I, uh, was helping this gentleman earlier."

"And I'm sure you did a wonderful job." Sylvia turns her back on Jane and picks up William's book. It's that book of poetry by Robert Browning.

Jane catches his eye and mouths, "I'm sorry."

William clears his throat. "You have quite the horror section here. That's pretty impressive."

Sylvia rings up the book. "Yes, it's a favorite of the English teacher here in town. I try to make sure I always have books for his classroom available. $15.66 is your total."

William pays, and reluctantly, Jane walks the short

way to the office door just behind the pastry cabinet. She lingers in the doorway, watching William, moving her eyes over him as he turns to leave the store. She can't quite watch his butt because of the bookshelves, but she can at least see him. At the door, the little bell goes off, and as he steps out, he turns back and smiles at her.

"I can feel you lingering there, Jane."

Jane jumps at Sylvia's voice, and her moment with William is over. She steps into the office, holding her chest as if her heart might burst out of it. She needs to breathe, to remember that she's at work in the bookshop, but what she mostly needs to remember are William's last words. He'd been browsing the horror section when she'd gone to the bathroom. It is a pretty good section in the store and a popular one. Maybe it's time for her to read some horror.

Chapter 5

Hope is a thin wire that holds the world up. Too much weight upon it will cause it to snap like the big fish that got away. Jane will always cherish the memory of fishing with her grandfather when she had clearly gotten a big fish that simply pulled harder than she could with her little arms. The fishing line could not withstand the struggle, or perhaps the fish found some underwater place to pull the string along so that it would break. Regardless, the string broke, and Jane's hopes and hook went with that fish.

Hope still clings to her, however, while she stands in the office of Paper Pages. Even though William is no longer here, he made that last suggestion about the horror section. She has a hope, an idea of a hope, that keeps her going through those tedious conversations with some of the book clubs in town. After an hour, she has the orders placed for the last book club and is able to get back to the store.

"Finished already?" Sylvia asks. "Sometimes those ladies do carry on, don't they?"

"Yes, they do." Jane hadn't noticed at the time, but it does seem that she rushed through the conversations a bit quicker than usual. It's that tiny hope at the back of her mind that keeps whispering to her.

Jane doesn't want to investigate in front of Sylvia; however, not because she doesn't trust Sylvia, but because this seems like something private that she wants to experience on her own before sharing with anyone else.

After ensuring that the entire place is tidy and greeting the customers who come in for their sweet treats or to find another book to add to their ever-growing pile, Sylvia calls it a day.

"Lock up behind you, dear. I've got to head to Guthrie."

Jane promises she will and waves her boss away as she leaves. Finally, with no one else around, Jane walks to the horror section. Even though nearly all of the books have black covers and a similar vibe, Jane knows the first one she will check. She lifts it from the shelf and smiles at the cover. A big, scary-looking house greets the reader. It's the kind of book all modern horror aficionados would be excited to read. The title has to do with selling the house. She's never read it, so she doesn't know who would be interested in buying a spooky house like that.

She opens it, and there, inside the front cover, is a small slip of paper. She grabs it, her heart slamming harder in her chest than it ever has from reading a horror novel, and slips the book back onto the shelf. The paper is a small flyer for live music that night in downtown Guthrie, not exactly what she hoped to find. She had this idea that she would find his name and phone number, she would call when she got home, and they would meet up for dinner.

Instead, there's music at an art gallery in Guthrie. Then the idea clicks home for her. He left the flyer because that's where he will be this evening. She knows the gallery, so she can't believe a full band would play there. But the advertisement says, "Special music by Bag of Bones." Surely if it were just an individual, they would put that person's name there, right?

She knows a little about these things, but she doesn't want to think about her experience in music. It still hurts too much.

Clearly, she has to go to this performance. She has to close up the shop, get home to change, and make her way to Guthrie. The idea of it terrifies and excites her. She jumps into action.

Chapter 6

Trying to look sensuous isn't easy, at least not with the wardrobe Jane currently has. She can't remember the last time that she needed to be alluring, but here she is now. She has to have something that will look casual and yet sexy. But she doesn't seem to have it.

After she closed up the shop, she rushed across town to her house, which isn't far, and she got started finding the right thing to wear. The small flyer lay on her bed next to some of the discarded outfits. She occasionally needs to glance at it to make sure this whole thing is real.

She grabs her phone and calls the only person who can help her in this situation, her best friend. "Martha, I need your help."

Of course, Jane does a video call with Martha. She needs her best friend to be able to see her outfit.

"What is it, Jane? Henry needs me to throw together a dessert for tonight. I don't know what to do, but you know how men are. He thinks I can just whip something up and hand it over to him." She sighs, somehow finding some air after that big story. Jane smiles.

They met at a Pilates class three years earlier when both of them were attempting to find a way to get fit in their later years. The class seemed ill-advised, so after discovering their mutual love for books, they left that and joined a book club that also included drinking wine.

They've been friends ever since.

"I'm trying to find the perfect outfit for tonight." Those words break through to Martha, who stops rambling and stares into the camera.

"Where are you going tonight? Why do you need the perfect outfit?" Martha, who has never known Jane to have a love interest, blurts out, "Who is he?"

Jane smiles; she can't help it. She can't hide anything from her best friend, at least nothing like this. "His name is, is, uh, William." Her cheeks burn.

"William? I don't know anyone named William."

"No, you probably don't. He's a stranger in town. He stopped by the bookshop, and, well, we had a moment." And for the second time that day, Jane giggles. She wants to cover her face for acting this way but manages to quell the embarrassment.

"Janey, look at you; you've got a crush." Martha laughs, and Jane does nothing to thwart her joy.

"Okay, Martha, so maybe I do. I've got to have your opinion, though. I need to know if this looks all right."

"Oh, you look lovely, darling." Her face disappears from the screen. "Henry, I've got to go."

"Go?" Jane hears Henry's voice from Martha's house. "Go where?"

"I'm going to go with Jane to meet this new guy she's got a crush on."

"Jane? All right. Get some ice cream or something while you're out."

Martha brings her attention back to Jane, who is standing with her mouth open. "I'll be over in just a few minutes, dear. Obviously, I won't need long to get myself cute. I always dress cute."

Jane sputters a response, but Martha has already ended the call. Jane reflects on how having a best friend can be both awesome and horribly stupid at the same time. She knows she's going to be glad to have Martha around, but still, she's frustrated that she didn't at least ask.

And that crack about always being cute—well, she is, but she doesn't have to remind Jane.

About ten minutes later, Martha is there, wearing a cardigan over the clothes that Jane could see in her cellphone screen. "You look cute," Jane says to her when she comes in. She says it with so much sarcasm she could be British.

Martha, ever stoic when Jane uses sarcasm, just pretends not to notice. "Yes, I know. Where are we going, anyway?"

"Well, I'm going to Guthrie to listen to some live music. Not sure what you're planning to do."

Martha pats Jane on the cheek like she's a little kid. "That's nice, dear. I haven't gone to listen to music in forever. Henry is more of a podcast guy, you know."

"I didn't plan on you going."

Martha smiles broadly. "Of course you did. That's why you called."

Jane wants to protest. Her first instinct is to tell Martha to go on home, but when she pauses to think about it, she actually does want Martha to come with her.

"Okay, you can come, but there have to be some rules."

"Well, go ahead."

"You cannot embarrass me in front of William."

Martha holds a hand to her mouth in mock surprise. "I would never."

"I know, but in case you feel the urge, don't. I would also like it if I could maybe have a moment with William, you know, alone. I don't know if there's anything to this or not, but I have to be able to talk to him to find out."

"Are you sure it's talking you're after?"

"Martha!"

The two of them laugh; any tension that Jane might have felt about Martha going with her leaves her body. They load up in Jane's car, and for the next twenty minutes, they enjoy conversations about their day, and then they pull up in front of the art gallery. It's in one of the downtown buildings that has been around since the turn of the 20th century. The front is all windows. Through them, Jane sees several patrons checking out the art, and there's William, wearing jeans, a button-down shirt, and his wide-brimmed hat. He looks, for all the world, like perfection.

Jane takes a breath and stares at him. There isn't a band, not even any drums, but there's William standing near the microphone. It can't be him, can it?

Chapter 7

Once when Jane was a small girl, her parents, who were together back then, took her to the Rio Grande Gorge Bridge outside of Taos, New Mexico. She loved it. On each side of the bridge, there was a sidewalk. Jane imagined herself as a tightrope walker when she walked on it. On one side, the cars clipped along right beside them. On the other was a deep canyon cut into the rocky surface. The wind carried on down the gorge like some ancient ghost haunting the jagged rocks.

She stared down at the abyss and water below the bridge. She held onto the railing, certain that her legs wouldn't hold her anymore. The feeling, while terrible, also excited her. She wanted to step over the railing of the bridge and fly out over those broken canyon walls; she could almost picture the way it would feel. For just a few seconds, the free fall would be beyond anything she'd experienced.

The same feeling of helplessness and of wonder flitters back into her as she looks at William. Just like when she was a child, she wants to jump, to feel the air rush up at her, and to see the jagged rocks come flying toward her. She wants to grab the man she's been thinking about all day and take him home. But another part of her wants to run, to get as far away from this place as possible.

While this fight carries on within her, she's

reminded why she's glad to have to her best friend around.

"Right, then," Martha says, "let's go."

Jane nods and opens the driver's side door, an out-of-body experience, like she is watching the motions on a movie screen. She steps from the car, walking forward on wobbly legs. The sidewalk stretches before her like the narrow aisle of a 747 on a much-needed bathroom break. And through the window, she watches as William walks over behind the microphone and picks up a guitar. The guitar works like magic on her. The idea that he's a musician thrills her and takes her back to what must be a different life, one where music was her everything.

"Is that him?" Martha takes hold of her arm as if she were taking her to a wedding.

"That's him."

"Hunka hunka." Martha produces the sound deep in her throat, so it comes out like the croaking of a bullfrog. Jane chuckles uneasily, relishing the brief diversion.

Right before he starts playing, William looks at her, she swears he does, and smiles. Then his hands begin to work the strings, and through the door, Jane can hear a quick chord progression, and she's sure she's heard the song before.

Finally, they reach the door. She's expecting to pay, but there's no one to take their money. She and Martha walk in. Paintings cover the walls, while sculptures and vases stand on shelves throughout the space. A few people mill about, looking at the art. Others are seated in front of the musician, chatting or bopping along with the tune. There are perhaps thirty people in there.

Jane gazes on William as he sings the opening bars of the song. His voice is a rich baritone, like a big vat of caramel being stirred around. She wants to taste it, the caramel, not his voice. That would be weird.

The song he's singing is definitely one she knows, and when he gets to the chorus, she beams at him. "Sweet Jane," he sings. The chorus is just a repetition of those two words, and somehow, they sound even better coming from William's mouth than Lou Reed ever dreamed about. Jane hesitates to sing along outside of the bookshop, but she doesn't hesitate to dance.

They might as well be the only two people in the room while he sings the song. They have their eyes locked on each other and have completely thrown away the key. Martha is there, somewhere, but for the moment, Jane has even forgotten her.

As he strums that last chord of the song, a few people clap, but none as enthusiastically as her. It's then that she realizes she's still standing just inside the door and Martha is tugging at her coat, trying to get her to sit down. For something nearing the hundredth time that day, her cheeks burn. She didn't act like this before she met William. He keeps his eyes locked on her and a smile perched on his face, like he can't believe she's actually there.

She doesn't want to seem too eager, so she sits on the second row. Clearly, the front row would make her seem desperate.

Martha sits beside her but is only there for an instant before she bounces back up and disappears deeper into the room. Jane hardly notices. She's back in the trance that is William, taking in his features and allowing her nerves the chance to finally cool down. He begins playing another song, one she doesn't recognize, and she listens as she has never listened to music before.

Martha returns holding two glasses of red wine. She passes one to Jane with a wide smile. "I saw they were pouring back there and thought we might as well." She takes a large gulp of the wine. "Henry would probably be mad if he knew, but he's not here, is he?" She's whispering to Jane, but she doesn't realize how loud her whisper actually is. Jane smiles at her and swallows some of her wine. She will never not be grateful for the calming effects of alcohol, though on occasion, she has been ungrateful for the lowered inhibitions that have resulted in questionable decisions.

"Not tonight, though," she says into her wine.

"That's right!" Martha pats her on the shoulder, and Jane is taken aback. She must have missed something that Martha had been saying, quite a simple thing considering that Martha is always talking.

The music and the musician claim all of her attention. After an hour of songs and some banter with the audience, William finally takes a break, setting his guitar aside and walking slowly toward her, a shy smile on his face. A young lady interrupts his progress, clearly hoping to fangirl over some song he sang. She's smiling at him and tugging at her hair.

"Oh, get out of here, you wench. Want me to go hit her for you?" By now, Martha is working on her third glass of wine, and her words are beginning to slur. Jane hasn't even finished her first glass yet, but now she takes another sip.

Finally, William breaks away from the conversation and walks toward her again.

"You found it." His hat is still in place. Down under his chin, she can see a chain that has a Star of David pendant on it.

"You left a good hint, Bag of Bones."

He tosses back his head and gives a full-throated laugh. "I'm not sure where I came up with that one. Several years ago, a club owner contacted me about playing, and that's the name I told him to put on the marquee."

"A bag of bones is what I feel like most of the time." She smiles at him; she hasn't stopped smiling all day.

"Hear, hear." He lifts his glass to his lips.

"What are you drinking?"

"Martini." He holds out the glass to her, and she can see the olive. "A gin martini."

"I do love gin. Alas, I'm having wine."

Miraculously, Martha has been quiet but chooses that moment to reassert herself into the conversation. "It's good wine, though. I'm on my third. Also, I'm her best friend, Martha."

Fortunately, William finds this hilarious and laughs along with her. "Pleased to meet you, Martha." He holds out a hand, and Martha almost misses it. This sets her to laughing.

They spend the next little while chatting and getting to know each other better. William enjoys Martha, while Martha enjoys the wine. She goes for another glass, giving Jane a moment alone with this mysterious man. "I didn't know you were a musician."

"Considering that we met just a few hours ago, I'm certain there are a great many things you don't know about me."

She places a hand on his, giving in to the sudden need to touch him. "I'd like to find out."

His eyes take on a thoughtful, far-off look, like he's just caught sight of the mountain he wants to climb.

Before he can say anything, however, Martha rejoins them.

"That man at the bar is the nicest."

"I'm sure he is. Do you really think you need another glass?" Jane wants to remind her how Henry feels about her drinking but decides to keep it to herself.

"Do you think you should be holding hands already?"

Jane jerks her hand back like she's just realized it wasn't a hand but a shark. Yet again, heat rushes into her face. William laughs.

Martha slurs, "I didn't mean it."

William drains his glass and chews the olive. "It's all right. I need to get back up there anyway. Is there a song I could play for you?"

Jane thinks about it, wanting to hear the perfect song. She toys with the idea of asking him to play one of her songs, but that idea shrivels up quickly. "I don't care what you play; just get up there and play it!"

"I can sure do that for you."

He jumps right into a song that she knows. She sings along, doing her best to stop from giggling like a swooning maid. The day turned out so differently than she could have predicted.

Chapter 8

Music has a way of carrying the listener to a different place and time. At times, the poetry that someone else has written and set to music transports the listener away from their woes and hardships. Finding solace in music is one of the greatest gifts given by the universe or the deity.

Jane feels that connection tonight, sitting on the edge of her chair and bopping along to the tunes that William sings. Somehow, each song that he performs makes him sexier to her. The way that he handles the guitar, his left hand moving deftly up and down the neck while his right plucks and makes the sounds, makes her want to see what it would feel like to have his hands move over her skin the same way.

She learns through his banter with the crowd that the set list is a mix of original songs and covers. She loves them all and sings along when she can. She is able to keep Martha from getting any more wine. After four glasses, though, Martha is quite the dancer.

At the end of the night, Jane waits for another moment with William while Martha makes friends with one of the locals, a young man who looks like he'd rather be anywhere than speaking to Martha. Instead of rescuing the kid, however, Jane makes her way to William.

"You owe me something," she says to him. He's

bent over his guitar case, lovingly putting away the Taylor.

"Do I?" He stands, brushing off his hands on his pants.

She nods. "We were interrupted earlier. At the shop."

He takes a step closer. "I think I know what you mean." His eyes dart around. "Here?"

She steps up to him, their bodies coming into the smallest amount of contact. "Why not?"

His hands are on her hips, and he pulls her closer to him. "You're sure?"

She smells the gin on his breath and has never liked the smell more. "I'm sure." Her voice is thick, so he closes the gap between them, and their lips meet.

Some perfect love song like "Unchained Melody" plays through her head, and everything seems to slow down. If her eyes were open, she knows she would see the world in black and white, and William would resemble a young Humphrey Bogart.

Too quickly, the kiss ends, and Martha is there, speaking despite no one listening to her. "I just had the nicest conversation. That boy over there, he's just the nicest. You should really hear what he has to say about this guy you like. All good things, I assure you. I just enjoyed talking to him and thought you would like to know about it."

Somehow, Martha doesn't even notice that they've just shared this important first kiss or that she interrupted it. Jane ignores her. "I probably need to get her home. Can I call you later?"

Disappointment etches his handsome face, but judging by the heat coming from his body, she's sure it isn't the kissing that disappointed him. "Please call me."

She gives him a quick peck on the lips, trying not to linger too long, then pulls away from him. "Come on, Martha, Henry is waiting."

"Oh, drat. He's going to be put out with me. I think I had a glass of wine, Jane."

"You did, dear." She pulls Martha out the door. She steals one last look into the shop and finds William looking back at her. He gives a slight wave, which she returns.

Jane manages to get Martha into the car. The one glass of wine didn't affect her nearly as much as the kiss; that's still playing on repeat in her head. The drive back to Crescent is mostly a movie of William with the soundtrack of Martha snoring.

Chapter 9

Teenagers always go through a stage of rebellion where they want to do things to fit in or have new experiences, and it's usually things their parents don't want them to do. They'll try alcohol or cigarettes or even experiment with sex. Or there's the rite of passage that every teen tries at some point: sneaking out.

Once, when Jane was in high school but before she could drive, she decided she would sneak out of her dad's house. Naturally, it was to see a boy, and it was in the hopes that the boy in question would like her the way that she liked him. She got as far as the edge of the driveway, where she would meet her friend Tina in her car, when the porch light came on behind her. It was the only time she ever tried sneaking out. And the boy in question ended up dating Tina.

Jane replays the memory of that night after she drops Martha off at home. Martha has sobered up a little during the twenty-minute drive, but not enough to fool Henry. Jane isn't worried about her, though; Henry has a good sense of humor most of the time.

"Don't you go sneaking off to see that boy now, Jane. You need your rest." Martha offers this expert advice as she's climbing from the car. Jane smiles at the idea of a woman her age sneaking off. Sometimes, living in a small town means one might have to sneak around a little bit more.

Jane waves goodbye to her and drives home. Her thoughts are consumed with William, with sneaking around, and with that bitch Tina stealing her man in high school. Honestly, she held a grudge against her for a long time, even though she helped Jane dodge a massive bullet, one that she got to take instead. That guy turned out to be a nightmare, and why wouldn't he be? Any high school boy who could leave his house any hour of the day and expected nice girls to do the same was simply asking for trouble. Tina got to have his baby, which he pretended to want until it was born.

Jane finds herself standing in her living room, her mind so preoccupied that she doesn't even register that she'd made it home, gotten out of her car, and gone through the front door. Her whole mind has been consumed with Tina. Thinking of her now, she's certain she has to do something to keep some other woman like Tina from taking William away from her. Her memory flashes on that young gal who giggled at him during the show.

She stands in her living room and then walks into her kitchen. She turns on the light, lets her eyes move over the counters, and then turns the light off and heads back to the living room. She sits on the couch. She stands. She sits again. She grabs a magazine she has sitting on her coffee table. She flips through it, letting the pages fall like water between her fingers, seeing nothing printed there. She tosses the magazine and sighs. Her lips couldn't be tingling more if she had kissed an outlet. She loves the way his lips felt, and she wants more. She grabs her phone, scrolls to his number, and stares down at it.

"He wants you to call," she whispers. Years of living alone mean that sometimes, she has to speak out loud so that someone will hear her. The spoken words reassure her that he did, indeed, want her to call. That's why she has his phone number.

She calls. Her heart jumps into overdrive when she hears the tinny ringing sound. Then he answers.

"Jane. I wondered how long you might take."

"I feel like a schoolgirl; I'm so nervous. It's been so long since I've dated anyone or called someone I'm interested in dating." She runs a hand over her face, glad he can't see her embarrassment. Her cheeks have warmed so many times today, she's surprised they haven't burned.

He chuckles, but it doesn't sound humorous. "I'm nervous, too. I'm not sure what kind of spell you put me under in that bookshop, but I've been thinking of you since."

She bites her bottom lip. "I'm not ready to go to bed yet."

"Me neither."

"Give me ten minutes to freshen up, and then I'll drive to Guthrie."

"Really? You'll come back here? I could come to you."

She takes one glance at her messy house. "No, I want to show you around the streets of Guthrie."

"Ah, if you insist."

"I do."

"Then I'll see you in thirty minutes."

"At the football field."

"Weird choice, but okay."

They end the call, and every ounce of nerves that Jane kept at bay during the call comes rushing back in with the end of it. Her skin is electrified. She can't believe she's sneaking out of her house to meet a boy. Okay, not sneaking since it is her house, and he hasn't been a boy for a good forty years, but the sentiment is the same. She freshens her makeup, runs a brush through her hair, and throws on a little perfume.

"This is it," she says to her quiet house, "I'm off to give this guy another kiss. Maybe more." She winks at herself in the mirror before she darts out of her house.

Chapter 10

The highways in Oklahoma are straight and flat. The occasional rise in the earth usually happens right when you need to pass someone, but other than that, it's an all-around simple drive. The highway between Crescent and Guthrie, however, is comprised of near ninety-degree turns every couple of miles. It's one of those roads that really tests the skills of the average Oklahoma driver.

The first time Jane drove it, she found the curves to be overwhelming, but with the years of driving them, she doesn't even notice them anymore. Tonight, she's thinking only of William.

Her heart races faster than the posted speed limit as she rolls into town. When William said he would meet her wherever she wanted to go, she suggested the Rock.

Downtown Guthrie features one of the more interesting football fields in the state, one that is sunken below street level into a naturally formed canyon with rock walls built up around it. Its presence creates one more quirky thing about downtown Guthrie. For some reason, while the sun is down, Jane wants to stand on the grass that won't see football players until the next day.

She parks her car around the side where a chain-link fence makes it easier to get onto the field. Rather than try to climb the rock walls, here she can just walk right in. She sees William standing in the middle of the field, the silhouette of his guitar hanging from his shoulders. She stops herself from running to him, but it's a near thing. She can just hear the chords he's strumming over her breathing. As she nears him, the music is louder, and she can make out the chords to an old song. He starts singing, and she laughs as she realizes what song it is.

"Is that 'Janey's Got a Gun'?" she asks as she gets close to him.

He stops singing and laughs too. "I couldn't resist. I thought 'Sweet Jane' had already been played out, and I couldn't think of any other songs about someone named Jane."

She stands there, smiling at him for a long moment, just taking him in. The moonlight reflects off of everything, and the gray in his eyes feels more pronounced. "I think you were meant to be looked at in moonlight."

"How poetic." He takes off his guitar and lays it lovingly in the grass beside them. He straightens and grabs her up. "Have any trouble getting out of your house?"

The huskiness in his voice and the heat coming off his body make her insides tingle. "None at all."

When their lips meet, the night sky becomes jealous that no fireworks will ever be quite as bright on its surface. Jane, so long out of practice, falls right back into it with the ease of breathing. Nothing seems awkward or strange. Their teeth don't get in the way, and their lips open at just the right moments. Sometimes, Jane would dream of the perfect kiss, and after all her long life, she's finally experiencing it in the middle of a high school football field.

When she steps away from William, she's gulping for air like she's been underwater. They stare at each other, both complemented by the moonlight.

"Well, that was unexpected." He leans down to pick up his guitar.

Jane panics, thinking it wasn't as wonderful for him. "What's wrong?"

"Wrong?" He laughs. "That I had to wait fifty-nine years to experience the best kiss of my life."

She laughs along with him. "You're fifty-nine?" She wipes the tears from her eyes. "I thought you were way younger."

He grows serious. "I hope it's okay that I'm older than you."

"Are you kidding? If you keep kissing me like that, I don't give a damn how old you are."

They both laugh again, but the sound of it is interrupted by a shout from the street. "What are you doing? You can't be out there!"

Jane jumps and turns toward the voice. She can see the cop car and the flashlight bouncing around toward them. "Cops," she whispers in a panic.

William says nothing but takes her hand and pulls her along after him. They run away from the cop, something Jane hasn't done in her life. They run like they're truly trying to escape danger. Jane laughs while trying to keep oxygen flowing into her body. She can't believe she snuck out to meet a guy, and now she's running from the cops with him. The warmth of William's hand surrounded by the cool fall air is enough to make Jane fall in love with the night.

Chapter 11

Like teenagers, she thinks again. How do they go from meeting in the bookshop to being chased by the cops in less than twenty-four hours? Jane is certain that if her father were still alive, he would be shaking his head right now. He'd never gotten so much as a speeding ticket, but here she is, William and his Taylor guitar on one side and her on the other, running as fast as they can out of the canyon of a football field. The flashlight follows them, but once they get outside the field, it stops. She has a stitch in her side and can't fully fill her lungs. He's laughing and breathing easily as if he does this sort of exercise all the time.

"Where do we go?" she asks once they clear the football field.

"We make the most of the night." He pulls his guitar over his shoulder and runs it diagonally down his back like some gunslinging musician from the past. She knows that Guthrie has never been a stranger to roving musicians like William.

She follows him, just a step behind, with her small hand in his. The simple excitement of holding hands with William rises up in her. She wants to laugh, and a part of her wants to cry. It has been so long since something good has come to her.

The streets of Guthrie are quiet. Aside from the paved roads and sidewalks, downtown Guthrie appears much like it did at statehood in 1907. Jane occasionally finds old postcards and pictures from the turn of the twentieth century and is always amazed how much it hasn't changed.

"Did you know that there's an old bar down here where Tom Mix was a bartender for about a year?" William asks. His voice breaks the silence, and Jane's thoughts flit away.

"That's really interesting."

"You don't know who Tom Mix is, do you?"

She laughs. "Guilty."

"He was an actor in early cowboy movies. Before he got his start in movies, he called Guthrie home for a short while. He was even a pallbearer at Wyatt Earp's funeral."

"That's not true, is it?"

William shrugs and keeps walking.

"Wait." She pulls her hand from his, and that finally stops him. "How do you know that?"

"It's referenced in the movie *Tombstone*. It's maybe one of the greatest movies of all time."

She smiles, adoring him. "And you've never fact-checked that movie."

He turns around and starts walking away from her. "I'll pretend you didn't say that."

She jogs to catch up, giggling. "I haven't smiled this much in so long."

He turns back to her. "And why not? You have a beautiful smile. Why would you want to rob the world of such a treat?"

Jane accepts the compliment and allows things to turn serious for a moment. "Come on, William, at our age, we're both single. Something unpleasant must've happened in the past to cause this, right?"

"Sure." He shrugs. "Without music and the occasional bottle of gin, I wouldn't have made it as far as I have."

"That's it exactly. And suddenly, I find myself being chased by the cops after experiencing maybe the best kiss of my life. Life hasn't been this exciting or so damn lovely in a long time. It's like we're living in one of those love songs I used to sing." She clears her throat. "I mean, like you sang tonight." She closes her eyes, but he doesn't comment on her slipup.

The quiet streets of Guthrie turn out to be a perfect backdrop for their night. They walk, hand in hand. At one point, William even pulls his guitar in front of him and strums a few chords, lightly singing to her. When he hits the chorus of "American Pie," she joins in, singing the harmonies. To his credit, he doesn't stop singing but raises his eyebrows. Jane sings and pretends he didn't notice. They dance around each other's awkward moments with the grace that only comes with experience.

They sing together for the remainder of the song, their voices melding perfectly together. When the song ends, Jane pulls a little ahead of William, not wanting to talk about it but knowing it's going to happen. She just couldn't resist singing that song. It has always been one of her favorites and one that she still sings when she's alone.

"You sing beautifully," he says behind her. She doesn't turn back to him but keeps walking. "Clearly this isn't something you want to talk about." He sighs, then strums the guitar. "I wouldn't mind singing another one with you. What other songs do you like?"

She slows, allowing him to come up next to her. "So many. I love music, but I have to tell you, if I'd known you were a musician, I would never have come to Guthrie. It took my best friend and a whole lot of bravery for me to even get out of the car once I saw you at the microphone."

She can tell that her response shocks him. In her experience, the guitar usually attracts, not repels, women. But here she is, contradicting the rules. "I know I'm a strange one," she says. "There are just some things I don't want to talk about."

He gazes ahead as they pass the post office again. She wonders what he's thinking, but she's starting to think that she's put her foot right in it. Like she just saw the largest, freshest pile of dog crap and has purposefully walked in it. She's not sure why she does this. The few dates she's gone on since coming to Oklahoma have all ended with her destroying her chances at a second date. Maybe there's a sabotage button in her that she just really enjoys pressing.

"You have an interesting way of answering questions, Jane." His gaze breaks from the sidewalk ahead to make brief and wonderful eye contact with her. "All I asked was what kind of songs you like."

She's amazed, really quite shocked, that he's not running away. "You heard me, right?"

He stops walking and turns to face her. "I heard you. And here's the thing: we all have a past. You said yourself that at our age, for us to be single, something had to have gone wrong in life. I get that something happened in your past, and maybe music has something to do with it. That's all fine. But we're here now. Tonight. And you have a beautiful voice, and I would be sad if we didn't sing together at least one more time."

She waits a beat before saying anything, just staring up into his gray eyes. Then she starts walking. "How about 'Landslide' by Fleetwood Mac?"

"Excellent choice." He pulls out a capo and pops it on the third fret.

She swallows, and her heart, which she'd only recently gotten control of, starts speeding in her chest again. "And I'll take the lead."

He doesn't say anything but starts playing the opening chords. She closes her eyes. It's been so long, and yet, she sings the opening words to the song.

Chapter 12

When Jane gets home from being with William, she sits at her kitchen table and writes in a notebook. "You know that feeling you get when you're on a roller coaster and it's making its ascent, and then you get to the very top? There's nothing there below you, just the wide-open space, and all you can do is hope there's a track there to carry you on. Then it tips over, and you're experiencing speeds faster than you've ever felt. That's what tonight was like."

She's thinking about those gray eyes and how she could have gone with him, gone to bed with him. But she reminds herself that it had been a while since she'd kissed someone and even longer since she'd stayed the night with someone. She decides to ease into this like a warm bath. Already she feels more exposed to him since she sang with him.

That is an excellent thought, so she writes it down.

She never wanted to be a writer, like a novelist or anything like that. But creative types always like keeping journals and writing down their random thoughts. It's the only thing that makes room for other thoughts sometimes. Plus, she enjoys journaling because it ties her to the world of writing that she loves. She does work in a bookshop, after all.

She thinks about William again and how she was so close to going home with him. Actually bringing him to her home would be the more accurate description. He travels a lot, he told her, and that means he stays with people he knows more often than not. It's not lucrative to be a traveling musician in these modern times, so he can rarely afford a hotel. He confessed that he's slept in his car on more than one occasion and even keeps a hammock in there for nights when he can set up in a park.

Thinking of him now takes her down that road of wanting to be with him but also reminds her that she's got to be responsible. No matter how much he made her feel like a teenager again, she can't always go around acting like a teenager.

She writes that down, wishing there was a better way to show emphasis when handwriting something other than underlining it. She often considers buying a computer so that she can properly use italics, but then she would have to trade the warmth of pen and paper for cold technology. And the journal outweighs the italics.

She still sits at her table nearly every day and writes words in her journal. It's not always a play-by-play of her day, but sometimes just poetic ruminations on her life at the moment. The thing that she hasn't done in years is write songs.

Once upon a time, she always had a guitar in hand and a pen and paper nearby. She had even made something of a career of it. Music, however, has taken a different role in her life. It's no longer the focal point of her creative endeavors; instead, she just likes to listen to it. She has about fifty vinyl records that take up residence in her living room, where she can enjoy them from time to time.

Tonight, though, William put music back in the forefront of her mind. She's been humming songs he sang at the show all evening, and she even sang, not just with him, but by herself. She didn't think she would ever sing again, not after her husband treated her the way he did. She doesn't want to think about him, though, not after William.

William even showed her one of his songs he'd been working on. He sang a lot of his original songs at the art gallery, but while they walked around downtown, singing and enjoying this new adventure with each other, she asked him, "Have you worked on anything new lately?"

He gazed at the sidewalk, that dimple popping into his cheek like a sinkhole. "I have an idea. See what you think of this."

She watched his fingers move through chords she knew well, a D major to an E major to an A major. She liked the rhythm, and then he started to sing. "I wanna drive down I-35 and find a place to feel alive." He paused, letting the last chord ring out. "That's all I have. Just a single line for the chorus." He shrugged.

"Sometimes," she said back to him, "the chorus is all you need."

The song stayed in her mind the rest of the night. She jots the words down in her notebook, writing the chords over the top of them as she remembers them. It may not be exact, but it is still pretty close.

She accepts the idea of playing guitar and singing again. She also wants to sing with William once more. She had so much fun, she might even consider singing with him in front of other people.

She writes for a while longer, then decides to go to bed. She's going to be worth nothing at the shop as it is, but then she remembers with a laugh how drunk Martha was and thinks her friend will have an even harder time tomorrow than she will.

Chapter 13

Jane leaves her journal on the kitchen table before heading to bed. She drops her phone on the nightstand and plugs it in to charge. She turns out the light and stretches out on the bed to relax. Her eyes close, and as sleep takes her, a song takes up residence in her head, one about life and the things she's struggled with. A melody forms along with a few words. She partially writes the song without moving, wanting to believe she's going to sleep. But the song is persistent, like it is some living creature that wants to get out of her. Finally, she gives up on sleep and sits up.

It's been years since she's even had the desire to play her guitar. She still has one and has moved with it, telling herself over and over that it's time to get rid of it, but she's kept it. She hasn't taken it out of its case since her husband more or less kicked her out, but tonight is the night. The song wants to be written, or at least considered.

She pulls the battered hardshell case out of her closet, wipes some of the dust away, and opens it. The golden body of the acoustic guitar smiles back at her, and she lovingly touches the strings. "Hello, old friend." She lifts it from the case.

Naturally, it is out of tune, and the strings smell old, but it doesn't stop her from shaping an E major chord and strumming it. She cringes at the sound; she may be out of practice, but she still knows the sound of an out-of-tune guitar. Her fingers move to the tuning keys and bring the strings back into tune like the last time she did it was yesterday. Some skills, like kissing, she's just never lost the ability.

She abandons the E major for a G major chord and gives it a strum. It was always one of her favorite chords to play. The feel of her fingers pushing into the strings reminds her of a different time. She almost puts the guitar back, abandoning the idea as foolish, but she takes a breath and rolls on.

G to D to C, slow and easy. She smiles as her fingers move from place to place without her giving it much thought. She doesn't have a guitar pick, just her fingers. The tips of her fingers on her left hand scream at her for pushing down on the metal strings. She ignores the pain and embraces the feeling. Without calluses, she can feel each string.

Tentatively, she hums along to the chords, closing her eyes to picture it. The key of G doesn't quite feel right either, so she switches to the key of C and finds her tune there. She smiles as her voice matches with the notes, and she gets lost with the music, allowing it to carry her.

"Right now, I'm haunted by the mistake of my past," she sings, the same words that brought her out of bed on this quest to begin with. "I'm hiding all my deeds behind this mask."

That line feels too true. Every day, she feels like an imposter. Even her best friend, Martha, doesn't know her story or the roads that brought her to central Oklahoma. The pain courses through her with that realization. Thinking of William and how she knows she could be vulnerable with him, a scary thought, she sings the next line. "I wish that you could climb inside these things I'm trying to hide. Why is pain the only thing that lasts?"

As soon as the words cross her tongue, she stops. The last chord rings through the room until she finally pulls her fingers off. Pain. She stares into the darkest corner of the room and thinks of pain and how, years later, it haunts her at the strangest times. She doesn't think of love as often as she thinks of the loss of love. She doesn't remember the sunny days as well as she remembers the storms. Singing that line, she realizes it. And she remembers what she loved and has always loved about songwriting: it can break down walls she didn't know she had and help her find her innermost thoughts and feelings.

She strums the C again. "Right now, I'm clawing at the demons in my head, reliving every single word he said."

She won't say what he actually said; the "he" in question is clearly her ex. It wasn't poetic and maybe hurts too much, but she can find a way to spin it. She thinks for a moment and sings, "I think it's time we take a break; this love is getting hard to fake. Everything about you I misread."

Reluctantly, she lays the guitar down and runs into the kitchen to grab her journal. She's tapped into something and has to write it down. Back beside her guitar, she opens the journal and writes down all the words. She likes the AABBA rhyme scheme. It makes her smile that it's almost a Swedish band name. She taps the pen on the page for a second, liking the way the words look. She'll need a chorus, but she's not sure just yet what that will be.

She grabs her guitar to play through the verses again. She sings with her guitar for the first time in so long it nearly brings tears to her eyes. She's been missing so much without realizing it. Other parts of her life creep up into her mind, her life before Oklahoma, and she knows she's missed more than playing guitar. She doesn't want to think too much about that life before, but music connects her to that past. She can't help but remember who she left behind.

Chapter 14

Saturdays are made for shopping. Once Jane would have sworn by that mantra. There was a time in her youth when going to the mall was greater than anything. But those were different days when malls actually had stores, and she had to leave the house to shop. Now, so many people shop from home.

But small towns love their local businesses, and Paper Pages is a favorite statewide. People come from all over to visit their shop and maybe even buy something. Jane is always impressed with the way that Sylvia manages to create a place that is appealing to so many people.

Jane is there before Sylvia on Saturday morning, having not been able to muster much in the way of sleep. She has a key, so she's able to let herself in and get things going for the day. She still remembers the day that Sylvia entrusted her with the key to the store. She had worked hard for it and had been proud when Sylvia had passed it to her.

She gets the lights turned on, the register ready, and most importantly, she's able to make herself a coffee. The smell of books mingling with the smell of freshly brewed coffee is as comforting as sitting on her dad's lap when she was a kid. Jane smiles at that thought and resolves to write it down in her journal that night.

The song she'd worked on the night before

continues to play through her mind. She's always loved the art of songwriting and how, at times, when she would write a song, it would play like a record through her mind, round and round. And here she is again, for the first time in years, hearing a song she worked on playing on repeat in her head. That part of her that resolved to never play music again is clearly dying away. She wiggles her fingers as she thinks of playing guitar again.

But first, coffee.

She sips at her coffee and flips through the booklet of new releases for the month of November. She's only got a week until those start showing up in the shop, and she wants to know what's coming. There are always those casual browsers who want to buy a book but need the direction of the bookseller to help them decide.

Books are the one thing that people will never have enough of. Even if they never complete their to-be-read pile, they can always talk themselves into buying another. And for Jane, that's not just an idea but something that she puts into practice. Far too many books are stacked beside her bed, with another healthy pile living happily on her bookshelf.

The door jingles open, and Jane lifts her head to see Sylvia come in the door, followed by her husband, Brad. Jane waves at them both with a smile. Brad is a big guy who comes around the store frequently to do random chores for Sylvia. She's pretty sure he's the one who built all of the bookshelves in the store. Jane wonders what kind of task Sylvia has for him this time. Normally, Brad makes a living as an elevator repairman. It's an intriguing trade considering the complete lack of elevators in the small town. What makes the job even more bizarre is that more than ten people in Crescent make their living working on elevators.

"Hey, Brad, what kind of work does Sylvia have you doing today?" She gives a big smile so that Brad will know that she's only teasing him.

He smiles back. "Oh, you know." He has a deep, booming voice, especially in the small shop. If she'd been feeling drained, that was the kind of voice that would wake her right up out of her stupor. "We might change up the seating over here on this side." He indicates the north side of the store. "Not sure why people don't want to sit over here."

Sylvia nods along, but she's clearly in a different place, probably contemplating what she's going to say on her social media page about the bookshop. She goes live most Saturdays to try to drum up more action in the store, but Jane is certain most people would still stop by even without the videos.

"That's not a terrible idea," Jane says. She notices some out-of-place books and works on arranging the shelf correctly. Brad shrugs his shoulders and pulls out his tape measure to check out how much space they have for seating.

The day passes pretty quickly with the energy of a Saturday crowd popping in and out, trying to find the perfect book, gift, or pastry. She needs another jazz tune, one that captures the lively energy like "Boogie Stop Shuffle" by Charles Mingus. She finds the record in Sylvia's meager collection and puts it on the small turntable at the front of the store. The jazz music brings a different life to the shop.

But Jane, even while talking to customers, can hear *her* song playing in her mind, and she wants desperately to finish it. The itch for creativity is challenging to ignore. The unfortunate side effect of the artists who make a living doing anything other than their art is that they have to stop pursuing their art for a while.

Brad measures around the Book Boyfriend on the bench in the window. Sylvia had the idea to build a person out of books and give him a face. She labeled it "Book Boyfriend," and loads of people take their picture with him. Now, though, it's causing Brad some grief to get around him.

Jane makes her way through the shelves, asking people here and there if they need help. She's able to locate a fantasy novel for a young man who "needed something that wasn't Tolkien." She also helped an expectant mother find some excellent children's books for her nursery. She makes her rounds, earning her paycheck, not knowing that her world is about to get rocked.

The bell over the door chimes, and a young man, maybe in his mid-twenties, comes in. She doesn't recognize him immediately since she isn't expecting to see him, but then it clicks, and she does know him. She could never forget her son.

Chapter 15

Once upon a time, Jane got married. Happily married, in fact. She'd been a young, foolish girl who fell in love with a man she believed loved her back. Naturally, now she isn't as sure as she once was. She learned through that process that relationships are not effortless. The idea of two independent people coming together to live under the same roof seems to go against nature. But she tried it. And failed.

It is because of that ex-husband that she doesn't play music anymore. And why she hasn't seen her son in several years.

Her husband and her son abandoned her, and she had nowhere to go. Her parents were both gone. Jane decided to drive until she found a place where she could drift along. It worked pretty well for her. She was able to disappear from everyone she knew and never see her jerk of a husband again.

But now, walking in the door of her small-town bookshop like he just came in to browse the new releases, is her son. She stares at him, wondering. She reached out to him when he moved out of his dad's house, but years of poison against her could not be undone with a simple phone call. She continues to keep tabs on him on social media, however.

There's a moment of brief hesitation when she's unsure of whether or not he knows that she's there. She smiles at him, and he smiles back, but there's an uncertainty behind that smile. She makes her way over to him. "Hello. Welcome to Paper Pages."

"Are you Clara Davis?" He's right there in front of her for the first time in years, and she wants so badly to reach out and grab him, pull him into a hug.

"I—I am." She swallows. "But I go by Jane now."

"Jane? Is that your middle name?"

"Yes." The word barely slips out on her breath.

"I am…I mean…my name is—"

"I know who you are, Roger. A mother never forgets." Her voice is gentle, but it quivers with emotion.

He smiles a tight, shy smile. "I heard from some people back home that you worked here. Not sure how they found out. It seems like you didn't want to be found."

Around them, the bustle of the store continues on. More customers come into the store, and with more than ten people in the small space, it becomes hard to shop, let alone have a conversation. She sees Sylvia glance her way, but Jane knows that she'll understand.

"Come back here." She indicates the area at the register.

She goes around the counter, and he sits on one of the low stools. She pours some hot water into a mug and rips open a bag of peppermint tea. She drops it in the hot water and lets it steep.

"What brought you here, Roger? I was under the impression that I would never see you again." She slides the mug over in front of him.

He plays with the string on the bag, moving it around and around in the mug. "Recently, I started to piece some things together from the time that you left."

He shrugs. "The stories Dad would tell me growing up started to not make as much sense. Then I found records that the lawyer kept for my dad, and I read through them." He blows out a sudden puff of air. "None of it lined up or made any kind of sense. I decided I wanted to find you."

A customer comes up to the register with four or five books in her stack. Jane notices the new H.B. Berlow novel; she hadn't even realized it had been released. She rings up the lady and piles the books into a bag. They make their pleasant exchanges, and the lady leaves. When Jane turns back to her son, he's removed the bag from his tea and is sipping it.

"How did you find me? I mean, I'm not mad that you did, but I wonder."

He sits back on his stool and contemplates, not her, but his tea. "I asked around. Obviously, I couldn't ask Dad, but I knew there were some people around town who knew you. Eventually, I found Grandpa's, your dad's, obituary. I called the preacher who spoke at the funeral. He told me I could find you here. Since I'm your son, he told me."

Jane, touched, wipes a tear from her eye. "You went through a lot of work."

He nods, takes a sip. "Why didn't you?"

"Excuse me?" The smile on her face slides off like she just stepped in a wet spot on her carpet.

"Why didn't you do a lot of work to come back to me? I don't understand why you just left me there. I mean, life wasn't terrible with Dad most days, but I would've liked to have my mom around. I missed you."

Jane can't stop the tears from flowing now. Every single word he says to her, she's thought hundreds of times before. She wants to rush around the counter and hug him, but at the same time, she's unable to move. She can't make up for years lost, and to get him to understand, she would have to unpack all the trauma of her life before she left. She also doesn't want to blame him. To lay so much on a fifteen-year-old would be cruel. She gave up so much of her former life just to get away from her husband. Strangely, her son has walked back into her circle the day after she rediscovered music. Hopefully it's only the good things that are coming back from then.

"Jane," a soft voice says behind her, "are you all right?"

Jane turns and finds Sylvia standing there, her face full of concern. Jane smiles at her, trying to keep the tears to a minimum. She doesn't want to cry while she's supposed to be working, but she also didn't want to leave her son behind when her husband gave her the boot.

"Sylvia, I would like to introduce you to my son, Roger." Jane steps out of the way so that Sylvia can fully appreciate him. Sylvia's left eyebrow arches while the other lowers. She spends a moment scrutinizing Roger while the silence hangs. His brown hair hangs limply down over his forehead, and his white t-shirt is slightly wrinkled. He has longer limbs and more wrinkles on his face, but she can still see her son there. She has a sudden desire to pull him into her lap and read him a story. She misses him so much and had no idea until now.

Finally Sylvia says, "I'm pleased to meet you. I didn't know Jane had a son."

Roger clears his throat. "We haven't seen each other for some time."

Sylvia nods and turns back to the shop, leaving Jane

and Roger there alone. A customer comes up and needs help finding a book. Jane reluctantly leaves her son to do her job. The next hour flows in the same sort of way: her conversation with Roger being interrupted by a needy customer. She loves her job and loves helping people, but she does wish it wasn't so busy with all these people today.

Right when these thoughts enter her mind, Sylvia pops up and says, "Why don't you take off? You can show your son around town. There's no reason for you to be here. I can make Brad work a little, too. Let's face it, he's never going to figure out the seating over there."

Brad has been measuring the same spot for the last couple of hours. Even though it is what she wants, terror comes over Jane at the thought of being alone with Roger for more than a few minutes. She's not sure what they're going to talk about. She swallows and nods.

"Roger, the boss lady is letting me go. Would you like to go with me?"

Roger stands. "It was lovely to meet you, Sylvia."

"Likewise." Sylvia's smile doesn't quite meet her eyes, and Jane is surprised. Sylvia is always so genuine with people, but she must have other things on her mind. Jane turns to leave the store, and Roger follows her.

Chapter 16

Showing her son her house is not how Jane expected the day to go. She thought she'd help some customers, daydream of William, and possibly finish that song she'd stayed up too late working on. William still frolics at the back of her mind, but she can't focus on him at the moment. She gives Roger a tour of the house, what little there is, and finally settles in the living room with him. She only has a recliner and a loveseat. She offers the recliner to Roger so that she can face him while they speak.

"It's been years since I last saw you, Roger. And out of nowhere you pop back into my life. There has to be a reason."

Roger lifts the glass of water that Jane got him and takes a sip. "I want to know why you left. It's been ten years since you and Dad split up. I accepted his story of it for so long, and now that I'm older, I wanted to hear your side of the story."

For the second time that Saturday, the tenderness in Roger touches Jane. She would like to give him what he wants, but she also doesn't want to talk about Benjamin "Benny" Rigdon. She wants to have completely forgotten him and live her life pretending that he never existed.

Roger clears his throat and takes another sip of water. It brings her back to the current situation.

"Yes." Jane can't remember how to sit casually. "I fell for your dad when I was only twenty, and I didn't know any better. He's twelve years older than me, and I believed all his promises about love and music and everything."

Roger leans forward on his elbows, eyes ablaze like a kid on Christmas morning. "I remember you used to sing and play guitar. God," he shakes his head, "I'd nearly forgotten all about that."

"Me too." Jane smiles, the bitterness creeping into her voice. "I don't want to speak ill of your father. Ugh, that sentence sounds like it came from a made-for-TV movie. Maybe it did."

"Go on, Jane. I want to hear."

She notices he didn't call her Mom, and, though it stings, she can't blame him. "I don't know if he ever told you, but he was married when I met him. I was that— what do the kids call it these days? Oh, side piece. I lived the cliché of a naïve, young girl falling in love with a married man who made nothing but promises that turned out to be lies."

Jane hasn't smoked a cigarette in years, and when she did smoke, usually it was only when she was in a bar, having a drink. But she could go for one now, if only to have something to do with her hands. She needs to do something. She runs her hands through her hair, then kneads them over and over in her lap. She didn't realize how difficult this would be.

"The time we spent together was so magical up until the point when we got married. Things changed so quickly after that."

She stands, not even realizing she was going to until she does. "This isn't easy, Roger. I've never talked to anyone about this before."

Her phone chimes. She grabs it and sees a message from William. Her heart flutters, and she tries not to smile when she sees it, but for the briefest of seconds, she feels like the only person in the room. She swipes at the screen and reads his message. He just left Paper Pages. He came to see her before he leaves Oklahoma tomorrow. He wants to see her.

This, at least, feels more like normal ground. She knows how to handle William coming to see her. And of course, she wants to see him too.

"Jane, are you going to finish?" Roger's voice brings her back.

"I will, I promise, but I have a friend coming over." She types her address into the phone and hits Send.

His eyebrows raise, but he doesn't protest. He did, after all, stumble into her life today without any prior explanation.

She says, "Let me freshen up, and I'll be back out. You can watch TV or something."

She doesn't wait for Roger to say anything but runs off to her room. She needs Martha to come over and help her, but then she'd probably have to explain more of her life than she's ready to. She also doesn't want William to see her like this, though he did meet her in pretty much the same state the day before, and that went just fine. She changes shirts and quickly applies some foundation and a dab of perfume before returning to the living room.

Roger takes one look at her and says, "Friend?"

She can't stop the blush that bursts onto her cheeks. "No one asked you."

She opens the door just as William is walking up the sidewalk to her door. He still wears his fedora, but he's left his guitar back in the car. Today he's wearing a simple T-shirt and a pair of jeans that hug him in the right place. The smile on his face is one that illuminates the darkest parts of Jane's day. She didn't realize how much she needed to see him until this moment. The rehashing of her life with Roger's father really started to ruin her day.

"Hi, William." She opens the door, her smile for him already in place. "I wish I'd known you were going to be here." She realizes she could say the same thing to her son sitting in her living room. "It doesn't matter, though. I am glad to see you."

His smile dims. "Are you all right?" There's real concern in his voice, and she could kiss him for caring.

"I'm fine." She takes a breath. "My son is here. I, well, we have a lot of catching up to do."

"Oh." William's eyebrows shoot up his forehead. "How long has it been?"

Jane gives a humorless laugh. "Ten years. He was fifteen when I left. When I was forced to leave."

"Oh," William says again, and she can't blame him. She'd probably say the same thing.

"Well, come in. You might as well meet him."

William's smile returns, but there isn't any humor in it now. It's a sad smile, one that hurts Jane's heart to see. "I don't think I'm ready to meet your family yet."

"Oh." Now it's Jane's turn. She isn't surprised, as she would probably feel the same in his position. But damn if it doesn't hurt. "I understand."

She steps off of the porch and hugs him, not letting herself think about anything else, just his warm body pressed against hers. She can feel the hard muscles in his back, and a flare of desire lights up in her that she has to quell.

"Ah, hell," he says into the side of her neck. "We might as well do this."

She steps back and looks into his face. "Do what?"

He sighs. "Not sure what you've done to me, Jane, but I really like you. I am too old to pretend otherwise. If I'm going to be thinking about you all the time, I might as well get to know all parts of you."

She arches an eyebrow and manages to keep the blush out of her cheeks as she says, "All parts?"

William turns red and snickers. He diverts his eyes from hers. "Well—"

She cuts him off before it can get too personal out here on the porch. "Come in, then."

He takes her hand, and she leads him into her small house.

Chapter 17

The small living room looks different now that William is with her. She notices the chipped paint in the corner, the small cobweb bobbing on the wall, and the dust collecting on top of the TV. She cringes at the thought that her house might not be clean enough for him, but a quiet voice in the back of her mind whispers that he normally lives out of his car or on other people's couches.

"Cute house." William's voice is full of honesty and joviality.

"Thank you. You mean that, don't you?"

"Of course."

Roger stands from the couch when they come in, and Jane can't help but feel pride at her son's proper manners. She watches as the two of them shake hands.

"Roger and I have been catching up. Would you like some coffee or tea, William?"

"Coffee would be great. Roger, do you mind if I keep you company for a few minutes while your mom makes some coffee?"

"That would be fine," Roger says. Jane leaves the room, certain that everything is about to go wrong.

Her kitchen is right next to the living room, and it isn't difficult for her to hear what William and Roger discuss in the next room. Unsurprisingly, the conversation is mostly about her. She hears the way

William asks about her, but the two men are not only strangers to each other but also strangers to her. She met William for the first time yesterday, and she hasn't seen Roger in ten years. She's not sure what Roger could possibly say about her.

"I haven't seen her in so long, but from what I remember, she was a good mom. Up until she left. Sometimes, she wasn't around, but when she was, she was always good."

Jane scoops some coffee into the filter and gets the coffee pot going. She never got into the whole single-cup thing. It seems a waste of plastic to her. Also, she never cared much for pouring hot water over the coffee grounds, since that's the whole purpose of a coffee maker.

She pulls a couple of mugs from the cabinet and waits, the gurgling of the coffee maker not quite blocking out the sound of their voices from the next room. Her heart rate quickens when she hears William ask, "Why was she gone sometimes?"

She doesn't want the conversation to turn to her music, not yet. She wants to be the one to tell William that she's a musician. She clatters the two mugs together, thinking for a moment that she could drop one to bring the two men running into the kitchen. Men are always looking to help a distraught woman. But then she wouldn't have these mugs anymore, and frankly, that would be a waste.

She steps into the living room quickly. "Roger, do you drink coffee?"

"Uh, yes. But I probably don't need any."

She nods. "And, William, do you want sugar this time?"

He shakes his head. "Black and bitter." He smiles, his arm draped over the back of the loveseat, his legs crossed casually. He looks like this is the only place in the world he wants to be. She's thankful that she talked him into coming in, if only for more time to see him.

She stands there, her eyes darting between the two men. Men. She realizes the weight of the word as applied to her son, the baby whose diapers she changed, the kid she walked to his kindergarten classroom, and the small boy who needed her help doing some math homework in third grade. She wasn't always a great mom, not always present, but when she was, she tried to be great to him. In the end, none of it mattered since she wasn't there for a third of his life. A tear rolls down her cheek as she stands there.

"Jane? Are you all right?" She pulls herself out of her reverie. She can't fix the last ten years, so she might as well quit worrying about it.

"I'm fine. Let me get the coffee."

Back in the kitchen, she gets a cloth from the drawer and fills it with cool water. There is no point in worrying about what Roger would say. She runs the rag over the back of her neck. William will find out one way or another. She struggles with the idea of leaving her son. She can see the damage it did to him, the pain she caused him. She didn't want to think about him because it hurt her, too. And now here he is. Tears sting the corners of her eyes, and she wipes them away with the cool rag.

This week had been going so well. She'd been working, enjoying her small home, and finding joy in a book she'd just gotten. Life had been simple until William had walked in. Things got ridiculous when Roger walked in. Maybe I shouldn't go back to the bookshop. That strikes her as hilarious. It seems the only place where she can find happiness in her life recently. Well, there or in a book.

Maybe the bookshop is to blame. All those strange occurrences that have happened in the past—maybe the bookshop brought these people into Jane's life just so that she would be tortured and come out a better writer.

She drops the rag in the sink, fills two cups of coffee, adding a little sugar and cream to hers, and then heads back into the living room. Roger is leaning back in the recliner, while William is on the edge of his seat, listening intently to everything that Roger is saying. When Jane enters, the conversation halts, and William looks at her, a knowing grin on his face. She sits on the loveseat—tries not to think of it being called that—with William.

"Roger was just telling me about your life when you were still living at his home." William takes the coffee and sips it. Jane always gets her coffee from the bookshop, which is supplied by a local coffee roaster, Rural Route Roasters. She's never had a bad bag from them, though she does prefer the medium roast.

"Oh, really?" Jane sips her coffee, pretending to be completely uninterested in the conversation.

"Good coffee." William takes another sip, and Jane grins, feeling that she at least did this right.

"Thank you." Her eyes dart between Roger and William until she can't take the silence. "What have you been telling William?"

Roger laughs. "Just some of the things about life before you and Dad split up. Those were different days."

"They were indeed." He hasn't answered her question, so she sips her coffee.

Energy courses through William like he's been struck by lightning. He can't wait to speak and finally blurts out, "You're a musician?"

Jane closes her eyes, but a small smile slips onto her face. "I am." She opens her eyes and nearly explodes with laughter at the look of pure joy on William's face.

"When were you going to tell me? I mean, we spent so much time together last night, and you just listened to me play. You play guitar? Piano? Do you write songs?"

She covers her mouth to hide the laughter. "My, you're excited."

"Of course I am!"

She doesn't tell him everything, just that she's a guitar player and has dabbled in songwriting. William sits in awe of her, nearly bouncing as she talks.

"You have to come with me tonight." He nearly cuts her off to get these words out.

"Come where?"

"I have a show in Oklahoma City, a small club in Bricktown. You have to come." He directs his attention to Roger. "You should come, too."

Roger actually smiles. "I haven't been to watch anyone play music for a long time. That sounds great."

With that decided, she has to once more change her clothes and get ready. She spends far too long picking an outfit, deciding not to call Martha for her advice, though her friend will need to hear all about this new dilemma later. Finally, she's ready. She steps into the living room, and when William looks at her, she knows she made the right choice in clothes. His eyes go wide, and she can see the desire in them.

"Ready?" she asks.

Chapter 18

Two nights in a row of live music isn't at all how Jane saw her weekend going. True, it would have been much quieter, but this is absolutely worth every minute of it.

William graciously gives Roger and Jane both a ride, knowing that he'll have to drive them back to Crescent when the night is over. He seems to be cool with it, so Roger and Jane load into his small SUV. There is just enough room in the car for the three of them. Along with the clothes and tools of the trade, William also has boxes of merch for his shows. It's a tight fit for the three of them.

They ride to Oklahoma City and enjoy the company. Roger makes a few requests for songs to listen to in the car, so William finally passes his phone back and tells him to control the soundtrack. Jane enjoys being around William in this no-pressure situation. She would love to kiss him again, and possibly more, but for now, she's content. Roger really knows his music, blasting through The Ramones and following that up with Tom Petty. She's impressed but then remembers that she probably influenced him while he was growing up.

They all sing along with the songs, but then Roger plays one that Jane and William, the old people in the car, don't know. Clearly Roger is a big fan, so they don't say anything. The song is by a rock band called The

Gaslight Anthem, a pseudo-ballad called "Get Hurt." The words of it remind Jane so strongly of her divorce from Roger's dad that she is forced to look out the window to distract herself from it. When the song is over, Roger says, "That song helped me a lot when you left. It's about the lead singer's divorce."

"Is it?" Jane has to wipe at her tears before turning back to him. "It's quite a beautiful song." She doesn't correct him whenever he refers to their divorce as her leaving. Clearly, his father has been in charge of the narrative, so she allows it. She also never finished telling him about the end of her marriage, so he can be forgiven.

"Yeah, it is." With the phone in his hand, he scrolls through some other songs and gets them going. William catches Jane's eye and mouths, "You okay?" She nods and squeezes his leg. She appreciates having someone who cares about her.

Highway 74 has some roadwork going on, so there's a bit of a slowdown once they hit the I-44 interchange, but it doesn't take long to get through it. The city is quiet for a Saturday night. They pass a few cars here and there, but there aren't any major traffic jams outside of the road work. William chooses to exit at 23rd Street for the relaxing drive into Bricktown. Once they're off the highway, they roll the windows down, and the unseasonably warm air wafts through the car. Still, Jane is glad she brought a jacket on this excursion. It seems warm, but the breeze chills her skin.

Roger plays the song "Bohemian Rhapsody" by Queen, and everyone in the car belts out the lyrics so they can hear each other over the roar of the wind. It's the feeling of being in contact with other people through music while wind rushes through her hair that causes

Jane to realize just what she's been missing for all of these years since she gave up music.

Long before she's ready, they've arrived at the venue, that small blip on the side of the alley in Bricktown. Although it's early, already Bricktown is moving like a living thing. People walk here and there, up and down sidewalks and side streets. Most of them are clearly not going to the club where William is playing, and none of them are dressed for the weather, no matter how unseasonably warm it is.

William has a parking spot in the garage next door to the club. He pulls in and throws open the driver's door. "I guess I'll only have to make one trip since you two are here with me."

"We'd be happy to help," Jane says. Roger nods his agreement. That's how Jane finds herself schlepping a guitar into a club for the first time in years. Roger carries a box of merch, and William carries his bag that holds his harmonicas and his other necessary equipment. Jane leads the way. One thing she learned in the early days of gigging was that she never had to search for the owner if she walked in with an instrument; somehow they would always find her. Having a guitar just creates a sort of presence.

"How are you folks?" A middle-aged, balding man, presumably the manager, comes over to them, hand extended like he can't wait to find out who they are.

William steps up next to Jane so that the man can see him. "Hi, James." He has that warm smile back on his face, part Cheshire cat, part fox. It makes Jane's heart jump every time she sees it.

"Oh, William, I didn't see you there. Got an entourage tonight, eh?" He nods, placing the hand that had been extended to Jane on his hip. "Well, you know what to do. Need anything? Just holler."

"I will." William moves them over to the small stage right next to the door.

"Played here before, huh?" Jane lays the guitar case on its side so he can open it. She longs to see the guitar again, and the thought of opening the case puts a tingle into her fingertips. She has a song to finish; she needs to remember. Right now, though, she is ready to hear William play again.

"James usually lets me pop in whenever I'm in town. I haven't been back in three months, so this is lovely. Makes at least something on this trip feel like home."

Jane stands and watches him get out his guitar and harmonicas. William's words bounce around in her head, trying to get her attention. The part about him not being back around for three months jumps up and waves at her. She sees it, her heart cracking when she acknowledges it. Maybe he'll come around more to see me?

Roger sets the box down and asks William about what to do with the merch.

"There's a table right over near the bar. It's a great setup, as people who want to buy a drink have to stand by your merch table. Sometimes, they feel totally compelled to buy a shirt while they wait for their drink."

"That's brilliant." Roger says, "Want me to set it up?"

William sits quietly, working on his guitar stand. His jaw is set like Roger just asked if there's anyone he can kill for William. Jane understands. There's something sacred about a musician's quirks. They can get stuck in their ways, and anyone stepping in to mess that up can cause problems. But William surprises her. "Sure, go ahead."

Roger walks away with the box, leaving William and Jane alone for the moment. "That was sweet of you. I know you wanted to do it yourself."

He nods. "I need to learn to let people in. We shouldn't turn people down when they want to help us; otherwise, they may not want to help when we need it."

"Sage advice."

William gets his guitar out and strums it. He smiles as he places it on the stand. "It might be true, too, or maybe I just wanted to be alone with you for a minute. You look wonderful, and I'm excited for the opportunity to kiss you again."

Heat rushes through Jane's body. "Then get over here and do it already."

He does, his passion taking Jane's breath away. It's every bit as wonderful as it was last night. When the kiss ends, the first words that come into her head come out of her mouth. "I needed that."

"Good. I did, too."

Once his gear is ready, they make their way to the bar for a drink and to make sure Roger is setting up the merch correctly. He has some t-shirts, stickers, patches, buttons, and even a CD.

"Don't sell those much anymore. People don't even have a way to play them like they once did."

Jane lifts it and studies the pictures on the back. "Is this ten years old?"

"Yes. I have newer music, but it's all in streaming."

They get drinks and talk as the place slowly fills. Jane's heart hammers harder in anticipation of the music. Finally, William stands and makes his way to the stage.

Chapter 19

Jane can still remember her first concert, one her dad had taken her to when she was quite young. It was a Tom Petty show and probably what got her most interested in playing music herself. She loved the movement of the band, the way that the songs brought different personalities out of everyone in the room, and how for days she had a ringing in her ears that reminded her how much the music lingered.

Since then, she has been to far too many concerts to count. This one, though, with Roger by her side and William up on the stage singing his songs, she thinks could be in her top five. The intimacy of the small bar allows a closeness to grow between her and Roger. The shared experience of the music does more for them than simple words would. The gin goes to her head again and makes her sing every time she knows the words, and also when she doesn't.

She gets distracted by a patron reading a book. She knows better than most how people who love books will read them anywhere, but here? With this man singing?

The distraction forces her to think about the bookshop and home. There's been so much activity in her life lately that she hasn't had the time to think about the bookshop. She once heard someone say, "Find a job that you enjoy and you'll never work a day in your life." At the bookshop, she's found that to be true. There are books and pages and people. All of it is better than she ever thought it could be. And yet, here she is in a club, listening to a man she's known for a day belt out beautiful songs that stir her heart in ways it hasn't been moved. She wants to weep and laugh at the same time. So, why would she be thinking about the bookshop now?

At the end of the song, she claps. Roger comes back with a second beer and another gin & tonic for her. She's cheerful after the first and eager for the second, but then, that cheerful feeling changes to dread abruptly.

Up behind the microphone, William says, "Ladies and gentlemen, thank you for being here tonight on this beautiful October evening." Everyone claps. There is a good crowd, a number of them fans of William's that are here to hear him play. "I have had a blessed life, as you all know. But recently, and by recently, I mean yesterday." The crowd laughs, and Jane's heart speeds up a couple of notches. "Yesterday, I found one of the biggest blessings while in a bookstore. And I know what you're thinking, but I assure you it wasn't a book." Obviously there's no way he's not talking about her. She squeezes her hands together in anticipation. "Her name is Jane." He pauses, allowing the name to echo out over the room and into the silence that follows. He chuckles to break the silence. "She's probably going to leave me after this, but I'm not too worried. I'm her ride home." The crowd laughs. They're having a great time listening to him talk, and she's simply stuck there; she cannot leave or disappear. "So right now, I'm going to pull her even further into the conversation. Jane, would you mind coming up here?"

There it is. She has one of those out-of-body experiences, like she's no longer responsible for her own actions but is watching them happen in a movie. She imagines, as she stands and moves toward the front of the club, this must be what a book feels like when it's pulled from the shelf and whisked away. She's carried off by legs that don't belong to her.

She steps up on the stage, every eye on her, but the only eyes that matter are the ones hers are locked on. She tries to smile at him, but in her nerves, it probably looks like a grimace. "Hi," she whispers, but the microphone picks it up, and it moves around to all the people there.

"Ladies and gentlemen, Jane." He lifts his hand toward her, and the crowd claps and whoops enthusiastically for her. Despite her nerves, something clicks in her, and she remembers all the times, the hundreds of times, she stood on a stage and wooed a crowd. She waves and smiles, and she owns them.

William scoots over to the side of the mic to allow her the space. She steps up to it, heart hammering in her chest. "Good evening." The microphone delivers her voice to everyone in the place, and to her, she sounds like herself, the self she's been missing. "I'm happy to be here tonight."

William leans forward next to her, and her skin tingles at his presence. "I learned today that Miss Jane here was once a singer." The crowd cheers. Since many of them are regulars at William's shows, they've never seen him do anything like this before, and they're excited. "Jane? Would you like to sing tonight?"

Yesterday she would have thrown up at just the thought of singing again, but William calms her and makes her feel alive in new ways and old. None of the anguish shows on her face. "I'd be happy to sing."

The crowd cheers, and they haven't even heard her

sing yet. William plays the opening notes to that Fleetwood Mac song they sang last night. She closes her eyes and thinks of the first words. Her body sways in time with the music, and she leans into it. She lets William play through the intro an extra time before she opens her mouth to sing. And it's like she's transported to a different time and place. She's young again, finding the joy in the strum of a guitar or the needle running through the grooves of a vinyl record. It's like she's meeting an old friend or slipping on a coat she hasn't worn in years and finding it still fits.

Before she's ready, they reach the end of the song, and she belts out the final notes. It chills her when the crowd reacts at the end. Like a fresh summer rain on the warmest of days. Like the first sip of a cold beer. Like finding love when there's no way love could exist.

William claps right along with the crowd. She waves and turns to leave the stage. William says into the microphone, "Ladies and gentlemen, wasn't that a treat?" They cheer, many of them making eye contact with her as she moves toward her seat.

She sits down next to her son and breathes. "Was that okay?"

Roger leans in and wraps an arm around her. It's the first physical contact he's given her, and it sends warmth through her. "That was grand."

She sips her cocktail and allows herself to live in this moment. She spirals into happiness. A few people stop and speak to her as they make their way to the bar. Words that she hears and doesn't hear at the same time. For her, the act of standing on a stage and performing again changes her. Her mind swirls, and she wants the good to last.

Naturally, it can't.

Chapter 20

Growing up, Jane can remember hearing phrases about good things happening in threes. Or bad things. Even celebrity deaths would come in trilogies. Even the word "trilogy" is a much more common word than "pentalogy," for example. People just always like things that come in threes.

With the good things that have been happening to Jane—meeting William and being reunited with her son—she is sort of hoping for another one of those good things. It couldn't possibly be a *bad* thing, could it? But then it is. In the very same place where the good things happened.

The show continues on just as it had before she sang. After her moment on the stage, however, the music delights her in a different way. The old flame for songs flickers once more inside her chest. Maybe music can mean something to her again.

On the way home in the car with William and Roger, she's in a whole different world. Everything makes sense. Even Roger seems to be feeling optimistic about all of it. It is the kind of night she will think about for the next several years, one of those I-wish-I-could-go-back sort of nights.

When William drops them off, he walks her to the door. Roger goes inside the house with a quick "Good night," giving them the time alone.

"Thank you," she says to William. "Everything tonight was exactly what I needed." And they kiss, the kind of kiss romantic movies wish they could show on screen, the kind that makes those involved lighter than air.

"Where are you off to now?" She keeps one hand on his chest, the other wrapped around his waist. Her arms attempt to keep him there within reach, but she knows he must go.

"I have to be in California in two days, then Arizona with a stop in Santa Fe before I head to Colorado Springs."

"I wish you didn't have to go."

"I know what you mean. Seems like a terrible time to get interested in someone."

She hugs him, putting her head against his chest and taking in the smell of him. "Santa Fe sounds nice."

"Haven't you ever been there?"

"No."

"It is beautiful. Plus, I have a friend who lives there and lets me crash in his guest house."

"Guest house? How fancy."

They laugh and spend more time talking about things that are only important to them. It keeps them together for the fleeting moments that they have left. Finally, with one more kiss, William darts off into the night and onto his next adventure.

The next two days, Jane spends with her son. Roger asks no more questions about why she left despite the fact that she hasn't finished telling him. She believes they will be able to overcome the past and have a strong relationship going forward.

Roger took off a week of work, planning on

spending time tracking down Jane and getting answers out of her. He said he didn't expect that he would enjoy spending time with her the way that he did. On Monday they make a trip to the city to enjoy some local cuisine like Empire Slice House in the Plaza. She takes him into a record store, and they spend way too much time trying to make sense of the maze of shelves. Each of them buys at least a hundred dollars' worth of vinyl.

So how do all of these good things come to an end? Jane believes when she wakes up on that Tuesday morning that it won't. She'll roll into the bookshop, and things will continue to be great. But that's part of what makes bad things bad: they come out of nowhere.

The Tuesday morning at Paper Pages goes very much the same way as any ordinary morning at the bookshop. Bowl Cut pretends to write. Whole Grain Muffin gets her muffin and coffee. A couple of extra high school kids pop by. At one point she finds a book on the shelf where she'd been sure she had checked before. The store sometimes has a mind of its own, always revealing new places to store and find books.

And then it happens.

The bells above the door jingle, and the door opens. There in the frame of the door stands the man she'd run from all those years ago, the one she'd abandoned her son to escape, the one she'd hoped to never see again: Roger's dad, Benjamin. Though it has been ten years since she last laid eyes on him, she knows him. She's had nightmares about him, that he might show up in her life one day, but she always hoped they were just nightmares. Yet, here he is, older but no less real.

"Clara." It's not a question but a simple statement. He says it like she's a set of keys he's been searching for and suddenly remembers where he put them. His smile is false good cheer, and it roils her stomach. Somewhere on her back, a scar prickles with the memory of the man.

She doesn't respond, just stands like an animal caught in the headlights of an oncoming car. All thought leaves her head. He's here, and no matter how many times she blinks, he doesn't go away.

"Imagine my surprise when I called my son, and he didn't answer his phone. I checked his location. I wondered what the hell he could be doing in Oklahoma, and I realized there's only one reason he'd be here. He's been asking people about you, I've heard. It wasn't hard to find you once I got to this…town." He looks like the idea of the town makes him want to vomit. His suit probably cost more than all the books in the store. "I gave up looking for you a long time ago. Leave it to that little bastard to be the one to find you."

Those words finally break through the nightmare. "Don't you call him that. He's ten times the man you've ever been."

"If only you knew."

Benny smiles, his teeth perfect and straight. She wants to punch them; she wants to run. The warring emotions are tugging her in opposite directions. She notices, as she stares at him, that his once-sleek black hair has some streaks of gray in it and his temples are mostly white. Instead of making him look older, it makes him look better, somehow. But like most men of a certain age, he's sporting the same haircut he's had for the last twenty-five years.

"Benny, please leave. We have no business. You kicked me out, remember?"

He takes a step forward. There are no customers in

the shop, and the street looks pretty quiet. It's just the two of them. That thought terrifies her.

"I kicked you out, yes, but I didn't expect you to leave, to disappear. I still had plans for you."

"I know. Why do you think I left? Why do you think I haven't picked up a guitar since I left? I want nothing to do with you or the beautiful things that are tainted because of you."

He doesn't say anything, but his hand slides into the inner pocket of his suit coat. He pulls out his phone and thumbs through it for a moment. Then he lazily turns it toward her. It's a cell phone video of her singing the night before. She can hear her voice through the tinny speaker. He turns it off and puts his phone away.

"Your son posted that online last night. You should encourage him to not do things like that if you don't want me to know about it."

She's shaken. She wasn't expecting anything like this and didn't even think about Roger posting a video. She's forgotten that young people are always taking videos rather than living in the moment. "He doesn't know that I've been hiding from you."

"Clara, you need to be more careful."

She edges back around the counter where she's left her phone. She's not sure what the local police force can do for her, but she's hopeful that they can at least run him off so she can get away. Maybe, the thought jumps into her head, she can chase after William and go on the road with him. She grabs her phone.

"Hand me that before you make a big mistake." He holds out his hand, and part of her, the part that stayed with him for so many years, almost does. One thing she became aware of after he kicked her out is that she was better off without him. He broke the spell he had on her. She realized she didn't need him, and more, she didn't want him. She's fought so long to overcome those pathetic instincts he'd built up in her, making her feel like she needed to do everything he suggested.

She holds tightly to the phone, her heart nearly beating out of her chest. She's scared but refuses to be intimidated by him. She swipes to open the phone and dials.

"Clara, please, you're making a fool of yourself. All I want is to talk to you."

He holds his hand out for the phone. She has a shock when she realizes he said, "Please."

"No." She's just about to push the button to call the police when the door to the store opens and her hero walks in.

Chapter 21

The door flies open behind Benny. Well, not really
flies. That's just the way Jane pictures it happening: the
door opens and a hero emerges from the streets, ready to
fight the antagonist of Jane's story. The hero in this case
is William, probably not wearing a shirt and sporting
more muscles than most men his age could. Naturally,
her hero turns out to be a small white lady named Sylvia.
All she has to do is step through the door, and Benny's
cool fades faster than a desert winter.

"Good morning, Jane." Sylvia's voice comes from
behind a stack of books. Jane drops her phone and rushes
out from behind the counter.

"Let me help you with that."

"Oh, nonsense, dear, I've got it. But maybe this
gentleman could close the door for me on his way out."

Jane stops. How does Sylvia know Benny is in there
with them? She can't possibly see him over the books.
And to call him out like that, basically dismissing him
from the store, is an incredible thing.

Benny turns back and sneers in her direction before
exiting the building. All of the air returns to Jane's lungs.
It's like she's been standing on the moon instead of in a
bookstore. She watches him go, secretly hoping he'll get
hit by a car as he crosses the highway. When she turns
her attention back to the shop, Sylvia is standing right
next to her, her hands surprisingly empty.

Jane jumps. "Hi. You're not supposed to work today, are you?"

"Oh, you know, I needed to be in the bookshop, surrounded by my friends." She indicates the shelves, and Jane knows exactly what she means. "Are you okay, dear?"

"Okay? Yes, I'm fine."

Sylvia nods like she said she wasn't fine. "I understand if you need to go home."

"No, I'm fine, really. I should probably text Roger, though."

"Oh, is your son still around?" Sylvia turns to a stack of books that she starts to shelve. It might be the books that Sylvia brought in, but Jane could swear there were no books there. She's worn out; that is the only explanation.

"He is. He's staying this week. We're catching up."

"I see. Did you know that John Grisham was born in Jonesboro, Arkansas?"

"What? I...I guess I didn't know that." Jane walks back to the counter to grab her phone. She swipes open the lock screen. The phone number for the local police stares up at her from the screen. Seeing that reminds her of how close she came to actually calling. The fact that she didn't proves how much Benny can still control her. She shudders.

She sends a quick text to Roger. —*Hey, just saw your dad at the bookshop. Wanted to warn you that he's in town.*—

She hits Send before she has a chance to consider things further. She sighs. She doesn't want to think about Benny being in here, tainting another thing she loves with his presence. That part of her that wanted to run from him continues to want to run, but a bigger, stronger part wants to stay and force him out. She's made a home for herself here in this little town, and she doesn't want to run away from it, not this time.

Her phone chimes. —*He's here? Why?*—

She writes and erases her message four times before settling on, —*Looking for you, I guess*— What she wants to say is in the erased messages. She wants to tell Roger that his father is here to torment her, to take her back as a prisoner so that he can exploit her as he once did. Roger probably isn't ready for that. She's dropped some hints over the past few days, but mostly she's played nice. She has a lifetime of Benny's poison in Roger to work against, and she knows it won't be an overnight transition.

Her phone chimes again. —*Shit. I'm sorry, Mom.*—

She smiles at that last word. At some point the day before, he started calling her Mom, like it was what he'd called her all along. She finds comfort in the fact that this grown man still sees her as his mom.

—*I'll be fine. He's gone for now.*—

She sets her phone back down and grabs up her notepad to see what random books Sylvia has written down on it this week. Half the time, they don't sell the books on the shelves but special-order books for people to buy. She starts typing them in the computer. She gets lost in the work until the list is completed and all the books are ordered. It's always satisfying to cross something else off of the to-do list. Surprisingly, it also clears Benny from her mind, at least a little. There is still that frightened part of her that wants to scream, but with Sylvia there, she isn't as scared.

She checks her phone and sees that she's got a

message from William. Seeing his name instantly makes her smile. He's thinking of her, and that means more than the words on the screen. She writes him back, just a quick message to let him know he's also on her mind. She doesn't reveal the terrible news of Benny being in town. She wants him to believe she is safe and that life is nothing more than sunshine. In other words, she doesn't want him to worry about her.

The day carries on in more or less the same fashion but without Benny. She decides that when she leaves work and gets home, she needs to tell Roger some things. With her ex-husband showing his stupid, ugly head, she'll need to tell her side of the story.

Chapter 22

Few things in life can make an artist feel more alive than when a person tells them they appreciate their art. Whether that is a painter, a writer, a sculptor, or a musician. That last one has always struck home with Jane. When she first learned to play guitar, she spent entirely too much time dreaming of someday playing for people. She got so into the dream that while in high school she set out to do just that. Since she was too young to go into a bar, she went to a coffee shop. They weren't as big then as they are today, but that meant that only the really serious coffee drinkers went to them, and they generated a vibe. The first show she played, she was so nervous, she forgot to play three of the songs she'd practiced. But she loved every minute of it.

The best, though, was after it was all over, when she'd packed her guitar and was drinking her "pay" of a free cup of coffee, a stranger walked up to her and told her he liked her voice. "Do you write songs, or do you only play other people's?" he'd asked her, still holding her hand from when he'd shaken it. She didn't get a weird vibe from him, so she allowed it. When she answered that she had but didn't play them in public, he simply said, "Pity" before walking out the door.

It was the kind of interaction that spurs change. She'd been stuck dreaming and needed something to push her out of the dreams and into the real world. She would never get famous singing other people's songs, she decided, and she sat down to work on her own. The next year, she played one for her high school talent show.

At first it was like a terrible experiment gone wrong. Everything that she tried to write or wanted to write came out sounding like a little girl wrote it. And, as Jane thinks of it now, she basically was a little girl. It wasn't until her dad died that…

But she doesn't want to think of that, not yet. She tells Roger all of this as they sit down to dinner that night. She makes spaghetti because she remembers him loving it as a child, but as it turns out, he merely tolerates it as an adult. At first she's sad for the missing years but reminds herself to let it go. There's nothing that can be done for it now. She wants to be present, to live in these moments, getting to know her son once more. While he hasn't asked about her departure from his life again, she knows he wants to, and she's been bracing herself to actually tell him.

Through all of it, the dinner and the conversation, the two of them know that Benny is out there, close by. They know he's going to show up at some point, and they're waiting, without realizing they're waiting. To avoid the presence of the man not in the room, she grabs her guitar after dinner. With the dishes cleaned and put away, something she usually puts off, they've run out of chores to keep them busy. The guitar will provide a lovely distraction from it all.

"Do you remember this guitar?" she asks as she pulls it from the case.

He stares at it, unable to take his eyes off of it. "Of course. But when I was really little. I'd half convinced myself that it wasn't even real."

She nods. "I didn't play as much the older you got. And you didn't ask me to as often."

"Didn't I?" He thinks about it. "I'm sorry about that. Teenagers tend to be the worst humans."

She laughs. "They do."

She strums a chord, a C#m, and lets it ring. It's always been one of her favorite chords because of the feeling behind it. She can always hear that chord and know the mood of the song instantly. She runs through a few chord progressions to allow her muscles to remember the action on the strings.

"Can I play something for you?" She doesn't open her eyes but focuses on the words she wrote a few nights ago. She hasn't had the time to finish the song, but lyrics keep popping up in her head, things she wants to say, and she has them jotted down on all sorts of different pieces of paper, even toilet paper. She's not sure why she had a pen with her in the bathroom, but she couldn't stop the moment of inspiration, so she went with it.

"Of course you can."

She opens her eyes and sees her son laid back on the loveseat like he's home, which warms her heart. She wants him to be able to relax around her. She strums the first chord of the song and starts singing. She does pretty well remembering the words as she goes along. She's always been proficient at remembering her words she's written. She takes pride in that.

She sings the first words again, and the first line resonates around the room and through the two people sitting there. "Right now, I'm haunted by the mistakes of my past."

She lets the last chord ring out and pauses. "Guess I didn't think about that before I started singing it."

Roger's mouth bends into a half smile. "It's all right, Mom. Go ahead."

So, she starts again. She allows her voice to carry her through the first two verses, knowing them in her heart. She realizes as she sings that the reason the words come out so easily is because they're so true.

In the chorus, her fingers find the placings for the F major chord, and she sings, "I wish that I could tell you I was wrong when I said that I am not that strong." She's been thinking of the words, of what she would say next, for three days. "I poured all my pain into a song to help me find a place where I belong."

She plays through the chord progression of the verse a couple of times, then chances a glance at Roger. There are tears on his face. She stops playing. "Honey, what is it?"

He shakes his head and wipes at his face. "I remember so well listening to you play and sing; it all just came flooding back. And the words to that song. I feel like you're crying out for forgiveness in it."

She takes her hand from the neck of the guitar; the temptation to play is too high. She crosses her arms on the body of the guitar and studies him. "Maybe I am. I've been working on it this week."

They share this moment of clarity between them.

The moment ends when there's a knock at the front door. Not a gentle tapping, but a deep pounding that chases the song out of the house. She jumps and nearly drops her guitar. While they ate, while they talked, and while she sang, she allowed herself to forget about the existence of Benny.

"I know you're in there, Clara, Roger. Open the door. We need to talk." Benny's voice carries all the authority he's always managed. She stands, ready to obey him, but finds that strength she had earlier.

Gently, she puts her guitar back into the case, not wanting Benny to see it. "He won't go away, will he?"

Roger shakes his head. He doesn't look frightened, just sad. When she comes back to the living room, there's another knock at the door. It's amazing to her that she can hear the frustration in that knock.

She walks over to the door and reaches for the handle.

Chapter 23

Jane stands in front of the door after putting her guitar away and stares at it, willing Benny to go away. The fact that he divorced her and put her out proves the kind of man he is, and now here he is, trying to put her through all of it again. She sighs, throws another look back at Roger, and opens the door.

Benny is an attractive man, even now, and she hates herself for thinking it. There were tender moments with him, times when she felt like he really cared. But now she knows that she was just foolish. It's strange how people can learn the truth about a situation, and suddenly, everything makes more sense. It wasn't until he forced her to that she realized she could have left him at any point.

"Hello, Clara. May I come in?"

She waits at the door, unsure of what other choice she has.

He steps through and smiles at Roger. "Hello, son."

Roger appears ashamed of himself, and Jane isn't sure why. She remains there, a stranger in her house, as she realizes something is happening that doesn't include her. Her eyes dart back and forth between her son and her ex-husband. An unexplained fear creeps up her spine.

"You did well. You can stay for this, or you can go ahead and take yourself home."

The sound of Benny's voice in Jane's house makes

her skin shriek like it's been doused in cold water. She hates everything that he's saying, and as the words slowly sink in, she turns to Roger. "You set me up?"

Roger won't look at her but continues to stare down at the floor. Finally, he nods.

The slight movement of the head barely takes any energy for him to muster, but it shatters Jane. Everything she thought she'd been building the past few days, and now she's learning that it was a farce, all a ruse orchestrated by Benny.

"I was amazed at how quickly he agreed to find you and come here. He wanted to make you believe that you two could reconcile the past." Benny chuckles. "He couldn't actually forgive you, you know?"

"Why?" She doesn't want to cry, but the tears sting her eyes and slip down her cheeks. She wants to be numb to this, another hurt put on her by Benny, but he used their son against her, and she can't stop that pain.

Roger addresses the floor. "Coming here was Dad's idea. But I did agree. I thought you were a deadbeat mom and that you deserved to be treated this way." He sighs and finally makes eye contact with her. "Obviously I was wrong."

Jane stands there, eyes darting between the two men. Benny still has the smile plastered on his face just like he did when he handed her the divorce papers. As she contemplates the trap she's walked herself into, Benny pulls out his wallet and produces five hundred-dollar bills that he passes to Roger. "I don't want to forget what I promised you."

Rogers stares at the money in his father's hand, and to his credit, he actually hesitates before he reaches up and grabs it.

"Five hundred dollars?" Jane asks. "I thought I might be worth a little more." She wipes at her face, allowing the swelling anger to take away her pain.

Benny actually laughs, a darkly sinister thing. "So, Clara, tell me, have you been writing any songs?"

Jane chooses not to answer. She could never hide anything from him. His smile widens. "I thought you must have been. When Roger sent the video of you singing, it was what I'd waited for all these years. You see, people want more music from you; they need it. And I am more than happy to supply it."

Jane shakes her head. "That part of my life is over. You saw to that, you know."

"Indeed. Roger, I've changed my mind; you need to go. It's best you not see any of this."

Benny doesn't look away from her as he speaks. But she doesn't want Roger to leave. Even if he betrayed her, it was because he didn't know her, something she hopes she can change. But right now, if he leaves, awful things will happen. Benny never was a decent guy behind closed doors. She has no reason to believe that's about to change now.

"Please don't go, Roger." Her voice is soft and fragile like a newly hatched bird.

Roger stands and faces her. She sees the boy she raised, the one she loved, and the one she left all mixed up in there. But then, she sees the man he's become. He does look like a younger version of Benny, but there is a kindness about his eyes that Benny has never had. He must've gotten that from her.

Roger steps between her and Benny. "Dad, I think you should be the one who goes."

The smile that has been plastered to Benny's face

since he walked in the door suddenly falls away, and she sees the anger she's all too familiar with. "Roger." The name comes from Benny's mouth in a near growl, like a dog warning another about their property.

Roger doesn't back down. "I know you've spent months, maybe even years, preparing for this moment. But I've spent ten years listening to you say bad things about this woman, and she's shown me nothing but kindness the last few days. Maybe if you'd gotten here right after I did, as you promised you would, I wouldn't feel the way I do."

"I was detained."

"Like you always seem to be." Roger's anger surprises Jane. Maybe this moment was a long time coming. "You need to leave. I want to talk to my mom to hear her side of things. Maybe after that, you can come and plead your case to her, but not without me."

Benny opens his mouth to say something, but before he can, Jane shouts, "Just go, Benny. Clearly, you're not wanted here."

Somehow, he manages to put the smile back on his face. "Fine. I'll go, but you must know that I will be back. You cannot get rid of me; no matter what you tell my son about me, he's still mine. And don't forget that money he has in his pocket. He sold you before; he'll sell you again."

With those last remarks, Benny leaves. Jane moves past Roger to close the door and slide the deadbolt home. She's breathing hard as she turns back to her son. "Thanks."

Roger flexes his fist. "Thank you. I've been needing to put him in his place for a while."

"I need a drink. Then I'm going to tell you

everything."

She moves to the kitchen to pour a glass to ease her nerves and build her courage for what she needs to say.

Chapter 24

Working at a bookstore was never quite the dream for Jane. But when her dream failed and her marriage broke, she needed a way to make money. The bookshop became her safe haven, a place where she could be herself and learn to speak to people. She'd grown accustomed to speaking into a microphone to large groups, but she had never mastered talking one-on-one. The bookshop taught her that.

She hadn't landed the job immediately upon arriving in Oklahoma, but she had discovered the store as soon as she rolled into town. She felt drawn to it the same way her customers always are. Working in customer service has helped her with her communication skills. Once she got comfortable asking people about their day, she learned she could carry on a conversation with a complete stranger just by learning a little about their favorite genre or author. When she sits down beside Roger, these skills that she's perfected in the bookshop will come in handy.

Still, she needs assistance from a glass of bourbon. Normally, she drinks it on the rocks, preferring the melted ice to water it down. But tonight, she needs her liquid courage neat so as to retain every drop of spunk that the bourbon can provide. She downs three fingers' worth in two large gulps and braces herself against the burn in her chest. Once, while in Louisville, she tried some different brands of bourbon on the Bourbon Trail, and the proprietor of one told her that the burn is called a Kentucky Hug. Now, she enjoys the warm embrace from the state of Kentucky as the alcohol moves through her body and up to her head. She comes out of the hug braver.

She sits beside Roger on the loveseat. "Benny said that you wanted to hurt me, but you claimed it was his idea. Yet, you still did it." He drops his head down. "No, you need to look at me. If I'm going to trust you, it's going to take more than you throwing him out of here."

He lifts his head and brings his eyes level with hers. She sees worry buried in them. "It was his idea for me to come here, to be reunited with you, and for him to step in. He was supposed to be here just a couple hours after me." He runs a hand through his hair. It stands at an angle before falling back into place. "I came because I wanted to hurt you. I felt abandoned by you, and I wanted you to feel some of that."

She places a hand on his knee to support him and to try and comfort herself. She suspected that was why he went along with it, but hearing it still hurts.

"I didn't think you wanted me around. I'm sorry."

"Of course, I didn't want you around. What fifteen-year-old wants their mom around? But I still loved you. I wanted you to be there when I needed you. But you disappeared."

His voice rises and his cheeks redden. She allows his anger. She's been angry with herself plenty of times for the same reason. She can't be the bitter one now. She's been upset with Benny plenty of times, but she could never blame Roger.

"I was confused when Benny kicked me out. I had

nowhere to go, and I wasn't sure anyone loved me anymore. I'm not making excuses, and I'm not blaming you. I'm trying to help you understand."

He places his warm hand on top of hers. "Then tell me, Mom."

She sighs and keeps her eyes on his hand. "I will. I'll tell you everything that happened between your dad and me. You have heard his version, so this will just give you a more complete picture of everything that happened. What I want more than anything is for you to understand why I left and disappeared from your life. If you still hate me after this, I will understand."

Roger, bless him, tries his best not to look too eager as she says all this. She thinks about getting another drink before beginning but decides to rely fully on the glass of ice water currently forming a moat of condensation around it on her coffee table. While the water won't help quell her fear, it will allow her to keep her wits. She pictures her boss and remembers what Sylia told her while training her at the bookshop.

"Never picture your audience naked," she had said. "That will just make you uncomfortable or encourage you to make bad decisions. What you should do instead is pretend the customer is one of your family members, someone you are excited to speak with."

It was good advice, and here she is actually speaking to a family member.

"Once I get started, Roger, I won't be able to stop, so save all of your questions until the end."

He smiles and nods.

She takes a breath and begins, "Back then, I was known as Clara…

Chapter 25

Back then, I was known as Clara. I didn't adopt my middle name until Benny kicked me out. I wanted separation from everything Benny had touched, and that included my name. I'd been playing music for several years at the time that I met Benny. I'd gotten quite the name for myself playing clubs in L.A. and Hollywood. The crowds really started to manifest. Mostly, it was the bands I got the chance to open for, but eventually, people started coming back to see me. I managed to get a few more musicians on board, and we had quite the band going. It started to become achievable, you know, the whole American rock and roll dream.

We started getting the attention of some important people, and I could feel things moving fairly quickly. I was nearing my 21st birthday when I met your dad. I should have known then that it was a foolish idea. Sorry, I'll try to not include my retrospective insights. But sometimes we do things in our youth that the world warns us against. From after-school TV specials to our parents, we get all the warnings we need to be well-adjusted people. In youth, though, we are quicker to make our own decisions, to shoot first and ask questions later. I really thought I knew everything.

Benny was a good-looking man who showed a lot of interest in me. It helped that he seemed to have everything together and have connections in the music industry at the same time. It could have been a passing fling, but he kept coming to shows and hanging around afterward. It wasn't until we'd been dating for a few months that I found out he was married.

It's not every girl's dream to meet a wonderful man, date him, begin to fall in love with him, and then find out he's married. I should have left him then. Sorry, I know I said I wouldn't do that, but let's face it, I'm going to. Here's the thing: I did leave him when I found out.

It was a Saturday afternoon. I had a show that night, a big one, and I wanted to spend some time with Benny before the show. He'd told me he would be busy, but no one is too busy for an afternoon coffee, right? That's what I told myself on the way to his house anyway. I'd never been there, but I'd managed to get his address out of him one night as we'd casually hung around my apartment. I found it quickly, but I wanted to make sure it was his before I went right up to the door and knocked. I sat in my car for a few minutes, you know, sort of casing the joint, waiting to see what would happen.

I probably had my suspicions that he was cheating on me. He'd done a lot of the classic secretive behaviors, like never inviting me to his place. I didn't, however, suspect that he was actually cheating *with* me, not on me. When he came out of the house on the porch, his wife followed him. I watched as she grabbed him and they kissed, right there on the porch. I've never been one for confrontation, so I didn't just jump right out and cause a scene. Instead, I started my car and drove off. As I went, I honked my horn so he would see my car.

He had the decency to wait a couple of days before contacting me. I had to cancel the show that night. I was inconsolable. My drummer called to check on me. We were always close, and I appreciated our friendship, but still, I lied to him about why we canceled. I was just so ashamed.

By the time Benny came by, I'd dealt with most of my feelings the way I normally did: I wrote some songs. I wrote some of my favorite songs by getting out what I was feeling. I wasn't happy to see him when he came by, but I think a small part of me had wanted him to do exactly that. He won me over just by showing up.

He said all the right things to me. He sobbed about his loveless marriage and how, when he met me, he hadn't planned on it turning to love quite as rapidly as it had. He'd wanted to tell me, sure, but those first days of a relationship are always the easiest, and no one wants to bring up hard things. I fell for everything he said to me. When he assured me that he'd hired a lawyer and would proceed with the divorce, I all but gave him the keys to my life. I was smitten.

Do you know how long you have to wait to get married after a divorce? Six months. I know because that's how long we waited. The honeymoon was wonderful. Even after all the years, I remember how I felt on that trip up to Seattle. I'd never been in love like that before. I guess that's why when we got back, I signed all the contracts to make him not only the manager of my music but also the executor of any and all future contracts. A few months after he became the manager, he fired the whole band and said I was better off without them. We'd really started playing some more-substantial shows and opening for bigger bands. I had some record companies showing some interest. I didn't want to fire my band since this was what we'd worked for for so long, but Benny convinced me it was right.

I couldn't even answer the phone when my drummer called after that. He wanted an explanation, and I couldn't give him one. All I can hope now is that he somehow forgave me since then. I've been too terrified to reach out to him.

After that, I really did have success, but of course, it wasn't quite the same without my band. And there was Benny, always urging me on to record more, to play more. When I actually got the break he wanted, we had our own tour bus, just the two of us, while everyone else had to ride in a van. I didn't want to acknowledge the problems with all of it. The one time I actually did get brave enough to ask him about it, well, he hit me. It wasn't hard. But who am I kidding? He shouldn't have done it. It wasn't the first time and wouldn't be the last. But it was the first time I felt truly alone.

The worst was after an awful show in Colorado. We'd had a couple of hits by then and had more people coming out. My whole performance was off. I wasn't allowed to even meet with the fans before he had me back on the bus to beat me. He took his belt off, and when I tried to get away from him, I felt the buckle slam into my back. I still have the scar. Of course, he promised to never do it again.

He started to isolate me from everyone I knew. Then the abuse increased. I've read about abusive relationships since, and ours was a textbook example. I didn't have anyone to turn to. My parents were both gone, I had no siblings, and I was sure I had no friends after Benny.

And yet, I loved him. That's the hardest thing for me to admit. I really did love him, and it angers me knowing that.

Ten years in, we had you. You weren't planned, though I did like the idea of having a child; I just wasn't sure I wanted a child with him. I missed my period and knew, but I held back the news, actually using it to my advantage the next time he tried to hit me. Roger, you were the one thing that saved my life. After you were born, I thought he would start loving me again and really make up for lost time.

But he didn't. He never touched me after you were born.

My career ended when I had you. I loved being your mom; I never want you to doubt that. Your father, however, wasn't a fan of me focusing more on you than on music. And since he no longer abused me, he had to find different ways to hurt me. He did that by taking you away from me. He hired a nanny and paid her to intervene whenever I wasn't focused on my music.

You have to understand that I had everything I wanted at that time in my music career, and I didn't want it anymore if I could simply be your mom.

I felt dried up by the time you hit your double digits. He manipulated you against me, isolated me, and did everything he could to ensure I would sit by myself and write the next hit song. I did, for a while, but then I just couldn't anymore. The guitar, my once-closest ally in the war of life, became revolting to me. I didn't even want to be in the same room as it. Depression took me down a dark path, and I thought a lot about suicide.

Benny finally decided there was only one way to get what he wanted, and that was to divorce me. I begged him not to. I didn't know what would happen out in the real world, but I didn't want to find out. When he presented the papers, with that smug smile on his face, I signed, and I left. I remember coming to your room and asking if you wanted to go with me. Obviously, a terrible choice to give to a fifteen-year-old boy. You had stability at your father's, and I was going to live in my car.

I don't blame you for the choice you made; it should never have been your choice in the first place.

After I left, all the years of pain and abuse I'd suffered melted away. I found freedom and hope for the first time. His big plan backfired. Once I was gone, I disappeared as completely as I could. I don't own the rights to my songs, so he gets any money that comes in from them, but I don't care. I found this little town in Oklahoma, and I got myself a job.

Chapter 26

Jane sits back on the sofa, her energy entirely spent. At some point, Roger had refilled her glass of water. She takes a sip of it now, her dry mouth grateful. She doesn't look at her son, and she's sure he isn't looking at her. It's a lot, the whole story laid out like that.

Finally, Roger clears his throat. "That clears up a lot, Mom."

She finally chances a glance at him. He's not crying, but he does have tears in his eyes. She does too.

"I'm sorry that I didn't know," he says. They sit like that for several moments, absorbing the silence. Jane has used all the words she knows, at least that's how she feels.

"He never mentioned the abuse?"

"No, never."

"Coward."

He chuckles, and the sound of mirth in the small room helps relieve the tension.

A knock at the front door startles them. Jane jumps up. "He couldn't have come back, could he?"

Roger jumps over to the window that faces the street and peers out. "It's not him. A different car. I can't tell what kind, though."

Jane takes a deep breath, her hand on the knob. What else could the day throw at her? She decides to find out and opens the door.

Martha stands on the porch and smiles at her. In the chaos of the last few days, Jane hasn't called her best friend. The sight of her friend is like the clouds parting to reveal the glory of the sun.

"Martha, come in! What are you doing here?" She holds the door open, and Martha comes inside.

"Well, I've texted you about thirty times and haven't gotten a response. I thought maybe you died or something. Well, hello." All of her words fall out on top of each other, and then she spots Roger. "Who is this?" She gives him a pinch on the arm. "I guess I wouldn't respond either."

Jane chuckles. It is delightful to see Martha. If she'd given it any thought, she would have called her much sooner. "Martha, this is my son Roger."

"Son? So, is he single?"

They both laugh. Roger, the poor kid, stands there looking a bit awkward.

"Roger, this is my best friend, Martha. Sorry about her. She's a bit much, though totally harmless. She could never cheat on Henry."

"Well, I don't know about that." Martha puts a hand on his bicep. "If I found the right guy."

Roger turns slightly pink.

"Okay, Martha, that's enough." She pulls her friend away from her son and into the living room, where they sit. Roger hangs back, watching the two of them. "So, as you can see, I've been busy."

"I'll say," Martha says, "I didn't even know you had a son."

Jane takes the time to fill Martha in on the past few days since they watched William's show. She leaves out the part about singing in the club. And just briefly mentions her ex-husband showing up. Mostly what she focuses on is Roger and the fact that they're repairing their relationship. On top of that, Jane feels an overwhelming sense of relief at having shared her entire story with Roger. Probably sharing with anyone would have been good, but the fact that her son understands her better helps a great deal.

"So you gave your ex the boot when he showed up?" Martha leans forward, a stern look overtaking her face. "Tell me, is he dangerous?"

Jane acts surprised. "Why would you say that?"

Martha takes her hand, her eyes solemn as they lock onto Jane's. "Dear, as you've been telling me these stories, I've paid attention. Something about him makes you really uncomfortable. Like you don't even want to talk about him."

Jane sighs. "Am I that obvious?"

"Maybe not to others, but I've known you for too long."

"Nine years?"

"Well, you know what I mean."

The two of them laugh, and the weight that Jane carries lightens a little more.

"Why don't you pack a bag?" Martha asks. "Really, if he's come by once and promised to come back, it would probably be better to simply get away from here. You can stay with us. I've got that guest bed that hasn't been used in years, not since Ryan stopped coming around." She turns to Roger. "Ryan is my son. Our daughter, Jean, still lives in Crescent. We see her often, but Ryan moved on up to Kansas City. I always thought he was too good for the small town. Now, he thinks he's too good for his parents."

Roger clears his throat. "Small towns are pretty intriguing. I think most people just want to be where they aren't. Does that make sense?"

Martha guffaws. "It does indeed. I like him, Jane; he's a wise one."

Jane nods and can't help but smile at the compliment for her son. "I guess I could come stay with you, if it's not too much trouble. Roger, what will you do?"

He holds up his phone. "I'm going to start by turning off my location so Dad can't find me. Maybe I'll hang around here, just in case he does come back. I can, I don't know, tell him you left town or something."

Jane doesn't like this idea at all. If Benny thinks that Roger has sided with her, it might make him dangerous toward her son, something he's never been before. She would rather he just leave town and go back home. She says as much.

"You want me to leave?"

Martha stands. "For your own good. Don't you see? Your mom is looking out for you. All this time, she's given up so much, and now, she's giving up more. She's trying to keep you safe."

He sighs. "You would take care of her?" He directs this question to Martha.

"Of course. I usually do anyway."

Jane fights back tears at the support these two show her.

Roger walks over and kneels in front of her. "Mom, I'm sorry about the years we lost, and I'm sorry my dad is an asshole. I didn't know he was married before you or that he abused you. He always made it seem like you were the bad guy, that our broken home was all your fault. Hearing your side of things, I just can't believe him anymore. I'm sorry it's taken this long. I hope that we can work through this and you can be my mom again."

Overwhelmed, Jane doesn't speak but buries her face in his shoulder and cries. The whirlwind of a week has brought her two good things and one bad. William is wonderful, but a repaired relationship with her son is worth so much more than any other good thing she's experienced. She even starts to believe that it doesn't matter that Benny came back into her life if it means she connected to her son.

Finally, she gets control of herself and pulls away from Roger. "Thank you." Her voice is husky and full of emotion.

Roger slides a hand into his pocket and pulls out the five one-hundred-dollar bills. "You should take this." He has tears in his eyes again.

"No, I shouldn't. That's your money."

He continues to hold it out. "At what cost, Mom? I think it's yours now."

She sees what he's doing and what this means to him. Reluctantly, as if the money will sting her, she reaches for it. Once she's taken it, Roger says, "You have to understand that when I agreed to Dad's demands, I thought I was doing the right thing. And I wanted to make a little money on the side. It was a win-win situation, right?"

Jane smiles and nods. "I can't blame you." She holds the money in her hand as she hugs him one more time before he leaves. "I promise I won't let us be separated anymore."

He nods and walks out of her house.

A part of her wants to sit down and cry some more, but she knows that she doesn't have time for that.

Chapter 27

Martha begins harping on Jane about contacting William as soon as they get to her house. "You just had this fantastic weekend with him, and he would probably like to know what's going on. Roger agrees."

"You spoke with Roger about this? When?"

"While you were packing. Just send a text. I know you don't want to bother him."

Jane pulls out her phone and stares at the screen. Without waiting, Martha grabs it and starts typing. She hands it back. "There. He'll call you when he can."

Jane takes the phone back, slightly annoyed with her friend. Still, the spare room Martha loans her is adorable. Jane's been in here before, but not for long. She didn't consider what it would be like to actually sleep in here. She quite likes it. Martha stays with her for a while, keeping up her running commentary of stories and thoughts. Finally, Jane feels settled enough to sit back on the bed and relax.

Martha stands. "Well, I better check on Henry."

"Thanks, Martha. Not sure I could ever repay you for this."

"Not sure that you'll ever need to, dear. That's what friends are for."

Jane closes her eyes just as her phone rings. She sees William's name there. She smiles. "And thanks for this, Martha."

Martha laughs. "Of course, dear."

The packing was easy, as was leaving her house. The hardest part was waiting to hear from William. Sure, she was only on the other side of a small town from her house, but it still felt more like a vacation than an actual abandonment of her entire life. She did have experience with that after all. But here, at last, is William's name popping up on her phone. She slides the tip of her finger across the answer button.

"Hello?"

"God, it's good to hear your voice. I didn't realize how much I missed it. Have you ever been desperately thirsty but didn't realize it until you got that first taste of water and your body reacted in a way that reminded you your body needs water to live?"

She giggles and appreciates the fact that she hasn't giggled in years, but somehow William does this to her. "I don't have any idea what you're talking about."

"Alas," he sighs, "it is the curse of the poet to be understood by only a few."

"How was the show?"

"Intimate." He doesn't hesitate when he says it.

"Is that a poetic way of saying…"

"Small? Yes. There were maybe twelve people present, but we had a great time. Every single person left with something because we all felt a connection to the music. At least, I think we all did. In other words, it was quite good."

"I'm so glad to hear that. I have to tell you, though, my cheeks hurt."

"Are you smiling too much?" he asks.

There's her giggle again. "I am."

"Me too. And as much fun as all of this is, you texted

me earlier and asked me to call. So, here I am calling. I'm sure there's a more serious reason for us to be trading pleasantries, unless I'm reading into things again."

It's her turn to sigh. "Martha told me I should probably fill you in on things. I wasn't sure, so she took my phone and texted you."

"Ah, Martha. Tell her thank you for me."

"I will. I already have, for me, several times."

For the next few minutes, the conversation turns to the ex-husband. She doesn't go into a lot of detail about their marriage, just enough for William to understand that she doesn't feel safe in her home since he showed up. She doesn't quite talk about her music career, not yet. Still, she says enough to give Benny's motivation. Ultimately, she wants William to understand her, understand everything about what's happening in her life. She's only known him for a short time and can count the number of times she's kissed him on one hand. And there's the fact that as she gets older, she doesn't have time on her side. She needs to pursue the good things in life as they come.

"This is a lot, Jane. Do you feel safe at Martha's?"

She's impressed with the response. Instead of bailing on her, he's asking about her safety. "I do. He has no reason to know anything about Martha or where she lives. And I had the foresight to leave my car at my house."

"Good. I'm sorry that all of this is happening to you. And do you still trust Roger?"

It was inevitable that she told William how Benny found her. She left out the part about Roger getting a wad of cash from his dad, though. "After we talked for a while, I think he understands me better."

119

"I have to ask you something. I hope it's all right. I was going to wait until I saw you again, but since we're on the phone talking about such heavy things, I thought I'd go ahead and broach the subject."

Her hand grips the phone tighter, and she sits up. "What is it? You sound so serious."

"I am sorry about that, but it's not that big, I promise. It's that video your son filmed of you singing at the show the other night. See, I shared it on my socials." She tries to predict where he's going with this to brace herself. "I got several comments from people that recognized you." He pauses, letting that sink in. "They said you were a famous singer."

"Did they?" She tries to sound innocent as she says this. She's not sure how innocent it sounds.

He chuckles. "I searched your name and couldn't find anything. There are no famous Janes. Well, maybe there are. But none that look like you. I did a little more searching, and I couldn't come up with anything. I wanted to reach out to one of the fans who suggested that you were some famous singer, but then I thought maybe I'd ask you first. Does that make sense?"

Tears sting her eyes, but the smile stays pressed into her cheeks. "Oh, William, that's the most considerate thing a man has ever done for me in my life. Thank you for that."

"Well, I wasn't trying to be a hero or anything. I just wanted to respect you. If it wasn't something you wanted to talk about, I didn't want to pursue it."

To her surprise, tears fall down her cheeks. "Brace yourself." Her voice is full of emotion, and she has a moment to wonder where all of this emotion is coming from today. "I made a bit of a living as a performer for a while in the nineties. My middle name is Jane, and my maiden name is Davis. That's how I introduce myself. But I hit it big after I married Benny. So I used his name and my first name. I am, or was, Clara Rigdon."

She can literally hear William gasp on the other end of the phone. "You're really her? Clara?"

He sounds giddy. She doesn't want to talk about this, but his excitement makes her excited. "I'm really her. But please, call me Jane. I don't want to be her anymore."

"I don't know why." He chuckles, and she pictures him shaking his head. "Of course, you're Jane to me. I wonder what you must think of me, over here trying to play music in dive bars, and you've actually become famous for it."

"I think you're wonderful. If I could've made a decent living doing what you're doing, I would have. Things changed a lot after Benny came into the picture."

"It's not too late, you know. You can come out on the road with me."

A burst of laughter escapes her before she can get ahold of it. "Can you imagine?"

"I can." There's no humor in his voice, and she's touched.

"Thank you, William. I'll think about it."

They talk on into the evening, and she is reminded even more of acting like a teenager when Martha tells her good night, and she feels the need to whisper so as not to wake her host. But by the time she falls asleep, she's considering what William said about playing music with him. It's an idea.

Chapter 28

Freedom comes in many forms. Physical freedom is the most obvious one that people think about. But there is also the emotional freedom that comes with relieving the emotional baggage often carried around. The poets know that life will end in death, and the rest of the world knows that they'll be bringing plenty of emotional baggage with them to the grave. It's an inevitability.

But now that Jane's story is out, now that she has told her son and her new friend William, she's lighter. So much lighter.

That night, she sleeps like she hasn't slept in years. It's as if the night doesn't even exist. Her head hits the pillow, and her eyes close. A few seconds later, her eyes open to find morning sunlight just beginning to creep into the sky. She stands from the bed, stretches, and runs a hand through her hair. She glances into the small mirror on the wall and smiles. She pulls off her nightgown and pulls on jeans and a t-shirt before heading to the kitchen.

"You look like you slept well." Martha sits at her dining room table with a cup of coffee in front of her. "I don't know what I expected, but I didn't expect you to look so darn refreshed."

"Thanks for noticing, Martha. I feel refreshed. I could go for some of that coffee, though."

"Sure. Help yourself. You know where the mugs are."

Having spent her share of hours in Martha's kitchen, she does indeed know where the mugs are. She hums while she fixes her cup. She always likes a little sugar and a little creamer, French vanilla if it's available, in her coffee. And thankfully, her best friend takes her coffee the same way. The tune she hums is the song she's been working on. While she stirs the coffee and creamer together, she pictures the words for the next verse. She wishes she had her guitar here so she could work on it. She'll be damned if Benny ever gets any profits from this song, if she ever finishes it. Maybe she should buy a new notebook at work today to write the words in. *A new notebook is exactly what I need.*

Thinking of the bookshop, she decides to call Sylvia and explain, at least a little, about what's happening.

"Hello, Jane. I wondered if you might call today." Sylvia doesn't wait for Jane to introduce the topic. She just jumps right into it. "I'm probably right in assuming that your ex-husband is still hanging around the town, right? Right, well, we don't want him coming to the one place he knows he can find you." The line goes silent for a moment, long enough that Jane checks to ensure that she hasn't lost the connection. She hasn't even said anything yet.

"Don't you worry your head about it, dear," Sylvia says. "I think I know what to do. I'll get that taken care of, and you just show up to work like you normally do. We should be just fine."

"Okay, but Sylvia…" But she loses her chance to speak. This time the line is dead, and her boss is gone. She wanted to ask what Sylvia would do. She assumes that her boss will simply call the cops and make them aware of the situation, but most times they won't do much if there isn't a restraining order in place. Up to this point, Jane hasn't had a reason to get one. She's been off on her own and safe, and it never seems like cops care that much. But maybe small-town cops are different than in the big city.

She sits at the table with Martha and broaches the subject between sips of coffee. "I don't know what Sylvia's going to do, but she did seem confident. I'm certain there's not a lot she can do, but what do I know?"

Martha laughs and shakes her head. Martha, a few years older than Jane, managed to retire early, partly because of smart financial decisions when she was younger and partly because her husband had done pretty well with his career. Of course, Henry still works, which is why he isn't sitting in the dining room with them. "That bookshop," she says, and takes a sip of coffee.

"What about it?"

"It always seemed different, you know? In a town where very few businesses make it, and in an era where bookstores aren't exactly the top of anyone's list of places to visit, and yet, that bookshop manages. And quite well, from what I can tell." She sips again at her coffee. "My, that's good."

"It is." Jane sits quietly and thinks about the bookshop. Obviously, she loves the place and loves working there. She wouldn't want to work anywhere else. But then, there is the apparent truth that Martha pointed out. And it's a thought that Jane herself has had in the past. "They say that independent bookstores have grown in popularity the past few years."

"I know they say that. But I expect that's true in places like New York City or even Oklahoma City. But Crescent? I can't name three people who even know how to read."

They both laugh, knowing the stereotypes of their small-town neighbors quite well.

Jane isn't sure if Martha is entirely joking about the bookshop, though, and the thought of it stays with her as she drinks her coffee. Sylvia has always struck her as someone who knows more about what's going on than she probably should. Maybe Jane should just ask her about it? Probably Sylvia would just laugh at her, maybe even call her crazy. And maybe she is. She finishes her coffee and gets ready for the day. So much lingers around her mind as she dresses.

If Jane thought she felt relieved after speaking with William, Roger, and Martha, it is nothing compared to what she feels when she enters the bookshop. The smell of the books reaches out to enfold her like a hug from her mom. Calm overtakes her, and she has to fight back the urge to cry. This is better than the first dip into the pool when she was a girl and school had just gotten out. As she walks up to the counter, she lovingly touches the spines of the books she passes. She straightens the display shelf that showcases the recommended releases, hoping to entice prospective buyers. She even brushes the finger puppets of famous people. She finds them a bit annoying, though she does own one of Alexander Hamilton and one of Edgar Allan Poe. The rest are pointless.

The door is unlocked and the lights are on, but there is no sign of her boss. "Sylvia?" Her voice sounds large in the small space, though the books jump out and grab that sound, pulling it in so there is no echo.

There's no response, and again Jane wonders what Sylvia's idea is to ensure Benny stays away. Surely if it were the police, they would already be parked outside, watching the place. She trusts Sylvia, clearly, as she is at work, and it possibly is best not to ask questions about things that are done for your own good, but still, Jane can't help but wonder.

Once the store is open, she welcomes more of the regulars, slings a few pastries, and even sells a few books. She thinks of what Martha said about nobody in Crescent knowing how to read and chuckles to herself. While Bowl Cut is off in his corner and working on whatever he claims to be writing, she turns the guestbook around and takes a look at the names there. Sylvia keeps it right by the register so that the people who sign it are also the ones buying things. When she flips through it, she finds several people from far away. Every state that surrounds Oklahoma is represented, but so are many others. She even sees one from England. It isn't that the bookshop isn't worth visiting; it's more that Jane wonders how they even heard of it to visit.

"Hello, Jane, I didn't hear you come in." Sylvia's voice startles Jane, and she nearly throws the guestbook across the room.

"God, Sylvia, I didn't even know you were in here."

"Of course. Where else would I be?" She's holding a couple of books that have names on them. She passes them to Jane. "These two customers will be in later to get these."

Jane takes the books. "Didn't you hear me call when I came in?"

Sylvia seems distracted. "I think I would have heard that." She turns and walks back into the office. Jane stares after her for a moment. She accidentally catches Bowl Cut's eyes, and he shrugs. His attention diverts back to his laptop. Jane is still trying to find her footing when the bell over the door once more jingles. She smiles at the young man coming in until she realizes it's her son. The smile stays in place, but the joy slides out of it.

"Roger? What are you doing here?"

Chapter 29

After her mom passed away and before she found solace in her music, Jane would have a recurring nightmare where her mom died over and over. She would wake in the middle of the night, sweating and cold. Oftentimes she would scream until her dad came running in to comfort her. The nightmares would eventually pass when she started writing songs to get through the emotions. It was the best thing she could do for herself. But now, with her son standing in the store, she's reminded that some nightmares are harder to escape. Whatever sense of safety she felt from being in the bookshop and from Sylvia's promises is shattered by the news from Roger.

"Roger? What are you doing here?"

"I had to come back." His eyes are wide like he's been chased by a big dog. "I didn't even make it home. I got down the highway a bit and stayed at a hotel in Edmond. I decided I would stay there and do some thinking. This morning, I came back to town to find Dad and tell him to leave. It was a confrontation I wasn't excited about but knew would be necessary. He blew up at me when I found him."

Roger runs a hand through his hair, his breathing coming in tortured gasps.

"Come on and sit down. I'll make you some tea."

He looks grateful at the invitation and moves easily

over to the barstools. Jane gets the hot water into a mug and dunks the teabag in the water. "So what did you say to him?"

"I told him it would be better if he just left. I'm not sure what's going on with him, but it wasn't just anger, Mom. He looked terrified, too. He screamed at me to get away from him. He told me that I could move out of his house and come live in this 'shithole' if that's what I wanted to do." He stares down at the mug in front of him. She wants to comfort him, so instead of allowing the years to continue separating them, she walks around the counter and wraps her arms around her son. He leans into the hug, allowing himself to be held by his mother.

"Is he on his way then?" She speaks to the top of his head, his slightly curly hair tickling her nose.

"No. That's the weird thing. He should be here. He ran to his car and followed me as I tore out of there. I knew it was a terrible idea to come here with him following me, but I also didn't think it would matter. I wasn't sure you would be here, but I thought I could at least check." He turns toward the door as if he's expecting his father to walk through any minute. "I don't know where he went, though. But this does buy you enough time to skip town, Mom. I think you should. I would offer you a place to stay, but as I still live with Dad, that's probably not a great idea."

Jane knows that it took Roger a lot of time before he would refer to her as "Mom" again, but he still hasn't dropped "Dad" for Benny. She's thankful for the innocent kind of love she can find in her son, but she still feels a little vindictive and would like it—she has to be able to admit this to herself—if he started to hate his father along with her.

"I'll have to give it some thought, Roger. I'm not sure where I can possibly go. Plus, I need to work here at the store."

"Oh, go on," a voice says by the register.

Jane jumps and turns to find Sylvia standing there. She holds a paperback novel with her index finger, keeping her place in it. She looks like she's been standing there for ages, just casually reading a book and watching the store. "I can handle the store for a few days. Just make sure you come back."

"Sylvia, you have to stop doing that!"

"What do you mean, Jane? You really do need a vacation." She shakes her head and walks away, dismissing any more conversation that Jane might want to bring up.

She turns back to her son. "What should I do?"

Roger shakes his head. "Head to some place you'd like to go. Like your boss said, take a vacation." When she hesitates, he adds, "You have the money I gave you. That should get you where you want to go, right?"

She nods as she considers this. She has a savings account, but she is quite frugal with her money. She enjoys opening her bank account and seeing that money there. If she takes any out to spend, then it won't look the same. It makes sense to her.

He smiles shyly. "Where will you go?"

She stands, thinking for a moment. Naturally, she thinks of where William might be next. "I've always wanted to go to Santa Fe."

"Yeah, that could be good." He thinks it over. "I've always thought it would be interesting to see. Plus, it seems like there are always musicals making reference to that town."

She smiles. "Blame it on being exposed to *Newsies*."

They both laugh. Behind her, Sylvia says, "Are you still here? Go on. Just call me when you decide to come back."

Jane jumps again. Sylvia must be part ninja. "Okay, Sylvia, I'm going."

She grabs her things and heads to the door. Roger follows her. Once out on the small porch attached to the front of the store, they stop. Again, she doesn't hesitate. She wraps her arms around her son, pulling him into her. "I love you, Roger. Thank you for coming back. I'll see you soon."

She walks away from him for the second time in her life, cursing her ex-husband, not for the last time, under her breath. She pauses when she remembers that Martha gave her a ride to work. "Roger, could you give me a ride?"

They drive mostly in silence as Jane thinks about the things she'll need to get from her house. One of the most important things is the old guitar. She'll need to stop somewhere on the way to New Mexico and pick up some guitar strings. She loves the way her guitar sounds, but nothing beats new strings. Roger drops her off at Martha's house, and they say their goodbyes again.

Martha is delighted to see her when she arrives.

"You're off work already?" She's been cleaning and pauses when Jane comes in. "Good, I needed an excuse to stop vacuuming."

"No need to stop on my behalf. Besides, I'm not staying. I'm going on vacation."

"Vacation? Well, I wish you had told me last night so I could get ready."

"Well, it's not really a vacation so much as it is a

need to get away. Benny is looking for me."

Martha's eyes widen. "Well, maybe I should go with you."

Martha is the kind of woman that Jane has always had difficulty saying no to. Usually, Jane isn't mad that Martha is that way. She generally finds that having her best friend with her is better than being alone. But on this, she is adamant.

"I'm sorry, Martha. I would love for you to go, but I'm afraid that this has to be just me."

"Oh." Martha grabs a rag and starts wiping down the shelf near her.

"'Oh?' Why do you say it like that? What is it?"

Martha doesn't stop her dusting. "All you had to do was tell me that you were going to see William. I don't know why you can't be honest with me."

"How do you even know?"

Martha drops the rag and turns back to her. "Come on, Jane, isn't it obvious?"

Jane's cheeks burn. "I guess it is."

Martha wraps her arms around her. "I'm so happy for you. I just hope this crap with your ex gets situated."

"Thank you, Martha."

Jane grabs her things. "Can you give me a ride home?"

"Home? You sure that's a good idea?"

"I have to just grab my guitar and my car. I won't be there but five minutes."

Finally Martha agrees, and they load up in her micro-SUV. As they drive, Jane keeps an eye out for Benny. She's not sure what he's currently driving, but knowing him, it's worth more than any other car in town.

Chapter 30

"I should stay here, shouldn't I?" Martha asks as they pull up into Jane's driveway.

"No," Jane says, already reaching for the door handle. "I'll be fine. I'll text you when I leave, so you know I'm fine."

She opens the door and steps out. The sunshine refreshes her, though the hint of winter is in the air. Oklahoma can never decide what season it wants on any given day with the exception of July and August. Oklahoma knows summer.

"You're sure?" Martha is leaning over into the passenger seat.

"Yes, now go." Jane closes the door and walks away from the car.

Martha drives away, and Jane enters her house. She doesn't usually lock her house, but since Benny was around causing problems, she decided the night before that she would.

She takes a breath in her living room, enjoying the smell of home. She wishes she was coming here after a day's work, slipping into pajamas, and cooking some pasta. Alas, she's here to ensure the great evil in her life won't find her. She packs a few extra clothes and puts the bag in the living room. She goes back down the hall to collect her guitar. She packs a small tool kit that she'll use later to change the strings. She hums a little while she works.

When she walks back in the living room to drop the guitar off, Benny is standing there. She's not surprised, but she had hoped to be out before he got here.

"Hello." His smile is one a predator wears before sinking its teeth into the flesh of its prey.

She doesn't even pause. Though she is dejected, she knows her best chance is to surprise him. She walks right by him and out the front door. She heads to her car and opens the back door to throw her guitar in. She hears Benny's feet on the porch behind her but doesn't turn toward him.

"What are you doing?" She can hear the anger in his voice now. She still isn't sure what kept him away from the bookshop, but clearly it doesn't extend to her house.

"I don't have to listen to the man who kicked me out. I'm leaving."

In two quick strides, he makes it across the yard to her. His hand is on her arm, squeezing. "You're not going anywhere without me. Do you not understand that?"

The bravery she'd felt only moments earlier starts to crawl back into the dark interior. Jane wants to stand up to him, but Clara, the woman who had been his wife, quakes at the idea of shouting him down. Tears sting the corners of her eyes as she stares up at him. "Why can't you just leave me alone? You took everything from me."

He smirks at her and squeezes her arm harder, the tips of his fingers biting in so deep she knows her skin will bruise later. "I need money, and to make more money, I need you. Never thought I'd say I need you again, but here we are."

"And why do you need money?" Jane takes back

over for Clara, and the bravery starts to come back, but then Benny's other hand, the one not holding her arm, smacks her face. She cries out, and her head flies back.

"You don't need to ask me any questions."

She keeps her head down, not wanting him to see the tears that have spilled down her face. A warm trickle of blood slides down from her nose onto her lip. She doesn't touch it, doesn't want him to have that satisfaction. Her hair hangs over her face, obscuring it from his view.

"Now, you're going to move your guitar to my car. We'll get you a bag packed up and head back to my house. I'll book you some studio time. It will be like old times."

Again, the bravery comes back with a roar, and she spits the words out before she can stop herself. "Don't you have some new hussy to make music for you?"

He lifts his hand again but doesn't hit her. Instead, he holds it out so she can see. "No ring. I never married after you. I guess you were irreplaceable." He says it with such sarcasm, but if he didn't remarry, maybe there is some truth to it.

"Come on," he says and starts to pull her toward the house, but a car door slams behind them, and an authoritative voice says, "Stop!"

They both turn toward it, and Jane's face breaks into a radiant smile. She doesn't think about what the blood does to that smile, but she knows it is full of joy.

A cop stands there with his hand on the butt of his gun, the holster unbuttoned. A quick glance over to the neighbors tells Jane who called the cops. While most of the time having nosy neighbors can be annoying, today she wants to bake them a cake. She waves, and they wave back.

"This isn't over," Benny says to her, clearly trying his best to not move his mouth. She almost has to ask him to repeat himself.

"Ma'am, are you okay?" It's the one she thinks of as Tough Cop. He comes into the store occasionally and buys romance novels. But he has that standard "tough cop" look, complete with the buzz cut and the tribal arm tattoo. She does appreciate him calling her "ma'am."

"I'm fine now." She takes a huge step away from Benny and wipes at the blood on her face, trying to hide it. "But if you could please make sure he leaves my property. Maybe escort him out of town."

Tough Cop takes his handcuffs from his utility belt. "I could take him down to the station for a little while and make sure he doesn't bother you."

She thinks this over. "That's a solid idea, Officer." Fortunately, Benny parked his car beside her and not behind her.

"I'm sure that won't be necessary." Benny's hand goes into his jacket, and Jane knows he's reaching for his wallet, hoping to buy his way out like he always has before. But Tough Cop decides to earn his nickname.

He whips his gun out of the holster, leveling it at Benny, and shouts, "Sir, remove your hand from your jacket. Slowly."

The dramatic flare of this shocks her, but a quick glance at Benny lets her know that she isn't as shocked as he is. Clearly, he has never had a gun pointed at him. She fights the smile that threatens her.

"I was merely grabbing my wallet." Benny pulls his hand out, wallet in hand as proof. But he lifts both hands above his head. "I thought maybe we could come to an agreement."

"Weren't you just saying you didn't have any money?" Jane asks.

"Shut it, Clara; this doesn't involve you."

The officer holsters his gun and walks behind Benny. He places a handcuff over one wrist and pulls his arms behind his waist to cuff the other. He even gives him the Miranda rights. Benny is clearly upset, but there's never been a situation yet that he hasn't been able to handle.

"My wife and I were merely having a conversation." Benny's voice is one that would be at home on a 19th-century snake oil salesman.

"Don't you dare call me that," Jane says. She turns to Tough Cop and says, "I'm his ex, thank God."

The cop forces Benny to the ground. "Stay there." He then turns his attention to Jane. "Ma'am, did he strike you?"

She touches her face but doesn't answer.

"Would you like to press charges?"

"I, uh, maybe." She's never pressed charges on anyone before. "What would I need to do?"

"Just come down to the station, fill out some paperwork, and we'll have you on your way."

She takes a step back. "That's not necessary. I'm heading out of town anyway."

Tough Cop changes his stance. "I can only hold him for a couple of hours before we have to release him. If you fill out the paperwork, I can keep him."

"A couple of hours will be enough."

"Clara, please." She's shocked to hear Benny's voice that way. He's pleading with her, and when she looks at him, there is real terror there. She wonders again what is going on with him but decides to ignore him.

Tough Cop makes him stand and walks him to the cop car. "You're sure?" he calls back to her.

She nods and turns back to her house to grab her bag. She pauses in the bathroom to clean the blood from her face and apply a little makeup to cover the red welt from his hand. She catches her eyes in her reflection. She's never looked so radiant. She beat him today. She stood up to him. She watched him cower. But there was real fear in Benny's eyes that had nothing to do with her. She decides that she doesn't care, gets in her car, and drives away.

Chapter 31

The road between central Oklahoma and central New Mexico provides a limited landscape to the lonely highway driver. On that long road between home and Santa Fe, she realizes why she didn't play many shows in the Plains states back when she toured. Crossing the Rockies could be a painful experience, but then getting into the prairie, where civilized locals were few and far between, could be somehow worse. The coasts, where people tended to live, were definitely the better places to play some music. As she drives, though, she's able to not worry about traffic but can instead think about her life for a while.

The road stretches on; she passes through one town, then a smaller town. Then nothing. The prairie sweeps around her, and she can see for miles. She notices cattle and the occasional other car, usually going the opposite direction, but the random snatches of life are hard to find out here. It is a lonely road, and despite the joy she has at the idea of going on vacation, her heart grows sad.

She thinks of the first time that Benny hit her. The flat of his palm rocked her head sideways. They'd been joking, she thought, about what he might do while she was out on the road, out on tour. He'd worked to procure a solid tour manager, someone to plan everything that she could possibly need. She'd been having fun with him, feeling good about going out on the road, sharing her songs with the people out there. It wasn't the first time he'd abused her, but all the previous times could be blamed on grabbing her too hard or letting his anger get the better of him. Every time he begged for forgiveness, tears in his eyes, she gladly gave it, had already given it. She'd stood there that time, her hand over her screaming cheek, as she stared up at him. It was she who had the tears in her eyes this time. He hadn't smiled, not then, but she could see there wasn't a trace of remorse, embarrassment, or any of the things he'd shown before. That was the first time she saw Benny for who he truly was.

She turns on her car stereo and cues up a playlist on her phone. Some of her favorite sad songs by some of her favorite singers. She made the playlist right before she moved to Oklahoma, believing her life to be over. When he'd kicked her out and demanded a divorce, when she'd realized the money that came from her music all went to him, she thought she'd give up on it all. And what hurts the most now is the memory that it wasn't the loss of her music or the love of playing, but it was the loss of him. Even then, she loved him.

Those were dangerous days. What money she did have, she spent on alcohol, hoping it would numb the pain she felt. She sought solace in the bottle, like so many other brokenhearted singers had done before her. She was a cliché, and she knew it.

She sat in her car one night, staring up at the liquor store sign, knowing she would kill herself that night. It was all she wanted to do: drink until she fell asleep and never wake up. She reached for the door handle when something stopped her; some supernatural *something* in the cosmos calmed her. She decided not to go to the liquor store that night. She made the same resolution for a week or so before the thirst for the drink overcame her again. By that point, she'd been working in a diner, waiting tables, and making pretty good tips. Occasionally someone would recognize her, but by then she'd been going by her middle name. Without the fancy clothes and makeup, a different name can act as the final piece of the disguise.

The need for alcohol, she's learned, comes and goes, but it never quite leaves completely. She's managed, in her new life, to calm the need. She can even have the occasional drink without worrying about going on a bender.

The sun is already setting by the time Jane makes it through the Texas panhandle. She's seen maybe four cars in the entirety of Texas. She is secluded in a world all her own. She thought that living in a small town in a sparsely populated state would be the loneliest she ever felt, but there's nothing quite as lonely as a West Texas highway.

It was one of her patrons at the diner who happened to be visiting from Oklahoma, one of those tourist types who came out to see what an actual city might look like, the kind where it takes three hours to get anywhere, not from distance but from traffic. The thing that caught Jane by surprise was the kindness in the young Okie.

"This is fun," the gal had said, and "gal" was the only word to describe her, "but I am looking forward to home. There's nothing quite like an Oklahoma sunset."

Jane, intrigued, had talked with her for about twenty minutes about the state, one she'd only briefly visited during a couple of tours. Ultimately, it was the description of wide-open spaces and the way the gal smiled as she spoke, like she couldn't do anything but smile. That night Jane stayed up way too late reading about Oklahoma, the various facts about the Land Run, and the small towns along the way. She didn't want to live too far from a city, so she focused her searches on central Oklahoma, close to Oklahoma City. When she found the small town of Crescent, just forty miles north of the city, she loved it. The charming downtown bookshop cemented it for her, and within a couple of weeks, she moved away, leaving no forwarding address and, she thought, no one with any knowledge of where she was going. She believed that until her son walked into Paper Pages.

Out on the distant horizon, Jane can just make out the shapes of the Rocky Mountains. She smiles at them and offers a little wave. She's missed seeing a rise in the ground, the swell of the earth that signifies something so much older and harder to understand than just the flat. Often as she's driven across the Rockies, she's pictured what it would have been like to be one of the first explorers to see the majestic mountains. How impressive and nearly impassable they would have been.

Eventually, she slows as she pulls into Santa Fe. The city doesn't appear much bigger than where she lives. It has a quaint style about it, with most of the homes being constructed out of stucco in the adobe style. Even many of the businesses have taken the same approach. The city is dark, and its inhabitants have gone to bed for the night. She decides to find a motel and crash for the night. She needs a night alone after the whirlwind of the week she's had. She finds one that looks promising. She parks and goes inside.

Chapter 32

Every motel has a unique feel to it. But each one reminds the visitor that they are, in fact, just visiting. Every surface in the room is alien and unusual. Even the carpet isn't as warm or inviting as the flooring in their own home. She gets a room with two queen beds, not because she's expecting to have company, but because she wants to use the space for her bag and guitar. The only music store in town was already closed when she pulled in, so the new strings will have to wait until the morning. But that won't stop her from playing it.

After dropping off her stuff, she decides to try to find a little liquid inspiration. She drives around town, enjoying the sights of the buildings nestled into the beautiful silhouettes of mountains. The air has turned crisp up in the Rockies, and she wishes she remembered to grab a coat before she left Oklahoma. She'll have to buy something in town in the morning.

Finally, she pulls up in the parking lot of the liquor store and stares at the dark windows. She forgot what time it was, and she laughs until she can hardly breathe. The whole drive across Texas, she'd been reminiscing about the days when she'd been too drunk to stand, when she'd nearly given up her life. And now when she thinks she needs a bottle of bourbon to help her sleep, and maybe inspire the words she needs for the song, she can't get into the liquor store.

Tears stream from her eyes as she continues to laugh. Outside of her car, the kid closing the liquor store goes to get in his truck but stops when he sees her. The look on his face causes her to laugh even more. He walks slowly to her car and taps on the window, and she rolls it down, wiping at her eyes.

"Ma'am, are you all right?"

Her laughter is under control, though some words come out in gasps. "I think so. I just thought it was funny that the liquor store was closed."

He smiles at her, the kind of smile that only uses half of his face. The kid is cute with his long hair, but he looks like he tries too hard to look like he doesn't care. "I don't know why that's funny. Do you need something?" He glances around the parking lot. "I could maybe get it for you."

"That's really sweet, but I think I've decided I don't need anything. I'm just trying to find a place where I belong."

She means it as a throwaway statement, but it's the chorus from her song she's been working on.

"Are you sure you're okay?"

"I'm fine. Thank you. Always treat old ladies like this, and you'll go far in life."

She doesn't wait for his response but rolls up the window and backs out of the parking lot. Where do I belong? The question runs through her head over and over. Tonight, she belongs in Santa Fe; that much she knows. She should be back in her hotel room, drinking water and playing guitar. She heads back.

After a quick shower, she once more belongs to the human race. After a shower, she once more feels human after being in the car all day.

She opens her guitar case and stares down at the yellow beauty. She skips her ritual of running her hand over the strings, and she grabs the neck and pulls the guitar out. She holds it as carefully as she would a baby. She sits, crosses her legs, and places the guitar on one. She structures her fingers for a C major chord and strums it. She hums along and smiles.

She decides not to jump right into the song but to sing another to warm up her voice. She sings a Tracy Chapman song about cars. It's the kind of song that resonates even a little more tonight after being on the road.

After a couple more songs, she decides that she's ready. She clears her throat and once more plays the C major chord. She closes her eyes, allowing herself to picture the words as they have been written in her mind. They've stayed ever present, ready for her to be ready for them. And here she is at last, prepared to finish the song.

"Right now," she sings, "I'm haunted by the mistake of my past." The line takes on a new meaning as she reflects that since she wrote it, her ex-husband has come back into her life. There's a real mistake for sure. "I'm hiding all my deeds behind this mask. I wish that you could climb inside the things I'm trying to hide. Why is pain the only thing that lasts?"

As she sings these lines, she wonders who she was speaking to when she wrote the song. Clearly the words are meant to be for someone. Of course, like a puzzle piece sliding into the perfect spot, she realizes it. William. She smiles at the thought of him and finds herself wondering why she didn't call him once on the entire drive over here. She strums the chords a couple more times, but now that William is in her head, she knows she won't be able to write anymore until she talks to him. She *would* begin falling for someone right when she needs her whole focus on a new song. Naturally, without him, she wouldn't have pulled the guitar out in the first place. She sighs and grabs her phone.

A few swipes and the phone is ringing.

"Hey, you." William's voice slips right into her ear. Her face breaks into a huge smile.

"Hi. How are you?"

The conversation follows on from there. He's in Arizona for the night, playing at a club. As always, he's hoping to bring in enough money to get him to the next spot. They laugh a lot while talking, one of the magical things that happens in any new relationship where both parties connect instantly. It's a simple conversation, and then William asks how she is.

"Well, today was a bit weird. My ex came around again, and the police intervened."

"What? You had to call the cops?" Jane can't hear him spit his drink out, but it seems like the type of reaction that should happen there. She tries not to laugh as she pictures him, a spray of beer flying from his mouth like tiny, wet missiles.

"I didn't call them. The nosy neighbors saw what was going on and called them."

"Wow. So you've gotten away from him. Where are you staying tonight? Martha's again? Or did you get a hotel room?"

"A *motel* room." She giggles. "I'm in New Mexico. Staying in Santa Fe for the night."

"What?" Again, it seems like the perfect time for a spit take. "You're in Santa Fe right now?"

"Yes, silly. Didn't I just say that?"

"I'll be there tomorrow."

She smiles even wider. "I know. You told me all of your show plans, remember?"

"I do. Are you saying you came to Santa Fe to see me?"

"Possibly." She's suddenly nervous and doesn't know what to do with her hands. Her smile melts away as she smooths the bedspread next to her, then plucks at it, ruining the smooth planes she'd created. "I don't know how long I'll need to stay. But I'll be here tomorrow."

"Then I'll see you tomorrow?"

And just like that, the smile is back on her face like it had never been gone. She can hear in his voice that he's smiling too. "William? Are you nervous to see me?"

"Nervous?" He pauses to think about it. "I am. But more than that, I'm excited to see you. I haven't in days. There's something that has my mind continuing to wander to you."

"That's lovely." She moves her hand to her hair and twists it around her index finger the way she did in high school when she'd been flirting with a boy on the phone. "When you're here, would you want to sing a song with me?"

"God, yes! I would love that."

"Then it's a date. I'll see you then."

The phone call ends, and Jane lies back on the bed, staring at the ceiling and thinking of nothing but William. In her mind, she watches those piercing gray eyes staring out at her from under the brim of the fedora he always seems to have on.

She strums at the strings of her guitar, but her desire

to play has gone. Inspiration ebbs and flows, and she's in no hurry to finish this song. There are no record contracts, no big plans riding on her success. This song, she doesn't want to force. She thinks it will be better than anything else she's written if she'll just allow it to come.

Sleep overcomes her quickly after the long drive, and she allows it, closing her eyes. She doesn't even bother to get under the covers.

Chapter 33

Jane wakes before the sun is in the sky the next morning. She has no memory of where she is, but enough light comes in through the window from a streetlight that she can at least see a little. She moans and takes in her surroundings before remembering that she isn't in her house but in a motel room hours from her actual home. Once she remembers that, she calms, lies back, and drifts into dreamless sleep.

The next time she wakes, the sun is peering into her room through the sheer curtains. She doesn't try to hide her face away from the light but stretches out her arms toward it. She feels remarkably well rested, maybe better than she has in a while. Then she remembers that she's going to see William later today, and her heart jumps forward three beats. The excitement gets her moving, the need to get dressed suddenly overwhelming. But there's no need, not yet. Instead, she lies back on her pillows, pulls out her phone, and starts the dreary task of checking her social media to see if anything fascinating is happening in the world.

Checkout is at 11:00, but Jane is ready well before then. She's certain she could have the room for another night but thinks it would be better to see if there are any of those short-term house rentals available. It would be lovely to stay in a house. So she packs her guitar and her bag and loads them into her car. Fortunately, she's in

Santa Fe, and there's no shortage of things she can do in the small town. This is a place of artists and for artists, and so she'll thrive. But the first thing she does is find a breakfast place.

New Mexico has created a new take on traditional Mexican food. It's not quite Mexican, and it's not quite Tex-Mex, but it offers a twist on the culinary style. When she sits down for breakfast, she decides not to order anything she could eat back in Crescent, so she ends up with huevos rancheros with beans, red sauce, and fresh tortillas. The meal is a testament to New Mexican cooking. It tastes so fantastic she's tempted to order more, though she's not sure she'll be hungry again for a few days.

She spends the day after breakfast wandering Santa Fe and thinking of William. At one spot, there's a small group of musicians standing on the street corner, playing their songs. She finds a place nearby and sits, watching them. She's always been intrigued by the way people allow music to affect them, especially other musicians. The guitar player focuses on the strings, watching where his fingers are going instead of looking out at the crowd. He's an introvert if Jane has ever seen one.

The singer, however, puts on a show. He owns the crowd, the few who stop to watch. Most people walk by, trying to avert their eyes, but he sings to them anyway. He has a microphone running into a small speaker, and his voice, while not the best she's ever heard, rings out with confidence rarely found in amateur musicians.

The final musician is playing an accordion. His steady rhythms on it bring the melodies together and combine what the guitar player and the singer are doing to make some kind of sense. In fact, if it weren't for him, she would have moved on several minutes ago. But the accordion brings her to a stop, and she simply watches them.

After three or four songs, she decides to continue her meandering but drops a twenty into the guitar case in front of them. The singer enthusiastically thanks her for the contribution. She sees hers isn't the first twenty in there, but she wonders whether it is the first one a passerby has dropped in. She learned the trick in her younger years to put a few bills, especially large ones, in the case before she played so that other people passing along would think she was worth dropping the bills in for. It's a silly manipulation of the human psyche, and it always worked in her favor.

The breeze blowing down from the Rockies makes her skin prickle with goosebumps. She is reminded of the fact that she didn't bring a jacket, so she stops in one of the tourist-trap stores that sells New Mexico merchandise. She decides that while she's in New Mexico, she'll stick out like a tourist and purchases a neon-green Santa Fe hoodie that zips up the front. She looks rather silly in it, but she's warm. Sometimes, looks can be traded for comfort.

That afternoon, after a healthy plate of tacos and a beer in a tavern close to downtown, she gets a phone call from William. She wonders if her heart can handle the elation she feels every time he calls her. She smiles at the screen when she sees his name and answers the phone.

"Jane, you wouldn't be wearing a neon-green hoodie, would you?" His voice is bordering on laughing as he says this.

"Why would you ask me that?" She does laugh as she says it and looks around to see if she can spot her handsome man.

There, across the street, is a man wearing a brown leather jacket and a dark-gray fedora. She can't see his eyes under the brim of his hat, but his body is turned toward her, and she's certain he's looking her way. She gives a little wave. Over the phone, he says, "I thought that was you. I'll be right there, but I might be embarrassed to walk around with a tourist." She laughs, he ends the call, and he makes his way over to her.

There are moments in life that we all look back on as pivotal to where we ended up. Sometimes they are little moments that just help life feel more real. For Jane, watching William walk toward her, she believes she's in one of those moments. She tries to capture every little thing in her mind, as Wordsworth said, "food and thought for future use."

"I cannot believe you're wearing that," William says; the smile on his face shows the dimples she's been dreaming of.

She holds out her arms, allowing him to take in all of the glory of the sweatshirt. "Will you still hug me?"

"Damn right." He pulls her into him, arms wrapped all the way around her waist. Her body pressed into his is better than a drink after a long day in the sun. The smell of leather and bourbon hangs around him, and she breathes it all in.

Right there on the sidewalk in the Santa Fe Plaza, he kisses her. Tourists jostle them as they make their way around them, but Jane and William don't notice, only paying attention to each other's lips, their hearts beating next to each other. The stubble above his lip tickles her, but she doesn't pull away. She runs a hand through his hair and knows that for the first time in a long time, kissing is not enough. She's been stressed, worn down, and thrown out of her normal routine. She needs something more.

They pause for a few breaths, forehead to forehead. "I needed that." She smiles at him, eyes locked on his. "But I need more."

His eyes grow wide, and she feels something below his waist stir. "Oh," is all he manages to say.

She laughs and decides to give him a break. "That can wait. Do you want to get a drink or something?"

"Indeed." He doesn't seem to know what he's agreeing to, a glazed look in his eyes. She's happy to know she still has that effect on men, but especially on this man.

"Where should we go?"

He snaps out of his reverie. "Oh, I know a place, but I must warn you, the tequila flows pretty freely."

"Normally, I don't drink this early in the day, I swear, but while on vacation, I might as well enjoy myself."

William glances at the bottle on her table. "Too bad you started with domestic."

"What? I like it, okay? Nothing wrong with that."

He takes her hand. "Let me show you what a great drink tastes like."

As they walk, she glances at the tight jeans over his butt and smiles. This could be a fun vacation.

Chapter 34

There's no place quite like New Mexico. The cooking, as she has already experienced, is similar to other styles but somehow all its own. It has houses and buildings the way that other cities do, but again, all in the adobe style of their ancestry. Naturally, they treat tequila with the same sort of style, using some of the same ingredients as the country they earned their name from, but also putting a twist on it.

Tentatively, Jane sips at her cocktail that boasts jalapeño, among other things. The tequila is the first thing she tastes in the drink, but the Tajin chili powder on the rim helps disguise it. The drink is light, sweet, and cold. And there on the back end is the spice. Jane finds it delightful, and before she's quite ready, the drink is empty. Her head swims with the realization.

"That went down easy." She holds up the glass, and he smiles.

"It did indeed." He holds up his own; nearly half of the margarita he ordered is still there. "Are you ready for another one?"

She thinks about it, her eyes taking in the ice cubes and the small amount of chili powder on the rim. "I need to find a place to stay tonight. I didn't renew my motel, and I hoped to find a house to stay in for a couple of days. In other words, I'm homeless in Santa Fe."

For a time she really was homeless. She could have

returned home and moved in with her dad, but that felt too much like giving up. She had friends who would let her sleep on a couch, and occasionally, she could throw down a sleeping bag in the back of a venue for the night. She doesn't miss that, but damn, she really did love the freedom of the road and the music. She brings her focus back to William. The alcohol is ruining her attention span.

He runs a finger over the salt on his rim and places it in his mouth. He got a more-traditional margarita, claiming not to like spicy drinks. He contemplates something, maybe something to build up to. "You don't have a place to stay?" He takes a drink, a long one, and she allows her eyes to rove over his muscular chest and arms while his eyes are diverted. Finally, he puts the now-empty glass on the table. "Looks like I'm empty, too." He lifts his hand and motions for the waitress to come to them.

The inside of the bar is dark, but they have a candle burning on the table between them. It casts a warm light over them but causes the shadows around them to flicker. Occasionally someone enters the bar and allows the sun to come in for a brief moment. Without those random reminders, it would be easy to pretend the day had ended long ago. Or maybe the sun has gone and won't be returning. They each order another round of the same drink. She debates trying something different but decides not to. She found the spicy side of the sweet drink to balance it nicely. The waitress smiles at her when she slurs her words slightly. She seems young or old; Jane can't decide in the faded firelight.

When the waitress leaves, her eyes once more find William's. "I told you I have to find a place to stay."

"You definitely will as soon as we finish this second drink." His eyes are bright, and Jane realizes that he's scared. Her heart jumps up in speed again, just like it did when he called her earlier in the day. "Stay with me, Jane."

There is no mirth in his eyes, just nervous determination. Her heart flutters, and she knows that tonight, she won't be getting much sleep. She smiles at the thought. "Of course I will."

If she could be totally honest with herself, she would admit that this is exactly what she hoped would happen when she checked out of her motel that morning. Not that she wanted to be homeless again, but that this man, who she's starting to think of as her boyfriend, would invite her to share his bed, wherever that might be.

The mood around their little table has become serious but still exciting. When the waitress returns with their drinks, they do their best to acknowledge her. It's a monumental task to look away from William's eyes for even a moment. Her desire for him has risen to new levels, and a slight squeeze from his hand lets her know that he wants her, too.

They drink, and the alcohol helps quell the sexual tension that has become the third member of their party. She's thankful for that; otherwise, she'd be taking him to the bathroom for some privacy, and she doesn't want that to be their first time. When the glasses are empty and their heads are swimming, Jane stands. "Whoa," she says, putting a hand on the table for balance. "That second was stronger than I thought it was."

William laughs. "The power of a good cocktail. You probably need to get something to eat."

"I just ate." She glances at her watch and is shocked

to see what time it is. "Well, I thought I just ate."

They'd been in the bar for four hours. Two drinks in four hours? She shouldn't be drunk, but she certainly feels it. "Let's get some tacos," William says, taking her arm.

"I had tacos for lunch."

"The beauty of New Mexican food is that you can have the same thing for every meal of the day without having the same thing once."

She arches an eyebrow at him. "What?"

"You'll see. I know a great place."

He takes her hand, and electricity shoots through her. She wants him, and she holds to that feeling as they walk out the door.

The sun has drifted low in the sky so that not much is poking out over the Rockies. It creates a rosy haze over the street. The temperature has also dropped with the sun, and she's thankful for her tourist sweatshirt. It isn't quite warm enough, but without it, she would be miserable.

The two of them wander, hand in hand, like a real couple.

"So, am I your girlfriend?" She knows she's drunk, or she would never let those words out. She covers her mouth with her other hand, her eyes locked on the sidewalk.

He stops on the sidewalk, pulls her into him, and plants a kiss on her lips. The alcohol isn't as effective as his lips at making her lose herself. She kisses him until he pulls away. "You are my girlfriend if that means I get to be your boyfriend."

She laughs, and he joins her. They walk down the sidewalk and begin singing a Ramones song to disrupt the quiet night air.

Chapter 35

In New Mexico, the gift that keeps on giving is the local food establishments. Jane finds that as good as the tacos at lunch were, the ones for dinner are better, probably having to do with the tequila in her belly. Somehow food tastes better when she's drunk. She knows this from experience as a musician, of course, but there have also been times, here and there, where drinking made sense on a weekday evening. Random drunken activities always end with food.

Each taco she orders is different, ranging from beef to chicken to veggie. Each one has an array of flavors, and each one is worth the few dollars they cost. She and William are having a great time, eating and laughing over whatever makes them laugh in the moment. Drunk people tend to laugh at everything.

Time speeds by, and the only way that she notices is that the air gets even colder once the sun is down. The beautiful lime-green hoodie she'd gotten earlier is not enough to keep the chill off of her skin. When William wanted to sit outside, she was still warm from the active night. She hadn't realized how cold it would get outside. The restaurant does provide patio heaters that help, but they can't beat central heat or maybe a fireplace. Also, a warm bed would be nice. A warm bed with a warm person next to her.

"I might be ready to go." She rubs her arms to

emphasize the chill and not that she's ready to go to bed with him.

"Well, then, I guess it's time to head to my friend's house."

She nods, suddenly nervous. Her mind gallops along as she thinks of what's next, and ultimately, it settles on excitement. She hasn't been with a man physically in years. There was an unwise three- or four-night stand with a guy down in Edmond. It didn't last because she didn't feel anything for him. At the time of her life when she should have been sleeping with different men and experimenting with sex, she'd gotten married and been with that same man for a long time. So, sex, naturally, still makes her nervous.

It doesn't mean she's not excited, though. Nervousness and excitement often appear together, especially when it's a good thing. A promoter once told her that nerves just meant it was something she wanted to do well. He was talking about her music, but she thinks the sentiment is the same here.

They drive across town, Jane in her car and William in his. She didn't want to leave her car parked somewhere random downtown. She's glad that the tacos soaked up most of the alcohol in her system. Her car moves along at a reasonable pace, and her hands keep the vehicle between the lines. She drums at the steering wheel along with whatever song is playing on the radio. She tries not to think about kissing him, about his lips, his body, or what they are about to do. She tries but finds that her mind is going to think of whatever it wants.

They pull up in front of a small place out on the edge of town. It's an adobe, like all the ones on the street. William parks in the driveway, and she pulls up at the curb. She climbs out, grabbing her bag. She sees her guitar and thinks about grabbing it, realizing she forgot to grab strings again. Isn't it amazing that something that would have been paramount in her mind has slipped to the back since her divorce?

She meets William on the lawn, her bag slung over her shoulder.

"This is my friend Jonas's house. He's cool. You'll probably like him."

She grabs his hand as he pulls her along to the front door.

In the living room, they make small talk with Jonas. He's an architect, often working in Taos and Colorado. He's pulled his hair back into a ponytail, and he continues to lift his glasses to rub at his nose where the nosepiece rests. He's a pleasant enough guy, but the tension that's been building between William and Jane all day is nearly screaming from each of them. Finally, Jonas can tell what's going on, and he says that the guest house is ready for them.

"William, you know where it is. If you guys need anything, don't hesitate to ask."

He smiles and stands, shaking hands with Jonas. "Thank you for allowing us to stay, Jonas."

"Are you kidding?" Jonas also stands and pulls him into a bro-hug. "Everyone is going to be so excited for you."

William glances back at her and gives her a shy smile. "Not as excited as me."

They make their way through Jonas's small house. The insides are those mud-caked adobe walls. The living room has one of those fireplaces built right into the wall. Exposed wood beams decorate the ceiling, and everywhere she looks, there are woven blankets and cacti decorations. New Mexico is a lovely place to visit, but she's not sure she could ever embrace these decorations.

He leads her out the back door, the two of them holding hands, less for guidance than for connection. She is surprised to see a small house in the backyard. There's no pool back here, but he does have a patio that takes up most of the yard. Grass has a difficult time in New Mexico, so people will pave their yards or use gravel to cover them up. The patio is a lovely touch. Whoever built the house added different levels made from wood with seating all around. There's even a built-in fire pit out here. "This is quite the backyard." Her voice is as delicate as a dandelion so as not to disturb the quiet. As soon as they edge closer to the guest house, strings of Edison bulbs kick on and brighten up the whole yard. It elevates it into a magical place where one might expect to meet fairies. She takes a look back at the house and sees Jonas peeking out at them, a small smile on his face.

"So the house isn't much." He sounds nervous. "But it's a cozy place to rest my head in between shows. Jonas and I go way back. He's been a really good friend to me through all the things."

He hasn't shared much of his own past, Jane realizes. With the sudden reappearance of her ex-husband this week, she's been distracted from learning more about him. She makes a mental note to ask more questions, but later. Right now, she's got other things on her mind.

"You don't have to worry about me understanding. Remember, I've been a traveling musician, too, so I've slept in some strange spaces."

"I know that, but this is the closest thing to home

that I have. I really don't live anywhere, so this place means more than you could know."

She understands this is important to him, so all joking drops away. "I get it." She leans in and kisses his lips. They're soft and warm in the cooling twilight. "Just take me already."

And he does. He leads her into the small space that is basically one big room with a kitchenette and a bed. In the corner, she spies a door that must lead to a toilet. Thank God for that. She wouldn't want to run back into Jonas's place every time she needs to pee. She just manages to register these things as she crosses the threshold when he is on her. Their lips come together like they needed kissing to continue living. Jane manages to get William's shirt off, and she has a moment of panic when she's unsure what he'll think when he sees her naked. But she can tell exactly what he thinks of her when he slides his jeans down.

Their lovemaking isn't something that would look grandiose on the silver screen, but to her, it is exactly what she hoped it would be. His body feels right, and he finds all of the right places on her skin. Her climax is strong and a reminder of how much she's missed over the last few years. She bites his neck as he finishes, and they lean into each other.

Panting, he rolls off of her. Exhaustion slips over the room like a rubber glove, and the two of them fall easily into sleep.

Chapter 36

The morning sun streaming in through the windows seems more vibrant after such a lovely evening. At some point during the night, William got up to use the bathroom. When he came back to bed, Jane got on top of him, needing a second round of that wonderful feeling. The sleep afterward was slower in coming, but again, she didn't mind. Now that she's awake, she feels loopy. She knows there's a difference between not wanting to get out of bed because she's exhausted and not wanting to get out of bed because she doesn't want this naked man beside her to put on clothes.

Eventually, she has no choice but to move. Nature seems to always call in those morning hours. She runs to the bathroom without putting on clothes. The air in the small space is cold, and her skin screams at her. She chooses to ignore it, knowing that the bed will be warm for her when she gets back to William's side.

Her movement must have disturbed him because when she returns, he's standing in the kitchen looking through the fridge. He's pulled his underwear on, and suddenly she's all too aware of her nakedness. He looks away from the fridge when she comes out of the bathroom, and his eyes widen when he sees she's wearing nothing. She moves to cover herself. When she does, he closes the fridge and closes the distance to her in two long strides. He takes her hands away, eyes locked on hers. "You have no reason to be ashamed." He pulls her into himself, wrapping her arms around him. "You are a beauty."

She doesn't respond but merely allows him to take control. The muscle in his taut skin moves under her fingertips. She closes her eyes, taking in the smell of him. Finally she says, "I wasn't expecting you out of bed. You surprised me, is all." She lets go of him and steps back, holding out her arms. She's a woman of a certain age who also once bore a child. She knows her body is far from perfect, but there is also a thrill of allowing him to see her. The vulnerability and trust flowing through her in the moment are nearly too much to bear. She watches as he takes in her body, all of it, and while her eyes are locked on his face, he removes his underwear so that she, too, can see all of him.

It isn't long after that they are back in the bed, using it not for sleep but for the other, more important purpose. She once believed she would never love another man again. After their third time making love in that little house, she wonders if she's ever actually been in love before. *Maybe I'm experiencing real love for the first time.* It's like drinking cheap whiskey that comes in a plastic bottle for years and then discovering the top-shelf stuff. It's the kind of discovery that makes the previous stuff disappear.

After they get dressed, she tries her best to do something with her hair so it doesn't look like she spent the whole night having sex. It sort of works. William is all smiles and jovial boyhood, bouncing from foot to foot. She's not about to ask when the last time was that he was with a woman, but judging by his mood, she'd say it's been a while. Maybe longer than her dry streak.

Without much food in the kitchen, they head off in search of breakfast. Since he's in the area so often, he knows the perfect spot.

"So where is your next show?" She's finished her plate of huevos rancheros. The meal she'd had the day before was so good, she thought she'd have it again. It was the right choice.

William smiles under that fedora he always seems to have on. "Tomorrow. I'm playing up in Colorado Springs. There's a bar up there that has always been good to me."

From the way William talks about his shows, she can tell he's been doing this for a long time. She can't say for sure how long, but he knows the venues and has an idea of what to expect. She thinks about Colorado Springs, the mountains, the parks, and the beauty. "Can I go with you?"

He laughs, a vibrant chuckle that shakes the glasses on their table. "I was going to ask if you wanted to come. You beat me to it."

Smiling, she reaches for his hand. "I'll keep surprising you if you'll let me."

His eyes settle on hers, and he offers her hand a squeeze. "I'll let you." There's no humor in his visage. The fun moment from before turns serious, and her smile melts off of her face like the cheese dropping from William's fork. Her heart speeds up as she stares into those gray eyes.

Another night in New Mexico, and they do a lot of the same things. They eat, drink, and enjoy each other. There's nothing quite like a couple that has just discovered sex to remind themselves of the joy and excitement that come with lovemaking. They walk into a music store, buy some guitar strings, and each of them picks out their favorite guitar in the place. William grabs a big-bodied Gibson acoustic, while she grabs a Gibson Les Paul. "Is our choice of a guitar a representation of our choice for a lover?" She laughs when she sees his guitar choice.

They spend a little time with Jonas, talking about life in Santa Fe. He and William have been friends for over ten years, and it started during one of those times when William came through and played a show. He's been bumming around in Jonas's guest house since then.

The only big difference between night one and night two is they pause to play some music together. As vulnerable as Jane felt standing naked in front of him, she finds it twice as daunting to sit in front of him with a guitar on her lap, a song she wrote fifteen years ago bouncing out of those strings. Before she plays a single note for him, she restrings the old guitar. An excitement builds up in her as she watches her fingers deftly move over the tuning keys and strings. It's an activity she hasn't done in so long, but she hasn't forgotten it.

They sit across from each other, exposing different parts of themselves that are deeper than the skin they've enjoyed. They sing, harmonize, and find an overwhelming sense of self as they play together. Any time Jane even considered playing music before, she hesitated. All that is gone as she once more sings with William.

"Colorado isn't going to be ready for this," William says as they finally set aside their instruments and get into bed.

Am I going to be ready for Colorado? Jane thinks but doesn't say. She's seen the joy on William's face and

167

doesn't want to throw any shade of doubt there. Playing for him is one thing, but playing for a crowd is something entirely different. She doesn't want to say this, doesn't want to disappoint him, so she keeps her silence. Maybe she *can* play for people again, people other than William.

Chapter 37

While the highway between Oklahoma and New Mexico is essentially empty, the one between New Mexico and Colorado is loaded with other cars and has no shortage of beautiful scenery. Jane stares out the window, taking in every vista and view, and thinking back on the last time she visited Colorado.

She was still married to Benny, but it was after Roger had been born. She believed it would be her last time to play in Colorado. Fate always has different plans. She was determined not to play, but Benny had been trying to create a revival of sorts for her music. He had big plans, but one of the biggest parts of the plan was for her to write and record new songs. That was the part that she simply could not do, but no matter how much she told him that, he wouldn't listen.

She played that show to half the promised crowd. Those who were in the audience didn't seem to care that she was there. In the back, she could see Benny, drinking too much and looking frustrated. He got into a fight with the concert promoter that night, and the fallout from that all but ended her comeback. It was only two months later that Benny gave her divorce papers.

Now, with the Rocky Mountains looming out of every window, she's hopeful that Colorado will have a new meaning, that Clara will be gone for good, but Jane will be there to take her place.

They roll on up the highway until they reach the Springs. For a while, they drive in and out of towns without ever leaving a town. It's a lot like being back home in California, especially compared to the wastelands of the Texas panhandle. But seeing Colorado Springs brings Jane a bigger peace than she thought possible. She believed that seeing the city again would bring unwanted emotions through her worn-out heart. Instead, it's like she's a new person visiting a new city. At one point she can make out the giant red rocks of Garden of the Gods, the incredible park that delights even the oldest of travelers. Those rocks don't remind her of her ex-husband, but instead, of the beautiful creations around them.

They make their way to the Old Town, a quaint little downtown-type space that was once the hub of all life in the Springs. Now, it's an area where people who still like to shop in charming stores may go to find them. They pull up in front of a club called The Miner's Delight.

"This is it?" Jane's looking at the building. It's an old movie theater converted into a bar. The marquee is still there, but instead of the movie playing, it has the daily specials. She smiles at the list of cocktails. They have names like Iron Ored Fashioned and Fool's Gold Smash.

"This is it." He climbs out of the car and starts getting his gear out. She joins him. She grabs her guitar case, and he grabs his. He also has two boxes with CDs that he occasionally sells. "I'll come back for one of those. Sometimes, people buy them."

He holds the door open for her, and she steps into the darkened interior of a bar. It's not quite as dark as the place where they'd had drinks in Santa Fe. On the left is the bar, one with an overhead shelf for easy-to-reach glasses. The back wall is decorated with bottles of alcohol and a mirror. The wall decorations include pickaxes and mining helmets. She's just glad it isn't a *Minecraft*-themed bar.

The bartender looks like he might have been born around the same time as Roger. He brightens visibly when he sees William walk in the door. "Hey, Will!"

Jane smiles over at William, who takes the name in stride. "Jack! How are you?"

They step over to the bar, placing their guitar cases down. Jane holds out a hand. "I'm Jane." She wants to be upfront with this and doesn't want to be introduced as Clara.

The bartender takes her hand. "I'm Daniel." He chuckles at the look on her face. "Will here insists on calling me Jack. I guess it's a Tennessee whiskey joke."

They all laugh. William indicates her. "Jane here is going to join me tonight, if that's all right."

"Oh yeah? Of course that's all right." He grabs a glass. "Want me to get one started for you?"

"Not yet." William takes a look at his watch. "Maybe something to eat first."

"Cute kid." She picks up her guitar as she follows William to the stage.

The bar is in what turns out to be the snack bar of the movie theater. They enter the proper theater and find most of the original seating intact and the original stage up at the front. The first few rows of chairs have been removed here to make room for the standing crowd. The stage is large enough for a full band. Too bad they don't have one. There are two microphone stands and a guitar stand. At just the sight of the venue, Jane's heart quickens. It's a reminder that she's maybe chasing something worth pursuing.

They set up their guitars and do a brief sound check, adding two microphones to the mix for Jane. William has been here so often that "Jack" just lets him set up the sound himself. He runs up the stairs to the small room that probably once held the projector. He adjusts some knobs while Jane proceeds to check her guitar and microphone. "There will be a sound guy," William assures her as she watches him work. Being a traveling musician means being able to jump in at a moment's notice and do whatever it takes, like running a sound system.

Once they have the stage set and the sound check finished, the whole thing becomes a lot more real to Jane, and she has to acknowledge that she is going to get on the stage and allow a part of her past to become resurrected.

They eat in relative silence, choosing to dine at the small cafe down the street that serves hamburgers and fries. While there is a taco shop across the street from the venue, they'd had plenty of tacos over the last couple of days. Something about a beef patty on a bun with cheese takes Jane home, making her feel more calm.

"You haven't said much." He is all giddy excitement. He's made it clear how much he's looking forward to playing with her.

She shrugs. "I guess I'm nervous." Fortunately, those nerves do not make her lose her appetite. Only three French fries remain on her plate out of the large pile she'd gotten.

"That makes sense. You haven't played for a while."

"There's that. But there's also the fact that I don't

want to be Clara anymore, you know?" She sighs at the disappointment on his face. "I've worked pretty hard to get away from that time of my past. I don't want to be reminded of my ex-husband and that former life. But I also don't want to be ruled by that. I had some damn nice songs back then, and I don't want him to ruin that for me."

William smiles. "Do you want to play one tonight?"

Jane catches his eye. The weird thing is, she kind of does. She's been thinking about it all day, about the way one or two of her songs could get the crowd energized. Or at the very least, it would make her feel more comfortable.

"Maybe."

Sometimes, a maybe is all a woman will give, and any man with experience knows that sometimes maybe is good enough. He nods, and she can see at least one of his dimples. "Let's get back down there and have a drink."

Probably a little alcohol is what Jane needs to make sure her mind isn't too heavy with the past, with the life she once knew. They walk together, hand in hand, Jane feeling like the hand holding her now is the only thing keeping her from floating off into the stratosphere.

A few more people have come into the club now that dinner is over. A couple of guys sit at the bar watching some football and mindlessly eating peanuts. Jack once more smiles at them as they enter. William holds up two fingers, and for a second Jane thinks he's giving the peace sign before she realizes he's ordering a drink for her too.

"What are we having?"

"Jack makes the best whiskey sour. Probably has

something to do with his name."

Her face lights up at the joke. "That sounds good."

She learned a long time ago that she doesn't like straight whiskey, but she can sure put down some whiskey-based cocktails. With two of those Whiskey Sours in her system, she could practically dance and sing and maybe even melt a little. She decides to limit herself to one, at least for now.

Jack has opened the walls to the theater more so that people can sit at the bar and still enjoy the band. He's really made the place fantastic.

With drinks in hand, William leads Jane down to the stage. She drinks quicker as they approach it, but the drink doesn't seem to help her nerves much. She has an out-of-body experience as they step up onto the wooden platform. Someone else places her drink on the ground and picks up her guitar. It isn't her that strums it and makes sure it's still in tune. When she looks up and sees twenty or thirty people coming into the theater to watch, she comes back to herself. She might remember how to do this after all.

Chapter 38

The thrill of stepping onto a stage in front of a crowd is exhilarating and addictive. It's why so many people continue to tour long after the glory days are, in fact, behind them. It doesn't even matter if the people in the room want to hear their music or just want to have a beer. Jane has always found the crowd will respond if the music hits them, and that can be a wonderful moment for the performer.

She has long known the sensation but has forgotten the intensity of it until she steps up onto the stage next to William and grabs her guitar. The house lights are still on, but dimmed. It doesn't keep her from being able to see the audience. A few guys still sit at the bar, paying more attention to their phones or the TVs than to her or William. But other patrons have brought their drinks into the theater and have taken seats. Jane smiles at them, but she's not sure how friendly she looks.

Her heart is racing, but she knows this is right. It feels like her life has been moving toward this moment for a long time. And here she is, embracing it.

"Good evening, folks." William's voice booms out over the PA system. "I'm William, and this is Jane. But tonight, we're a Bag of Bones."

The people who have come in to listen clap, and William strikes the first chords of the first song. He takes the lead and pulls her along with him. Without warning, they're blazing through the setlist faster than her heart was beating at the start. She sings background vocals for him, her voice harmonizing with his in a beautiful intertwining of notes. He smiles at her, sings to her at some points, and takes her on a journey of song that she's thrilled to be a part of. She allows herself to embrace the music and to be embraced back. She appreciated his performance when she was in the audience in Oklahoma City, but being on stage with him brings a different energy to her system.

They take a brief intermission after the first hour, and Jane is reeling from the excitement. It wouldn't even matter if the whole room were empty. She's playing music again and can hardly believe it.

"You want a drink?" William's hand is on the small of her back as he guides her closer to the bar.

"Water. Just water. I don't think I'll need alcohol for the rest of my life."

The light in her eyes must be enough to convince him. He laughs, and she joins him. "It is good to be playing again, yeah?"

"Yes."

William steps away to get them some water. A stranger approaches her and smiles. "You have a lovely voice," he says. "I've seen William plenty of times around here, but not you. Where'd he pick you up?"

"Oh, you know. Somewhere on the prairie."

The man pauses, clearly wanting a further explanation, but she's not going to give him any. He sighs. "Well, you add a new layer to the music that is just incredible. I wanted to let you know." He smiles, not making eye contact with her, and Jane dreads what the next thing out of his mouth will be. "Can I buy you a drink?"

She cringes, but she also knows it was what he really wanted to ask. A part of her is glad to know that she's actually still capable of getting a man's attention, but it gets old playing for a bunch of men who always want to buy her a drink. At that moment, before she has to answer, William walks up and hands her the water. "Here you are." He smiles at the stranger. "Hey, man, how are you?"

"Oh, great, William! I was just telling Jane how great her voice is."

"That's great." William turns toward her and puts an arm around her, leading her away from the stranger.

"He seemed nice." She takes a sip of her water and relishes the cold that soothes her stale throat.

"They all seem nice until they want to buy you a drink."

She pauses and stares at him. "How did you know?"

"I overheard him. Come on, let's get back to it."

During the short walk back to their places on stage, she reflects on William and decides that she really likes him. Sure, she's been thinking of him endlessly for the past few days, and she's had sex with him a few times, but still, women have to make decisions. And she has decided to like him.

The second set features more cover songs by female singers, which means Jane sings more. She belts out the tunes, and the music turns her inside out and helps her to see the darkness within herself. She's transformed by the notes, the chords, and all along the joyous trip, William is there beside her, blossoming into more.

They compel the crowd to join them on the musical voyage they take them on. Most everyone in the bar is standing, dancing, swaying, and, of course, drinking. They abandon their chairs to get closer to the stage. A few people pull out their phones and film, but she doesn't let that bother her. Some might recognize her, but most won't. William is loving every minute of it, throwing in some fun banter between songs. She's not sure, but she's guessing he isn't used to this kind of attention in this club, and she's glad to be a part of it.

They play the last song, and she moves to put down her guitar, but before she can, William tries his best to ruin everything.

He says into the microphone, "We're going to play one more song to end the night. We haven't planned this, but I think the crowd deserves it. You all have been magnificent."

The crowd applauds. Surprisingly, few of them have vacated the area in front of the stage but stand there expectantly. She is convinced that the crowd never acts this way. She's smiling at William, but not a genuine smile. Instead, it's one of those smiles that women will use when they're confused by a situation but want it to end soon. She awkwardly holds her guitar and just stares at him.

"Have any of you ever heard the song 'When We Were in Love'?" As soon as he says it, her heart sinks. The affection she'd felt for him moments ago dissipates. She keeps the smile plastered on but knows where this is heading, and she's powerless to stop it. She's not the weak woman she once was, but she doesn't want to cause a scene in front of the crowd; they don't deserve that. And through all of her thoughts, the crowd cheers, screaming their assurances that they do know that song. She can see that several have already worked out where he's going with this. When he glances at her, she shakes her head, but it doesn't stop him.

"Well, everyone, some of you may have already guessed that the woman sharing the stage with me is the very same woman who wrote that song." William is all smiles as the crowd reacts to this. More people come into the theater area as he speaks. "Ladies and gentlemen, may I present Clara Rigdon?"

He sweeps an arm out toward her, and applause sweeps down over her. She can't help but smile and wave. She steps up to William and whispers to him, "Don't think you're not in trouble for this."

His smile falters slightly, but it is hard for her to be too upset at him in the moment. The room is electrified with excitement. She steps up to the mic, and it carries her "Thank you" to all in the room. "I don't go by Clara anymore. But it is true that once upon a time, I did." Once more the crowd erupts, making the room feel like it contains two hundred people instead of thirty. It electrifies her. She thinks back on that last show in Colorado, the one that ended her comeback, and wonders where all these people were then. "As William said, this song is called 'When We Were in Love.'"

She hits the G major chord, not waiting on William to take the lead. This is her song, after all, and if she's going to sing it, she's going to be in charge of it. The lyrics come back to her as if she'd sung them yesterday. "Sing a song about forgiveness, and tell me all the reasons why I should go ahead and forget all the ways you made me cry."

Several people pull out their phones to film her, but she's quite pleased to see the majority of the crowd is singing along with her. Joy isn't the right word for what she's feeling, but she's too busy singing to think of a better one.

Without her even realizing it, the song ends, and she and William are bowing to the applause before running offstage.

Chapter 39

The old theater has a backstage area where Jack has set up a small office that he uses for counting money at the end of the day. William leads Jane there by the hand, as the crowd continues to scream. Once he closes the door to the small office, she allows the excitement of what just happened to fade away. The betrayal comes slamming back into her as she recalls William introducing her by her first name, the name she wants to be separated from. Before she can say much, though, the door to the office opens, and Jack enters.

"That was crazy," Jack says. "Never seen anything like it here. You guys take a minute, and I'll set up a table where you can greet people and sell your stuff."

When they came in earlier, William hadn't even bothered setting up his CDs he'd brought in. He said that people usually just found him if they wanted one. Jack leaves them just as abruptly as he came in. Once they're alone in the office and the noise from the bar is once more shut out, anger seethes through her as she stares at William. He's smiling like a puppy. "I can't believe how well that went."

"You had no right." Her voice is barely louder than his breaths, but he hears her just the same. The smile falls off his face and is replaced by pure shock. She might have slapped his face, but it likely wouldn't have had the same impact. "You had no right," she says it again, then turns her back on him.

"Jane, come on, the crowd loved you." She hears the chair he's been sitting in squeak as he stands. The heat of his body comes so near, she could probably reach back and touch him where he stands.

"Don't." She's not sure what he's trying to do, but she's positive she doesn't want him to do it. "The crowd was having a great time without throwing my old name out there."

"Is that what you're upset about?" His hand lands on her shoulder. She jerks away from it.

"Of course that's what I'm upset about. You think I want everyone to know who I am? You think there's any way I'm not going to hear from my ex-husband again after that stunt?"

"I guess I didn't think of that."

"What did you think of?" She turns to him now and sees the pain on his face. A small part of her is distressed knowing that she's caused it. But she quiets that part down, not wanting to give in to the softness there. When he doesn't give an answer, she provides one. "You were trying to make yourself cooler. Trying to sell more CDs or trying to get more attention. I don't know, but you sure weren't thinking of me."

William won't make eye contact with her but stares down at the ground instead. Finally, in the silence that follows her statements, he says, "When will you be comfortable being you again?" He lifts his head, and his gray eyes lock on hers. "When will you let the past go and start living for yourself?"

"Let go of the past? Aren't you the one who just brought up my past? I was trying to live for myself."

She doesn't want tears to fall but instead wants to

stand there, stony-faced, showing him that she doesn't care about him, but then the tears do appear, one at a time. She stares at him, concentrating all of her anger and betrayal on him, but the tears make her feel weak. "Just…" She sucks in a breath, tearing her eyes from him and focusing on the ceiling. "Can you just leave me alone for a while?"

There's not a place for him to go in the small office, so she moves out of his way so he can see the door. "Jane, I'm really sorry."

She doesn't look at him, not while the tears continue to trickle down her face. "Just go."

Finally, to her surprise, he does. He doesn't say another word but steps out. When the door closes, she puts a trembling hand to her face and sits down in the single chair in the office. She doesn't let loose like her body wants but holds on, letting the tears fall slowly. She slams a hand down onto the desk, making a couple of pens jump.

She's alone, giving her the chance to think about things. She considers this whole thing from William's point of view and can see that he was just excited. He did wait until the very end of the set to introduce her as Clara. He showed some restraint. She wipes the tears from her face. As much as she wants to be angry with him, she has to admit that she had fun singing that song again. It was exhilarating having the crowd sing along with her. She would never have experienced tonight if not for William. Maybe there is something good here, after all.

At last, she takes a breath and lets it out slowly, allowing her muscles to slacken as she stands there. She nods once as if to reassure herself, and then she opens the door. William isn't there. She's guessing that he's gone up to meet with people. Well, maybe she'll make him suffer a little longer and stay mad at him. She shrugs. The night has endless possibilities.

She closes the office door behind her and makes her way back up to the front of the theater.

Chapter 40

Back in the main part of the club, Jack has indeed set up a table. William has taken his place there and is attempting to field the questions that are being tossed in his direction about her. She pauses and enjoys watching him squirm under their pressure. Jack is attempting to keep the order. She also notices that there are two glasses on the table that clearly contain Old Fashioned cocktails. The crowd begins to cheer the moment they spot her.

She doesn't make eye contact with William as she sits down at the table but keeps her focus on the people, the ones who are the reason she's even come out. She greets everyone with a warm smile and poses for pictures. Several people ask her questions about where she's been and what she's doing now. She gives vague answers that aren't really what they want, but it's enough. She even takes a few photos with William and the patrons who want a picture with her. William sells a bunch of CDs and shirts. No one knows that Jane isn't on the recording. She's certain they would buy it anyway so chooses not to say anything.

After a while, the crowd starts to diminish; people go back to their tables and finish their drinks. A few continue to cast eyes in the direction of Jane and William, but everyone has left them alone. They return to the stage to pack up their instruments. She carries her guitar case right out the front door, not pausing for

William. She knows that she's forgiven him, but she wants to stay resentful for now.

She stands on the sidewalk, alone. With the sun down and the mountains looming, the air has turned quite cold, and her skin breaks out in gooseflesh. She sets her guitar on the sidewalk and rubs her arms. It is a testament to her stubbornness that she could be inside where it's warm but is choosing to stand out here to prove her anger.

The cool mountain air makes her think of home, or what she's come to think of as home. A fall Oklahoma night is quite unlike a fall night anywhere else. She wishes she was there, enjoying the painted sunset and the light breeze. For a long time, Oklahoma seemed more like the prison that it once was for Native Americans and outlaws. But at some point, despite the politics, she found a true home there. She learned how much it helps to keep politics out of the conversation, especially since she still doesn't agree with most of them. But thinking of Oklahoma has her thinking about the people she's left behind. She pulls out her phone, ignores the slew of notifications at the top of the screen, and calls Martha.

"I wondered when you might call. I've just been patiently waiting, you know. Didn't want to interrupt your vacation." Martha doesn't even say hello when she answers the phone but starts in. Jane loves it and can hardly believe how much she misses her friend and the life that was nearly normal just two weeks ago.

"Well, Martha, things got…interesting."

"And what does that mean?"

Jane can picture her sitting in her recliner, Hank in the one next to her nearly asleep. "Well, I came to Santa Fe and, you know, found William."

"Oh, that kind of 'interesting.' I do remember that's why I couldn't go with you."

They both laugh, and whatever resentment she continued to hold onto disappears with the glee. Since she is on the phone with Martha, she might as well tell her what happened. She explains about the drive to Colorado and the show and how fun it was to play on stage again. "Then he introduced me to the crowd as Clara, and the crowd went from slightly interested to fully invested. It really felt like he did it to, I don't know, show off or something."

The chill air keeps reminding her how vulnerable her skin is. She rubs her left arm with her right, trying to use the friction to warm it.

"Maybe he did, Jane, but did you have fun?" Martha's voice is serious and gruff.

"Did I have fun? Well, yeah, I suppose I did." She answers cautiously, feeling like she's walking into a trap.

"Then what the hell does it matter if he wanted to show you off? That might be the sweetest thing you've ever been a part of, and you're outraged about it."

"But…"

"Don't start that. You need to stop and think about what you've come from, the marriage, I mean. You have to consider how different William is. If he didn't do it to hurt you, then I say you're still better off."

Jane stands in silence, absorbing all of this. She's not used to Martha showing this serious side. "Are you mad?" Jane asks. She needs to say something just to break the silence.

"You know what? I kind of am. If Henry took me out and wanted to show me off to his friends, I'd be delighted. Now, I know it isn't the same thing, but it sure seems like it is. Just enjoy the limelight like you once did. There's nothing wrong with it."

Jane sighs. "I guess I hadn't thought of it that way. I just really wanted to leave the name Clara behind."

"I suppose you wanted to leave your husband behind, too. Funny how the past can just keep coming back."

The door to the club opens behind her, and William walks out to stand beside her. "Thanks, Martha. I'll call you tomorrow."

She ends the call and turns to William. His eyes are wide, and a frown creases the bottom half of his face. He could have just found out that he has cancer. She pities him. "Hi," she says.

He doesn't speak but swallows and dips his head. She can hardly believe it, but tears are starting to well in his eyes. Maybe she doesn't pity him enough. "Can we put our stuff in the car? It's cold out here."

He nods, and they walk to where his car is parked in the lot across the street. They slide the guitars in and then walk back to the bar to get the rest of William's stuff. He's left it by the door for a hasty exit. Jack, behind the bar, yells at them when they come in. She doesn't want to wait for the conversation she needs to have with William, but Jack is looking earnest. They step up to the bar, where Jack can hardly be seen through the smile he's wearing.

"Guys, that was incredible. How would you feel about playing tomorrow night?"

The question isn't what she expected. Of all the things she planned to hear this kid say, this was closer to the bottom, if at all. "Tomorrow night?" She's thinking about what day of the week it is. She turns her focus to

William, letting him give an answer.

"We would love to, but we've got to find a place to stay. The plan was to head back to Santa Fe tonight."

"Santa Fe?" Jack says, looking serious for the first time all night. "You don't want to drive that far tonight. I tell you what. I'll put you guys up in a hotel room. One," he slides his eyes over to Jane, "or two? And you guys come back here tomorrow and play. I'll advertise the crap out of it, and we'll all make some money."

The excitement coming from Jack is palpable, and it is difficult to resist a free room instead of the nearly five-hour drive. And the promise of more money doesn't hurt. Jane knows firsthand what it's like to live out on the road and not know where the next meal is going to come from. It's a tempting offer.

"Let me talk it over with Jane," William says and turns toward her.

She doesn't give him a chance. "We'll do it. And that'll be one room." She arches an eyebrow with confidence, despite her warm cheeks.

"Really?" William's eyes widen. "You're sure?"

"Of course. But you're going to have to take me shopping for some clothes tomorrow. I didn't bring much."

Jack is watching the exchange with enthusiasm. He's too young to run a bar, but maybe it's just that she's too old to appreciate how old he really is. "Okay, Jack, we're settled. Get us a room."

Jack gets out his phone and starts tapping at the screen. Jane watches this with amusement and has to throw in a quip. "You know, when I was younger and I wanted a room, I actually had to call the place."

Jack doesn't even look up from his phone. "How

archaic."

Jane laughs; she can't help it. The word seems so out of place coming from Jack.

He puts his phone away. "I've got you a room, one with a king-size bed, at the Sherford Inn. It's on the northern side of the Springs, and it's quite attractive. I'd put my mother in there if she didn't want to stay with me."

Jane holds out her hand to him. "Thanks, Jack. I appreciate the opportunity to play again. Are you going to advertise that Clara Rigdon is back?"

Jack suddenly looks shy, but still holding onto Jane's hand, he says, "I was planning on it. But you tell me different, and I won't."

She meets William's eyes and holds his gaze as she responds, "No, go ahead. It's time I start embracing the past."

They walk out of the Miner's Delight with William's few boxes of merch to load in the car. "Does this mean you're not mad at me?" William asks as they climb in the car.

"I'll never tell." She keeps her face toward the window so he cannot see her face.

Chapter 41

The commute to the northern part of Colorado Springs is quiet. They have some music playing in the background, some 90's station, but it's not loud enough to really appreciate the tunes. She hasn't said anything to him about what happened and still has not clarified her feelings. He just drives, both hands on the wheel, eyes on the road like he's trying to pass his driver's test.

The silence finally gets to him because he randomly breaks it. "So, our first night in a hotel together." It's not a question, just a statement that leaves her wondering what he could possibly mean.

"Pull more stunts like you did tonight, and it may be the only night we have together."

He doesn't take his eyes from the road. It's difficult to have a conversation with the passenger while driving in the Springs area. There seems to always be some form of traffic. "Point taken, *Jane.*"

He overly emphasizes her name. She whips her head in his direction, a smirk on her face. "Going to play it like that? Think that's a good idea while you're driving?" She slides a hand up his thigh, right up to his balls. It gets his attention immediately. He sits up straighter, and his hands tighten on the wheel. She gives a squeeze, brief and just hard enough. When he relaxes, she gives a tighter squeeze, one that makes his eyes bulge out. She lets go and moves back to her side of the car.

William lets out a huge sigh. "Okay, truce. Remind me not to tease you while I'm driving ever again."

Jane laughs and relaxes back in her seat. She's tremendously exhausted and is grateful that they're only driving thirty minutes instead of the five hours back to Santa Fe. All the traveling she's done lately is getting to her. Add to that the nighttime escapades she and William have been experiencing, and sleep has struggled to keep up.

"I'll be happy to get in bed tonight," she says, her eyes taking in the city outside of her window. Unfortunately, the peaks of the mountains are best seen outside of William's window, but it's too dark tonight to see much anyway. She'll have a glorious view of them on the drive back to the club tomorrow.

"Yes, bed sounds great." He yawns, as if the idea of sleep had just occurred to him, and now he's forced to fight it back into submission to keep it from taking over him.

They make a stop at a store to purchase some necessary items like toothbrushes and toothpaste. Jane buys a nightgown that William assures her is adorable, but she thinks looks more like an old lady's. She doesn't remind herself that she is an old lady, at least not this time. They buy a few snacks, and at one point they chase each other through the aisles laughing. That nearly gets them kicked out of the store but makes them feel once more like the teens they long ago were. Romance and love can turn the clock back decades, if only for fleeting moments, allowing the oldest of lovers to feel like children.

The night ends in their hotel room. She feels like a queen as she settles into the bed that is as big as a prairie.

Jack wasn't kidding when he said the place was nice. The decor is modern with subdued colors that probably help patrons calm down when they enter the room. Despite being a hotel room, it feels like it was made just for them that night and that no one else has ever slept in it.

After enjoying the bed for long enough that she almost does fall asleep, she pops up and grabs her guitar case. She lays it on the bed and opens it. William, nearly asleep himself, arches an eyebrow at her. "Thought you were tired."

"I am, but I wanted to show you this song I've been working on." Her cheeks burn. There's something so intimate about showing another artist a work in progress.

"That would be awesome."

He gives her his full attention.

She plays. "Right now," she sings and goes through the two verses she has ready.

She pauses after the second chorus and shrugs. "That's all I have so far."

"That's great, Jane. The lyrics are really poetic. I like it a lot." His soft voice is genuine. "Where did you get the idea?"

She smiles, hoping to be poetic the way William always is. "I guess I was trying to, I don't know, search through the secrets of my soul."

"Now, that's poetic." He laughs and shakes his head.

She plays the verse chords and sings. "I'm searching through the secrets of my soul and learning I don't want them anymore."

"That's good," he says.

She sucks in a breath, hoping it will hold the next words. "Living through the past just makes me relive my mistakes. I need something new to fill that hole."

He nods. "Yes, that's beautiful."

She sings through the chorus one more time. There's more to the song, she's sure, but right now, she's spent. She replaces the guitar in the case.

"You're finished?" William's excitement is palpable. There's not a trace of exhaustion around him.

She nods. "I'm not quite ready to finish that one. Plus, I'm tired."

Her new nightgown is soft and comfortable, and she does have to agree with William, however reluctantly, that it does look cute on her. William crawls into the bed next to her, a smile on his weary face. "Are we good?" The words tumble out before his head hits the pillow.

Jane lightly slaps his arm. "Tonight was too fun to stay mad." She leans over and kisses him lightly on his warm lips. "I forgive you."

He sits up, excited. "Great, because I was thinking we could…"

"Not tonight, please. I am so tired I would probably fall asleep on you."

He chuckles. "I wouldn't mind. But you're probably right."

They snuggle up close together with the lights off, and despite what Jane said, she does feel a desire for him as she wraps her arms around him. But she is too sleepy. A deep breath later and sleep finds her.

Chapter 42

It's easy to forget life outside of bliss. In the moments with William since arriving in Santa Fe, Jane has forgotten about the real world. She's left everything back home behind with the exception of calling Martha the night before. So she wakes the next morning and checks her phone; she isn't surprised to find she has three text messages from Roger. Each one seems a bit more frantic than the last. She sits up in bed to read them, which causes William to stir.

"What is it?" His voice is heavy with sleep, which she finds endearing.

Jane doesn't have time to find him adorable, however, as she reads the text messages. "It seems that the patrons at the show last night have posted videos of me singing. My ex-husband is unhappy."

"Fuck him."

Jane nearly drops her phone, realizing that it's the first curse word that she's heard William utter. She'd nearly become convinced that he couldn't swear. "I would give anything to not worry about that man, but the thing is, he owns the rights to that song. To all my songs, actually."

William sits up in bed. "You're kidding. How did he manage to do that?"

Jane can't make eye contact with him. "I was young and dumb. I thought it was love." She sighs. "I don't know that I have enough excuses."

"So, what? He's pissed that you sang that song last night?"

"According to Roger, he's more than pissed. He didn't know where I went after I left Crescent. But now, he knows where I am."

"He knows where you *were*. He doesn't know we're still here."

She turns her phone toward him. On the screen is a flier advertising the show tonight. "True to his word, Jack is advertising. Roger sent me this."

The color drains from William's face. "Shit."

She's now impressed. That's two swear words she's heard from him. She's not sure why she isn't taking this more seriously, but maybe it's being with William that's freeing her mind. Maybe she just knows deep down that for any kind of freedom, she'll have to face Benny sometime. Maybe sooner is better than later.

"We're not going to cancel the show, if that's what you're thinking."

He seems surprised by this response to their dilemma. "Of course we'll cancel. He could show up tonight and cause all kinds of problems."

"That's true, he could; probably he will. But I'm tired of him. I hadn't seen him in years before this week, but now I feel haunted by him. It's like my life wasn't actually moving forward until now. And now that it is, he's trying to drag me back, and I'm not letting him."

She's struggling for her breath to catch up with her thoughts. Suddenly she's furious, not at William, but at that bastard of an ex-husband. Who does he think he is, kicking her out and then coming back and making demands of her?

"So, yes, we're playing that show tonight." She jumps up out of the bed and starts pacing. "He's not stopping me from rediscovering my love for music. He won't. And he can't stop me from playing the songs that I wrote." The last two words blast out of her, maybe a little too loudly.

"Hey, Jane." William's soft voice sounds even quieter in contrast with her own. "I know you're feeling a lot of passion right now, but it's early, and I don't want you to wake the neighbors."

Jane leaps like she's been goosed and holds a hand over her mouth. "I forgot we were in a hotel."

He's laughing, his whole body reacting to her moment of embarrassment. "It happens."

She laughs along with him, then grabs him and plants a big kiss on his lips. "We're playing tonight?"

He kisses her back. "We're playing."

The kissing becomes more physical as they lie in bed together. They're well-rested, frustrated, hopeful, bitter, and excited. It's a raging roller coaster of emotions.

She is sure that brunch was created for people who have nothing to do after a morning of lovemaking. They are high from the orgasms and ravenous from the exercise. Brunch gives one the ability to refill the fuel, and drinking a mimosa brings them down from that high. That has to be why it has suddenly caught on as one of the most popular times to eat now.

The restaurant is busy, but they manage to get a table back in the corner away from the morning light. They enjoy sitting across from each other, wearing yesterday's clothes like it's a joke only they get. The food is better than anything she has ever tasted. At least that's what she thinks, but maybe she's just that hungry.

They spend the afternoon shopping, trying to find the right outfit for what may be a large show for them. They hop from thrift store to thrift store and finally have enough cool items to make them appear somewhat attractive. And different enough from what they wore the night before so they won't look like eccentrics.

With that task completed, they decide to see the most important site in Colorado Springs: Garden of the Gods. The red rocks rise up out of the ground like fingers, a truly magnificent and mesmerizing sight to behold. They roll into the parking lot and walk up to the colossal red giants, their gasps of wonder heard every few seconds as they gain ground on the rocks. In her travels through Colorado, Jane never had a chance to see the Garden.

"Have you ever been?" She's holding William's hand, but he's leading the way, so she directs the question to the back of his head. He keeps walking but turns his head slightly to answer.

"Once. I came by here several years ago, but clearly I have missed a sight worth seeing."

When they get into the main part of the park, she stops and gazes around. "Where is the ticket booth?"

William pauses to face her. "What do you mean?"

"I mean, where do we pay?"

He chuckles. "Well, believe it or not, the park is free."

"Free? You're kidding?"

He takes her hand and walks her to what appears to be one of the largest rock formations. There, a sign can be found that gives all the information about the park, including the fact that it was donated to the city as long as it remained free for all time. Jane reads the sign several times just to make sure she's reading correctly. "Free." Her voice comes out in a near whisper, just loud enough for William to hear. He's all smiles as he looks at her.

"Pretty incredible, right?"

The rest of that afternoon, they find spot after spot to climb, run, and generally act like children. They go back to the car at one point to drive farther into the park to find a giant boulder that is seemingly standing without the interference of gravity. They hike along a trail, pausing every now and then to appreciate the beauty or to kiss. There's something about being in nature that makes her feel the emotion between them even more fully.

She sits for a rest on a large rock, staring down at the trees below. William continues walking, stepping up on another higher part of the red rocks. Jane pulls her phone from her pocket and snaps a photo of him. He looks like an explorer finding the land for the first time. She smiles at the picture, but as she goes to put her phone away, something catches her eye just below William. She sucks in a breath as she realizes that a mule deer is bedded down in the shade of the rock. His antlers curl up from his head, and his jaw works back and forth, chewing.

She lifts a hand, slowly, and waves it at William. Finally, he sees her, and she points below him. He takes off his sunglasses to see what's there. She watches as he pulls his phone out and takes a picture of the deer. She continues to watch him and wonders about the lives of deer out here in the wilds of Colorado. It makes her shiver. She is overwhelmed by the idea. The moment makes her think of another William Wordsworth poem where he said, "Dull would he be of soul who could pass by." How many others walked right by this area on their way from point A to point B and ignored the beauty of nature around them? Her soul takes a gulp of the sight before it and feels renewed.

She hopes that her music later that day will have a similar impact on the people coming to see her.

Chapter 43

The discovery of a creative outlet is life-changing and more addictive than any known substance. There is peace in the creative process that helps people deal with the darkest of days. Music, the writing of songs, and the composition of chords can bring a calm to the soul similar to what the Romantic poets described when sitting in nature. Wordsworth meant a viewing of the city of London when he suggested that someone who passed by would be "dull of soul," but the same sentiment is true of anyone who doesn't appreciate the creative process to its very core.

Creativity is beautiful, but then sharing that creation can likewise be wonderful. Getting to show a novel to a reader, a sculpture to an art lover, or a song to the listener, the process of presenting one's work is both terrifying and wonderful. It's a feeling that Jane will carry with her up onto the stage that night at the Miner's Delight. She'll be there because some people enjoy her voice or find meaning in her songs.

On the drive to the bar, she has the radio blasting 90's music, and she sings along to every word she remembers and makes up the ones she doesn't. William joins her, and the blending of their two voices is as beautiful as a teenager's first crush. At one point the music breaks and the DJ comes on, talking about local things going down. Jane tunes out the DJ until she hears her name, well, her former name.

"That's right, Clara Rigdon is playing tonight in Colorado Springs. She emerged from nowhere last night, taking the whole place by surprise. No one has heard from Clara in years; at the height of her career, she simply vanished. Suddenly, she's back and playing tonight at the Miner's Delight. If you loved nineties music, then you already know her. Get down to the Springs tonight and have a great time."

She turns to William, her mouth formed into a large O. His expression is a mirror of hers. "That was incredible, right? How did Jack manage to get word out so quickly?"

"I have no idea. Jane, this might be the biggest show I've ever played."

"Well, let's hope it's a good one then." She laughs to show that she's not nervous, but on the inside, she's screaming. She wanted this, she did, but now that it's actually here, the nerves start to come back. Nerves are pretty funny like that. "Let's get there!" William pushes a little harder on the gas, and they swing over into the fast lane.

Once they arrive at the bar, she's impressed with the number of people hanging out outside. They drive by, sort of slowly, to take in the twenty or thirty people out on the sidewalk. "It looks like the advertisement is working."

William heads to the end of the block and turns back to the right. Jack called earlier to tell them that with the number of people they are expecting, they could park in one of the private spots in the alley. William quickly finds the spot and throws the car into park. "Are you nervous?" He stares straight ahead, not looking to her to see her reaction to this question.

"Damn right I am. Being nervous is the best way to remind yourself that you still have a heartbeat. Can you feel it?"

He laughs and steals a glance at her. "I can. Thank you for this. Not sure I deserve it at all."

"If not you, then who?" She doesn't wait for an answer but leans into him and kisses his lips. "Let's do this."

They get out of the car, grabbing the two guitar cases from the backseat. She takes a lingering look at William, appreciating the white button-up shirt that he only has buttoned halfway. It has blue thread swirling through it and matches the maroon jeans he managed to find at one of the thrift stores. Of course he has his fedora to top it all off.

"You're beautiful." She says it without thinking. She's completely overwhelmed by the sight of him, and the words slip out.

He stops and smiles, sort of shyly, at her. "You think so?" He's not being silly but genuinely means it.

She nods, and he holds out a hand, and she takes it. They walk in the back door, past the extra cases of beer and the spare kegs. They also pass the small office where Jack let them hide out the night before. She isn't sure what she was upset about now, and she's glad she didn't chase this guy off.

"Hey, Jack, we're here." The two walk into the main bar, which is empty except for Jack and a couple of other guys wearing black shirts. Based on the size of them, she guesses they must be the extra security needed at events like this. Jack perks up when he sees them, a smile wide enough to compete with the Rockies on his face.

"Here they are! The heroes of the evening." He runs up to them and actually hugs them, both at the same time. His excitement bleeds into them, and her nervousness diminishes in the aura he's giving off.

"I don't know that we're heroes," she says.

"Sure, you are. We're going to open the doors in about two hours. You guys can go ahead and start setting up. As soon as you're ready, I'll get you an Old Fashioned mixed up."

"Don't you mean an Iron Ored Fashioned?"

Jack laughs, his head thrown back at the ceiling so that the sound bounces around the room. "You like that? I came up with it myself!"

Before she can respond, William interrupts, or his stomach does with a big growl. She says, "Hey, Jack, could you scrounge up some food for us? We sort of missed lunch, hanging out in the Garden of the Gods."

Jack beams at them. "Of course I can!"

They head back into the theater and start setting up the guitars and microphones. Jack talked his sound guy into coming in early so they could do an actual soundcheck. They run through a couple of tunes. Since the word is out that Clara will be performing, they work on a couple of her more difficult ones. It helps remind Jane of what she's given up for Benny. Just singing some of the words again makes her want to cry.

With the soundcheck over, the two of them set up the merch table with what little merch they have left. "It would be fantastic if I sold out of CDs. I probably won't order any more."

"Really? You don't think you'll sell more?" She grabs one and stares down at the cover. It's just a black and white photo of William in front of a brick wall, but it does seem like it must be at least fifteen years old.

"Everyone wants vinyl now. When I got the CDs, people were just starting to get into vinyl again. Now it's all the rage."

"So you think you'll get this pressed into vinyl?"

"Maybe. Or maybe I'll record a new record. That could be a lot of fun."

"It could be." She sets up a row of CDs. "What's stopping you?"

"Money." The answer is flat, but exactly what she expected. Money is the central thing that prevents creative people from being able to create. She was lucky to be able to record whenever she wanted to for so long.

"Maybe someday."

William sighs. "Maybe someday."

They eat their combination of lunch and dinner in one of the booths in the bar. Jack kindly ordered them sandwiches from the deli next door. The sandwiches, along with chips and two Old Fashioned cocktails, are in their bellies, so they are more than prepared for the show.

"Hey, guys," Jack says to them once they've finished eating. "I have quite a line out there. If you would like to move to the office, I can go ahead and open the doors."

"Planning to make as much money as you can on the bar tabs tonight, huh, Jack?" She arches her eyebrow at him, and Jack has the decency to appear embarrassed.

"Well…" He shrugs.

"We'll get out of your way." William stands and takes her hand. "Don't give him too much crap. I really like that kid."

"I do, too, which is why I give him crap."

The two of them head backstage, their laughter the start of the music for the night.

Chapter 44

In the small enclosure of the office, Jane finds that she can't take her eyes off William. "I'm getting old, William. I guess you already noticed that." She's not sure what she's going to say as she begins this conversation, but she allows the bourbon to work through her, giving her the guidance. "I want you to know that I'm excited about this." She runs an index finger from her chest to his, drawing an invisible line from her to him. "And I hope you are as well. But what I want to say is, if you're in on this, so am I."

Warmth rushes up to her cheeks as the words echo back through her mind. She's not drunk, but her inhibitions have lowered enough that she's able to say the things she's thinking. Words have sometimes escaped her mouth when her brain was off in the back room checking algebraic equations her high school math teachers made her learn. Sometimes it could cause unwanted results. Other times it worked in her favor, and she would thank that long-forgotten math teacher.

William takes a sip of his drink and sets it on the desk. Her heart speeds up a bump or two when he's looking away. She's certain he's going to deny her. But when he looks back up, his eyes are earnest, and she can see the emotion there. "I'm getting older, too," he says, his voice thick with emotion. "I'll be your guy as long as you'll have me."

After they kiss, they stand together with their foreheads touching, both of them knowing they've crossed an important threshold. Finally, William smiles. "Let's go get them."

The knock at the office door tells them that it's time. Jack's smile is bigger than it's ever been. "Are you guys ready? They're ready for you!"

Beyond Jack, Jane can hear the crowd. It's a low murmur, but one that means more than just a few dozen people have come out tonight.

She's been nervous before, but never like this. She can't feel her legs as they carry her to the stage. William's hand is in hers, and once more, she's like a balloon that he's holding down to the earth. The lights hit her, and she watches, half-blind, as her hand, no longer holding William's, reaches out for the guitar. All of it sinks into her, bringing her feet back in contact with the wooden stage. She can do this.

With that guitar strapped around her, she transforms back into that performer that she once was. The confidence washes over her like she's being baptized in rock n' roll. She steps up to the microphone, her guitar draped over her shoulder. "Hello. My name is Clara." The crowd interrupts her with cheers. She beams at them. "But you can call me Jane," she adds once the crowd quiets. They cheer louder for this.

At the other microphone, William says, "And we're just a Bag of Bones."

In their off time that afternoon, they'd rehearsed a couple of ways to begin the show, and that was what they finally settled on. Introductions finished, they launch into their first song and never look back. They don't just play the one Clara song tonight but work in several more.

She still hasn't finished her new song, so it won't be in the lineup. So, for now, she's back in the past, rocking songs she hasn't played in years, but the crowd is there with her, singing along to every word. It's like she disappeared, but her music didn't. They've just been waiting for this day to come back.

The first set ends, and she's sweaty but excited. Normally, she would have had an opener so she could just play one set. But William plays shows like this all the time, playing for three or four hours to ensure he gets the most money he can from the night. After one set, she's exhausted, but he's as excited as Jack about the show.

They head back to the office for their fifteen-minute break. "Can you believe how much fun this is?" William asks her. She giggles at his joy. She can't help it; he's just so childlike.

"It is wonderful." She thinks back on when she used to play, something she supposes that she'll always do. She once looked forward to playing every single note, every single song. A part of her awakens to the crowd and to the music, and she finds herself getting excited all over again about the prospect of playing more.

Jack shows up with a drink for them. "You guys are so great." The joy he'd exhibited the night before is at least doubled tonight. Probably because he's making a ton of money tonight. "Everyone wants to talk to you guys, to meet you. They're bombarding the bar, asking about you guys." He laughs. "And they're buying all the drinks! I've got my two security guys running the bar to help me. I've got to get back out there. Take your time!"

And with that, Jack is gone. They stand in the silence of the moment, the echoes of the words, and the renewed murmur of the crowd their only soundtrack. For some reason, she thinks of the bookshop and what song could be playing in there at this exact moment. Maybe something by Lou Reed.

She turns to William, wanting to ask him how he feels about the show so far, but before she can get the words out, his lips are smashed into hers and his arms are wrapped around her body. She returns the passion, kissing him in every way that she knows how. She pours her heart into it, showing him without words exactly how she feels about him.

He pulls back, keeping his forehead pressed to hers. His breathing is on par with having just finished a major workout. "Thank you for this."

"For what, exactly?" Their voices are whispers that come out between gulps of air.

"For coming to my show, for letting me kiss you, for giving me at least one great night of playing music. Do you know how long I've been doing this?" He lets her go, grabs his drink, and downs it. "I've been playing so long and never thought I'd play for a crowd like that. Oh, I dreamed it, but dreams only get you so far, you know?"

She's smiling at his mania. It's like he wants to say a lot but doesn't quite have the words for it. Or the words aren't enough. He sets the empty glass down and paces what little he can in the small office. "I've just always wanted shows like this. I've always thought about what it would be like to have the crowd singing along. Sure, they're not my songs, but they're yours, and you've let me be a part of it."

She pulls him back to her. "Take a breath, William. This is yours. Without you, we wouldn't be playing this. Enjoy it."

He laughs, a kind of maniacal burst that perfectly illustrates his state of mind. He kisses her, once, on the lips, and in that kiss, she can feel the love coursing through him. She could spend the rest of her life trying to make him as happy as he is now.

"Let's go play some more."

In response, he takes her hand, and she gets to lead him out to the stage.

Chapter 45

Jane and William, the Bag of Bones, are blazing through the second song of their second set when Jane sees him: that uptight prick who looks out of place in a bar like this. His black suit probably cost more than the entire liquor collection on the shelf behind the bar. When she sees him, she doesn't shy away. It's as if when she announced that she would be known as Jane instead of Clara, something switched inside of her. She doesn't feel as afraid of him now.

Their eyes meet as she sings the next song, one that she wrote about him. When they'd had a particularly rough patch, she'd written an apology in the form of a song that wasn't really apologizing for anything. He had been too dense to see it for anything other than another one of her songs, and when she wrote songs, he knew he could make more money. The apology had worked, but every time she sang the song after that, she could smile to herself, knowing that he didn't get it.

"I'm sorry for saying what I thought." The chorus of the song rings out over the crowd, several of them singing along. "I'm sorry for being what I'm not. I'm sorry for giving it all I've got." She realizes now that the only thing Benny heard in the lyrics of this song was the words "I'm sorry." She belts them out now, knowing in her heart that she's not sorry and never has been.

Benny hangs around the back of the crowd, not

getting too close to the patrons of this fine establishment. And as they near the end of the set, Jane knows some kind of confrontation is coming. She decides that she won't call for the bouncers and won't have them boot him out but will allow this to happen. She's tired of running from it. Before the last song of the set, she steps over to William. "Benny is here." His eyes widen and cast around the audience looking for him. "Don't worry about it. I just wanted you to be aware so you can be ready for whatever is going to happen next."

William sees she's serious and smiles at her. "I'm with you."

Their last song is a slow one that William wrote, one that drifts through the room, bringing everyone to a somber place. It's a nice way to end the set. Again, Jack walks them back to the office, a cocktail in each hand for them. They enter the small room, sipping at their drinks, the door closing behind them.

"How long do you think he'll be?" William asks. She can tell he's nervous, and she is too, but she also thinks she's ready.

"Just another minute, I'm sure." She takes another sip, and there's a knock on the door. She smiles. "Right on time."

She opens the door, and Benny is standing there. Up close she can see that he's not as put together as she assumed. Black bags hang from his eyes like a three-day hangover. His hair is disheveled, and his suit is wrinkled. "Benny?" He doesn't even smile at her; the cockiness and arrogance are completely gone. This doesn't look like the man she married.

"Hello, Clara." Half of his former charm comes into his smile, but she can still see the worry there.

"What is going on with you, Benny?" She steps back, really worried about this new man she's seeing.

He steps into the space that she occupied, turns that half-smile toward William, and shuts the door to the office. "I told you when I saw you last that I needed money. I wasn't kidding. I know you have new songs that you want to record, and I need that to happen. Now."

She shakes her head. "I don't have any new songs. I stopped playing. That's why you divorced me. Remember that?"

The declaration doesn't seem to affect him. "You've been out here with him, so you've probably been writing some songs in your free time. What are you not understanding?"

William steps up beside Jane. She can see the effort he has to put into this action, and she loves him for it. "We haven't had time to write songs. We've just been working on the songs for the set. It's not like we can just play without practicing."

Benny doesn't break eye contact with Jane. "You need to back down, William. This is between the two of us."

"I will not back down." She thinks for a second that he's misquoting a Tom Petty song. Before she can register that he's standing up for her, Benny moves toward him. Time slows, as it always does in a traumatic situation, but it also speeds up. One second, William and Benny are right beside her; the next, Benny has collided with William, who hits the desk and then the floor. Benny stands and runs his left hand through his hair, attempting to get it back into place. The other hand holds a bloody knife. Jane goes cold at the sight of it.

Her eyes find William. He has a hand pressed to his

side, where she can see blood spurting up between his fingers. She gasps. "What have you done? William, are you all right?"

She moves to crouch beside him, but Benny grabs her, holding the knife up for her to see. "I didn't want to do that. Listen to me." He slams her against the wall to get her attention. "I didn't want to do that," he roars at her, spit flying from his mouth into her face, and she's reminded of all the times he did this to her when they were married, all the times he bore down on her and screamed at her. "I just need some money."

She holds up her hands, not feeling the fear that she once would have, but at least understanding the limitations she has at the moment. She has to get out of this situation; then she can let the cops handle it. She has to approach it cleverly. "Benny, listen to me. I'm not lying to you. I haven't written any songs. I have started a new one, but I haven't been able to finish it. If you hadn't stabbed William, we could have finished our set, and you could have had the money from the bar. From the looks of the crowd, we would have made enough."

Rage boils up through his face. If she'd hoped her words would calm him down, she couldn't have been more wrong. He slams his hand into the wall beside her head over and over again. She's certain that he'll break the wall if he keeps going and prays that he will. That could bring Jack back and maybe save her from this. She can't believe that she had the chance to call for the bouncers and didn't do it. She thought she could casually dismiss Benny, but she wasn't prepared for the desperation in him. A man willing to stab someone is a man willing to do anything to get his way.

She swallows the bile that's worked into the back of

her mouth. She knows what she has to do. She doesn't have a lot of choice if she wants to help William. His life is dripping out of him. "I don't have any songs ready, Benny, but I can get one ready."

She closes her eyes. She swallows again to keep from crying. But the promise works, and Benny backs away from her. His smile is back in place, the one he always showed when Jane played for a sellout crowd. Just looking at him gloating makes Jane want to take a shower.

She kneels down next to William, who hasn't moved. "I'm going to go with him, William. Jack will find you and get you help. Do you understand?"

He nods but grabs her with one bloody hand. "You don't have to go. He needs you. He won't kill you."

She brushes at his face, tears welling in her eyes. "But he doesn't need you."

William's eyes grow as he understands what she means. She's going with Benny not for herself but for William. He lets go of her, his hand going back to cover the puncture wound in his side. "I think I love you, Jane."

She shakes her head. "Now's not the time, William." A burst of laughter jumps out of her mouth. "But I love you, too."

"How touching." Benny grabs her and pulls her up. "We have to go."

He pulls her out of the office, pausing just to make sure no one is in the hallway to find them. With one last look over her shoulder, she makes eye contact with William's gray eyes and keeps that image with her. She thinks she really does love him.

Chapter 46

The cold mountain air feels good on Jane's skin after the heat of the office. She walks willingly because she doesn't want Benny to touch her. The mad look in his eye has not left, and she still can't believe that he actually stabbed someone. Her heart is breaking at the thought of William sitting there on the office floor. She just hopes that he'll get the help he needs and that he'll forgive her for leaving him.

Eventually they make it to Benny's car. She climbs in, buckles her seatbelt, and stares out the windshield. As soon as they pull away from the curb, she pulls out her phone to call an ambulance. Benny snags the phone before she can unlock it. "What do you think you're doing?"

"Give it back. You got what you wanted; now let me call an ambulance for William." She's not sure what she's going to do when Benny gets them wherever they're going. She has no other song ideas for this man, and whatever he threatens her with will just make her shut down even more. She has no desire to work with him or for him. She just needs to make sure that William is safe.

Benny seems to be thinking about whether or not he'll let her call. Finally, he sighs and hands her the phone. "I didn't want any of this, you know. Why couldn't you just make it easy? Why couldn't you just give me a song without me having to resort to violence? You think I wanted to stab that man?"

She's not even listening. The moment she has her phone, she's dialing emergency services. When she finally gets through, she's relieved to learn that someone has already found William and an ambulance is on the way. "Are you all right, ma'am?" The voice coming through the phone, the dispatcher, sounds like a young female. She has a kind voice despite what must be an unkind job at times.

"Yes, I'm fine."

"Are you the woman who was with him? Did you stab him?"

Jane doesn't look toward Benny. She can tell he's getting nervous with every second she stays on the line. It won't be long before he takes the phone again. "No, I didn't."

"That's what we thought. If you'll stay on the phone, ma'am, I'll get you some help."

Before Jane can respond, Benny pulls the phone from her hand and tosses it out his window. "That's enough of that. I suppose he's going to get some help."

The rage springs up in her unbidden, and she finds herself wanting to scream. In the past, she never would have allowed herself. But she's no Clara, who would sit by and watch from the sidelines; she's Jane, and when Jane wants to scream, she screams.

"What the fuck is wrong with you?" The curse word feels necessary and somehow makes the scream seem louder in the small car. The car jerks to the left, and he tries to get control of himself and the car.

"Clara, calm down. You're acting crazy."

"*I'm* acting crazy? Have you looked at yourself

lately?" She considers grabbing the wheel and taking them off the road, but the likelihood of her getting killed with him is far too great. Besides, she doesn't think she's in actual danger since he needs her for something. However, after she writes a song for him, who knows if she'll be in danger then?

"I know this isn't ideal." Benny suddenly seems afraid of her, of her surprising outbursts. She's never spoken to him like this. Couple that with whatever is happening in his life, and she's certain his world is crumbling.

"Of course this isn't ideal, Benny! I was living a perfectly normal life, a fine life. And you had to come back and cause so many problems. As if being married to you wasn't enough. You had to come and destroy the life I had after the divorce as well." Fat, hot tears have started rolling down her cheeks, but she doesn't care. The fact that it's her anger bringing them on and not him makes her enjoy the tears.

He drives in silence, staring at the highway as the town disappears behind them. Jane stares at the yellow lines coming toward them in the car's headlights. She doesn't care why Benny needs a new song so badly or why he needs money. All she cares about is if she can give him what he wants, and maybe he'll let her go. A quiet voice in the back of her mind reminds her that the next time he needs money, he'll probably show back up. But she'll deal with that when it happens. That same voice reminds her that she thought the same thing when she saw him in the club. She didn't think he could stab a man.

Her anger dissipates in the silence of the drive, and she finds herself thinking of William and hoping he's all right. She hopes that he doesn't hate her for running off on him. The thoughts of him take her back to the highway with him when they drove north toward Colorado, the Rockies on their horizon, and none of this nonsense with it. William talked on that trip and told stories about being out on the road and how much fun he would have. "Sometimes," he'd said, "I just want to drive, you know? Take the highways, the interstates, whatever comes my way. You can find yourself on a beach or in a city, whatever." She'd thought it romantic at the time, the sort of romantic idea that highways deserve.

"I've gotten myself into trouble." Benny's voice is hoarse. He doesn't take his eyes away from the highway as he speaks, doesn't dart his eyes over to see if she's listening. "I'm afraid I've made some bad deals and have managed to make some enemies. If you can make a successful song, maybe I'll be okay. That's what I keep telling myself anyway. I don't have other plans."

"You don't have any other plans." He nods. She asks him, "What about the royalties from my catalog? Surely that's kept you afloat. I mean, I haven't gotten any of it, and I'm managing all right." The anger and bitterness start to slide back into her voice.

He shifts uncomfortably in his chair. "The royalties have slowed down. People don't seem to care about you as much as they once did. But a new song could change their minds."

"Yeah, I got it. A new song is all you care about. Did you see that crowd back there?" She points behind them as if the club is right there. "They cared."

"It's not enough."

He clicks on the radio to indicate the end of the

conversation. A song drifts over the inside of the car, and Jane, like so many other times in her life, allows the song to swirl over her, to carry her away. Of course the song that plays with that hated man right next to her is "Landslide" by Fleetwood Mac. She hums along and thinks about walking around Guthrie with William. Sometimes the best moments in life are the simplest, and she never realizes how important those moments are until they are gone.

She leans her head back. She doesn't know if she'll be able to help Benny with his problem, but she knows she'll try. Maybe she'll come out on the other side of this and be able to escape this man for real this time. With thoughts like those, she slowly drifts off to sleep.

Chapter 47

Jane wakes up in the middle of a city. Benny is talking on the phone, his voice rising to a level of manic she has only ever heard from him earlier when he stabbed William. She rubs at her face and looks around, trying to get her bearings. She's not sure where they are. She can still see the mountains, so they haven't driven too far, but currently, they're just sitting in the car on the side of the street. She dreams of home, of being away from this nightmare, of waking up inside of her bookshop after having drifted off reading a romance novel. Instead, she's still here.

"Where are we?" She's not really asking Benny but wondering out loud about her current situation.

"We're at the studio." He puts the phone down so he can speak to her. "I can't get the owner down here to let us in. He doesn't seem to understand the situation."

"You're on the phone with the owner of the studio, and he doesn't want to come down here? What time is it?"

"I don't know. Four or something."

She shakes her head. "What are you even doing?"

Benny goes back to speaking into the phone, really letting the guy have it the way he did with club owners back in the day. She continues to gaze around at the buildings around her. Her mind isn't quite awake yet, and she can't quite make sense of anything. Finally,

Benny hangs up.

"He's on his way. He finally came to see reason after all." Benny's smile is larger than any Jane has ever seen on his face. Or maybe it's just the weird shadows making his face look strange, but she's certain he appears demented. She is reminded of a tiger preparing to pounce on its prey. "Do you have any ideas for songs?"

I just want to go home. She thinks again of William saying he would drive anywhere, any highway, as long as it took him somewhere. She only wants to be driving on I-40 or I-35 at the moment. One of those highways taking her home. That sparks some memory in her head. Something William said, or sang, maybe?

"I've got an idea, but what are you going to do when the police come? You stabbed a man and kidnapped a woman, and I know I'm half asleep, but we didn't drive far enough to get out of state. Are we in Denver?"

"The cops can't find us. This is my only chance. You don't understand."

Jane shakes her head, understanding the situation better than Benny clearly does. She decides to speak no more on the subject but just wait silently until the sound engineer arrives to let them in. As she stares out the window, contemplating this stupid situation, she remembers the line that William sang to her. "I wanna drive down I-35." She thinks she can even remember the chord progression if she sits down with a guitar. It feels like betrayal, stealing William's song so she doesn't have to give Benny the one she's actually been writing. Surely William will understand.

A car pulls up beside Benny's. One lone man gets out, slamming the car door behind him. He walks up to the door of the studio and unlocks it. Before going in, he looks around, spots Benny and Jane sitting in Benny's car, and waves them over. Then, without waiting, he enters the building.

"There he is. Let's go!"

Benny hops out of the car and starts moving toward the building. Jane is a little slower, her thoughts still on which chord to start the verse with, but the chill in the air wakes her up, and she rushes to get to the studio.

Once inside, they make their way down a long hallway that is lined with photos of people singing and playing in a studio. There are a couple that she recognizes, but the rest are newer faces, people she wouldn't know if their music was playing right now. The carpet is plush underfoot, an orange-and-brown patterned floor that makes her think of the seventies. There's a faint odor of cigarettes and weed. They are in Colorado, where pot is perfectly legal, after all.

At the end of the hall is a large room made up like a living room. There they find the engineer, slamming things onto a counter. She is excited to see that he's making coffee. The chairs in the room look overlarge and inviting. She is so tired she almost wishes she could simply curl up in one and sleep. But life, oftentimes, is not fair, and this feels like one of those times. Still, the room has a homey feel that she just loves. The art in here showcases more bands, actual albums framed on the walls, and a fairly large TV.

"Go on, make yourselves at home. I'm not doing anything until I get some coffee." The engineer's voice is deep, full of sleep. Though bald, he does have a large beard that could use a brush, and the t-shirt he's wearing looks like he might have picked it up off the floor to wear in. Once the pot is brewing, he turns to face them finally.

He ignores Benny but smiles warmly enough at her.

"Clara, I'm excited to finally meet you. I wish it were better circumstances." He gives Benny the slightest of glances.

She reaches out to take his hand. "Nice to meet you. But please, call me Jane. I'm afraid the only Clara around here was married to this guy." She pokes her thumb in Benny's direction, which earns a laugh from the engineer.

"I'm Zack, by the way." He shakes her hand, and any temper he showed when he first arrived is completely gone as he speaks to her. Clearly that will not be the case when it comes to Benny. Zack doesn't look like a producer from the seventies but more like a middle school principal with his bald head and beard.

She lets go of Zack's hand. "Is there any way I can go in the studio? I'm not exactly sure what I'm going to record."

Zack nods along, clearly eager for her to enter the studio, until she says that last part. His face regains some of the purple it had when he was slamming things to make coffee. "Sorry," she says, hoping to stifle some of that anger. He doesn't look at her but turns his glare on Benny. Finally he huffs out a large breath and says, "Come on."

He grabs a mug and fills it with coffee from the still-percolating pot, something Jane always avoids. She's not sure why, but when she drinks from a pot that is still brewing, it's too strong. She follows him to another door. Benny starts to come too, but she turns to him and holds up a hand. "Stay here. I've never been able to write with you in the room, and you know it. It's not like I'm going to run away."

She doesn't wait for him but turns back to the door, following Zack. The door, as it turns out, leads right into the engineering room. It's not super large, but it's big enough to fit three or four people comfortably. There's even a couch. The soundboard faces a large window. The lights are still off in the actual studio, but as soon as Zack flips the switch, Jane sees a large room with instruments and microphones scattered around. It is the quintessential picture of a studio, and her pulse quickens as she stares into the room.

"This is wonderful." Her words barely come out.

Zack smiles, not speaking, allowing her to take in the surroundings. Finally, he breaks the silence. "It's exactly what I wanted a studio to look like. I worked really hard on it."

"You nailed it." She doesn't look at him but stares at the space she wants to be hers. "Can I?"

"By all means."

She enters the recording room. She ignores the grand piano, finding it beautiful but not her instrument of choice. Instead, she heads to the acoustic guitar propped up on a stand. The name Gibson is written across the top. The body of the guitar is large, but it fits perfectly on her leg when she sits down.

She's able to, for the moment at least, close her eyes and close away Benny and the reason she's in this room. Instead, she thinks about music and the reason she has always loved it. Then she poises her fingers to play.

Chapter 48

When Jane feels the pressure of the strings against the tips of her fingers, the weight and shape of the guitar in her lap, and the first chords of a song she's about to write, she can let the worry and pain from the past few hours fade right away. She closes her eyes and strums the guitar, knowing the placement of her fingers by heart. Forget Benny, she says to herself as her hands find the next chord; this is all for me and always has been.

"I wanna drive," she sings again, "down I-35 and find a place to feel alive." She pictures William singing that line to her. He didn't have an idea of where to go next, just that one line. She hesitates for a moment before singing more. "And I wanna be where the sand and sky meet." She strums the next chord and wonders what William would say next. She pictures him in the bookshop, buying that copy of poetry from Robert Browning. She smiles and sings, "And find the poetry of city streets."

She sings through the chorus a couple more times, really belting it out. After the third time, Zack's voice comes over the speaker. "That sounds great. Do you have a verse yet?"

Jane laughs. "Give me a second."

It takes longer than a second, but she is working with someone else's tools here. This guitar isn't hers, and neither is the idea behind the song. She's got to overcome that. Zack brings her a pad of paper, a pencil, and a cup of hot coffee. She thanks him, barely registering that he's there. She sips her coffee and writes three lines on the paper, takes another sip, and writes another three lines. She hardly blinks before the first verse is completely written. She reads over it, changes one word, then drops the pencil to replace it with the guitar pick.

She sings those lines, opting for a more mellow verse before hitting the chorus hard. Once more, Zack's voice comes over the loudspeaker. "That's great. Want me to start recording?"

"Not yet."

Another ten minutes of sipping coffee, writing words, and strumming chords, and she nearly has it. She looks toward the viewing window. "Zack? What do you think?"

"I think it needs a killer bridge to bring it home. But you're almost there. I know a drummer in town. Mind if I call him?"

Jane gives the thumbs-up, a huge smile on her face. For the engineer to go from pissed to excited enough to get another guy out of bed for this, she knows she must be doing something right. But she needs a bridge. Before the muse leaves her, she grabs the pencil once more and starts writing. The bridge comes with a little more difficulty, like a strawberry seed stuck between her teeth. She gets it eventually, but she feels like she's used every muscle in her body to make it happen.

"Zack?"

"Yeah?"

"I'm ready to run through it. Can you record it?"

"Got you."

Jane plugs the guitar in directly, grabs the headphones on the microphone, and steps up, ready to sing. She places her lyrics on the music stand and smiles to herself. She realizes that Benny hasn't been inside the studio to check on them. It's a mark of just how desperate he is that he hasn't been trying to control her at all. She wonders briefly what he's been doing out there by himself, but then she realizes that she doesn't care.

She strums through the chorus chords as her introduction and then mellows it out for the verse. "Some days waking up is hard when you've got nothing to wake up for. I just need to get myself away and go in search of a little space." She blazes through the song, singing each line as if she's been singing them for years. On the bridge she has a little trouble, but she makes it through anyway. She'll be able to solidify it when she actually records the song with the drummer. For now, she's just trying to get a demo of the song so she knows exactly what to do.

The end of the song comes at her before she realizes she doesn't know how to end it. She'd spent so much time making sense of the bridge that the song ending wasn't planned. She goes through the chorus and decides to go through it one more time, striking the chords instead of strumming them. She lets the music ring out and then ends it with a little background music and the final lines of the chorus. She loves it, and as soon as the chord is finished ringing out, she laughs. "That felt really good."

"That was great." Zack is giving her a thumbs-up from the control booth. "Want to take a break until Mark gets here?"

"Sure." She pulls off the headphones and sets down the guitar. The chorus of the song still runs through her head, and she hums along. She usually takes that as a strong indication that the song is effective when it gets stuck in her head. She hopes that others will connect to it.

She pauses, and the euphoria she's been feeling drips slowly away. This song won't be hers, she realizes, but instead it will belong to a woman named Clara. But mostly, it will belong to her ex-husband, like so many other parts of her life do. She squeezes her hands into fists at the thought of his smug face, the one that she will see when he hears this song for the first time. He will know instantly that it'll be a hit, and it will give him the money he needs to continue to survive. Despite the strength she wants to show, tears sting the corners of her eyes again. She clenches them shut, trying to stop the emotion. She stands there, her body rigid in the middle of the recording studio.

Breathe. Just breathe, and everything will be fine. She takes her advice, pulling the air in through her nose and letting it out. Little by little, she loosens her fists.

"Hey, are you all right?"

Jane opens her eyes and finds Zack standing there in front of her. She tries her best to smile. "Sure, I am."

"Well, you look a little upset. You just came in here and made a great song out of nothing, so I'm not sure what you would be upset about."

She shakes her head. "Me neither." The smile comes more naturally as she says this. "I'm going to get some water."

She steps past him, but he lays a hand gently on her shoulder. She stops but doesn't turn toward him. Behind her he whispers, "If you need help, just nod."

She wants so badly to nod, but instead, she sighs

deeply and walks on. She finds Benny nervously pacing back and forth in the lounge like he's waiting to find out if his wife and new baby are going to survive. When she comes in, he stops and just makes eye contact with her. In the moment, all of the anger and fear she's ever felt toward him or because of him come rushing back into her system. She steps right up to him.

"I just wrote the best song of my life." His face lightens at these words. "But I am not giving it to you. No, listen," she adds when he begins to protest. "You'll be just fine. When I release this song, it will generate interest in my music, and you'll be able to make money off my old catalog. That's the deal I'll make with you."

His cheeks redden, and she knows she's on dangerous ground. His voice is quiet when he finally speaks. "We're not here to make deals. I'm paying for the studio, so the song is mine."

"Then I'll pay for the studio. Zack likes me better anyway."

Her head slams to the right before she even knows what happened. Her left cheek explodes in pain, and a small trickle of blood runs out of her nose. He slapped her. Not again; she will not go through this again. She lifts a hand to her cheek and glares up at him. She can't control the tears coming out of her eyes now. "Get the fuck out of here." Her voice is soft and dangerous.

He stands there, staring in her direction, but his eyes are vacant. He doesn't act like he's going to respond, so Jane turns her back on him. Behind her, a small word escapes from her ex-husband. "Please."

She turns back to him to make sure she heard correctly.

He still isn't looking at her. "Please, Clara," he

swallows, "Jane. You have no idea how badly I need this."

She throws her hands up. "That's not my problem, Benny. You're not my problem. Not anymore." She jabs his chest with her index finger to drive home the point. And then she walks away from him. She doesn't look back, though a small part of her expects him to come running after her. She keeps walking until she reaches the door to the recording booth. With the door closed between her and Benny, she sucks in a wet breath.

Chapter 49

She leans against the wall, fighting with her emotions that want to betray her. She doesn't want to cry, but the tears flow anyway. Her cheek throbs, and her heart breaks at the thought that she's allowed this man to push her around for so long.

"Hey." The hand lands on her shoulder along with the word, and she's startled, ready to fight. But the voice is one of kindness. She turns and finds Zack standing there. Without waiting for an invitation or even stopping to consider the fact that she just met him, she falls into his body and cries. He wraps his arms around her and whispers all the kind words that one does to a crying woman.

After a moment, she's able to get control of herself. She steps back, wiping at her face. "I'm sorry." She's always apologizing for something, but she is rarely to blame.

"It's not a problem. I saw what he did. I came to intervene, but you seemed to handle it. So I called the cops."

Zack's bald head reflects the overhead lights, and he wears brown-lensed sunglasses, despite the fact that he's inside. She likes him more than she ever thought she could have. "You called the police?"

"Yeah." He shrugs. "There was clearly something going on between you before you got here, and then he hit you. I can't believe he did that."

She smiles, the same joy she'd felt at being on stage earlier coming back to her now. "Thank you."

"Let's go see if Mark is here yet. I called Travis, the bass player, and a guy named Bert to come play some lead. We're going to make a great song today."

Zack leads the way back into the lounge. Surprisingly, Benny still stands where she left him, as if he's stuck or there's a glitch in his brain. He definitely seems like someone just discovering gravity and how to deal with it. His eyes dart from Jane to Zack and back again. He seems worried and crazier than he did when he stabbed William.

"Why are you still here?" Her voice booms in the quiet of the room. She can't help it; she wants to scream at him.

Zack lays a comforting hand on her shoulder. "It's OK. Just let him be."

She does, turning away from Benny. She walks over to one of the couches and hopes it's as comfortable as it looks. As it turns out, it is. She feels exhaustion catch up with her. It's been a long day and a longer night. She closes her eyes, her breaths coming slower and slower. Soon, she's driving down Interstate 35, windows down and a strong summer breeze blowing through the inside of the car. She slides her hand out the window and lets the wind carry it up and down. Then she opens her eyes. She's awake again in the lounge of the studio. People are talking; that must have been what woke her. She turns her head to see two police officers speaking with Benny.

"Sir, were you in Colorado Springs earlier tonight?" The officer speaking is a big man, one who could crack Benny's head between his hands as if it were a peanut.

Benny is staring up at the officer, and clearly, he's terrified. Zack comes over to where she's sitting on the couch. "I'm sorry. I tried not to wake you."

"Are you kidding? I wouldn't want to miss this." Jane smiles at his reaction; the truth sinks into her then. She is excited to see him get taken away in handcuffs. She's not looking forward to a trial and being dragged before a jury to be judged and questioned, but she is excited for him to be taken out of her life permanently.

"I wasn't in Colorado Springs. I've been here for three days. Check my credit card statements. Actually, you'll need a warrant to do that. I want my lawyer." Benny's words come rushing out with barely a breath between the sentences.

The cop glances over at Jane. "A woman was taken from a club there, a woman matching her description." He points at her. "Then we get a call for a domestic disturbance here. You seem to have some violent tendencies. Now, asking you the question about Colorado Springs was just a formality. We have security footage of you walking out of the building with her. There's also some from a building across the street of you climbing into a car that matches the one out in the parking lot." He puts his hands on his belt, the way police always seem to be doing. Jane is impressed with how quickly they managed to get all that information on Benny.

The other officer pulls his cuffs from his belt and walks behind Benny. "You're under arrest."

Watching Benny get arrested and have the Miranda rights read to him rejuvenates Jane's frazzled spirit. She wants to cheer, to stand up and applaud the heroes in blue. Finally, the smaller of the two officers walks Benny out to the patrol car while the larger man approaches her.

"Ma'am?" He opens a small notepad. "Are you Clara?"

She doesn't stand up but allows him to talk down to her. "I am."

"There are some people in Colorado Springs that are worried about you. They'll be pleased to know that you're all right."

"I'm glad to know that people care about me. Can you tell me how William is doing?"

The officer once more consults his notepad. "He had to have surgery, but he'll recover. Good news for your ex out there. He'll get charged with assault and possibly kidnapping, possibly attempted murder, but at least it won't be a full murder charge."

Jane nods. "I don't really care what happens to him now. I'm just thankful for you coming along."

"Would you like for me to arrange a ride back to the Springs?"

The question surprises her. She stares past the cop, thinking about heading back to that club. She pictures William sitting in his hospital bed, a series of tubes running out of his body, smiling despite the pain. She thinks about her guitar and the fans she left behind. There are likely news stories about her random disappearance from the bar. While she longs to see William, there is a certain allure to the song she's been working on. Behind the cop, a big, bearded guy walks in carrying a black rectangle, presumably a bass case. Behind him, a blond guy in tattoos comes in carrying a snare drum.

"Ma'am?"

Her attention snaps back to the officer. "Hmm?"

"Do you need a ride back to the Springs?"

She sucks in a breath and makes a decision. "I don't think I will yet. I've got some unfinished business here. Thank you, though."

"You are welcome. And can I just say that my wife is a huge fan? Could I maybe take a picture with you? She won't believe me otherwise." His smile is huge. Jane obliges, of course. Taking a picture is the least she can do for this hero. She stands, wraps an arm around the officer, and he snaps a selfie. "Thank you so much."

She smiles. "Tell your wife to be on the lookout for new music."

He actually laughs like he can hardly believe he gets to be the one to share this news with her. "I will. Thank you."

With the police officers gone, the studio once more transforms back into a studio, complete with a carnival lineup of musicians. She catches Zack's eye. "Thank you. Are you sure these guys know how to play?"

The two newcomers stop and scoff at her. Zack just laughs. "They know how to play."

The bearded guy throws in, "We didn't expect to come upon a crime scene."

She lets loose a laugh. Zack introduces her to Mark and Travis. They proceed to set up their gear in the studio, and finally Bert walks in. They start playing their instruments way too loudly, and Jane loves every minute of it.

"You ready to start?" Zack asks her.

She nods and smiles. "I've never been more ready."

She dives into the song. The guys that Zack brought in find the natural groove to the song, and they remain there. It's the kind of immediate chemistry that makes her wish this was her actual band. They blaze through the song, working and tweaking it. She finds the little bits she wasn't pleased with at first, and she polishes those. The song begins to live and breathe on its own, and she's the Dr. Frankenstein behind this new creation.

They play through the song five or six times to ensure everyone knows their parts. Then they record the drums. Mark is a machine, and he gets the drums down in one take. The bass is next, also in one take. Bert tries a few different licks with the lead, and Jane plays the acoustic along with him. His solo on the song scorches a part of her soul she didn't know still needed rock n' roll.

After all that, they take a break. Jane steps into the bathroom and splashes cold water over her face.

Chapter 50

Jane smiles at herself in the mirror. A single droplet of water hangs from the end of her nose. A few more dot her face, and maybe with the makeup washed away she looks older. The last few hours have been among the best she's had in a while. Her ex-husband is gone, possibly for good, and her song has come out better than she could have imagined. And seriously, at the beginning of the day, the song barely even existed. Now, it's complete. She took something from nothing and made it beautiful.

The chorus of the song continues to ring through her head. "I wanna drive down I-35." To her, the best songs are the ones she wants to hear over and over again. Or they're the ones she doesn't have to listen to to actually hear, as they just play on repeat in a never-ending loop in her mind. That's how this song feels to her.

She turns the tap back on and splashes another handful of water on her face. It feels that good.

She walks back into the control room and asks Zack to borrow his phone. He seems uncertain until she says, "Benny threw mine out the window. I need to call William."

He gladly hands it over. She thinks for a few minutes, trying to remember William's phone number. She's always been decent with numbers since she grew up in the age of physical phone books. It takes her two tries, but on the second one, William answers.

"Hello?" The voice is weak, but unmistakably his. William.

"Hey, you. How are you feeling?"

"Jane? Oh god, how are you?"

"They have you on some drugs?"

"Very good ones." He chuckles, and it's so wonderful to hear his voice.

"Sorry I didn't call sooner. Benny tossed my phone. I had to borrow one."

"No problem. I've been out for the last few hours. What time will you be getting here?"

"What?" She presses the phone into the side of her head, and her heart rate speeds up. "William, I…"

"It's just that the police said they'd bring you back down here. They said they found you in Denver? That right?"

"Yes, that's right."

"So you're on your way now? I didn't think it would take this long. Are you close?"

"William, I'm not on my way." She says it in a rush, in the hopes that he won't cut her off again, so it comes out more intense than she intends it to. "I stayed here." She wants to cry. That good feeling she'd had, splashing water on her face, flees like mice before a cat.

"You're not on your way?" He sounds completely flabbergasted. "You stayed there. You saw what happened to me, saw him stab me, and you didn't come back when you could have?"

She can't stop the tears that slip free. She'd been so focused on writing the song, on recording it, yet she hadn't thought about William hardly at all the whole day. She'd been just living it up in the studio while he'd been completely alone in the hospital. "I'm sorry, William. I guess I got carried away. I just knew that you'd understand."

William gives a slight groan but doesn't raise his voice. That's something that Jane could probably handle better. Yelling she understands, but the quiet disappointment just hurts a little more. "Sure, I understand." He sighs. "You're off in Denver having a great time while I'm just wasting away in the hospital. I would rather be in Denver, too. Wait." Silence falls over the phone, and Jane strains to hear what he's going to say next. Only then does she realize there is music playing all around her. It's the song she's been working on all day. It's at the end when she sings the chorus a couple of times. She closes her eyes.

"Is that my song?" The disappointment dissipates, and the anger that she had hoped for comes through the phone. "You recorded a song I wrote?"

Her voice is barely more than a whisper. "You'd only written one line. I finished the rest."

William's bark of laughter has no humor in it. "So because I hadn't finished it, that gave you the right to steal it?"

"Benny demanded that I put a song together, and I didn't have any ideas. Your song was the only thing I could think of."

"What about the song you've been working on? What about your song, Jane?"

Shit. She'd forgotten that she'd told him about her song. "William, I'm sorry, but I couldn't let him have that one."

"I guess it doesn't matter now, does it? He's not going to get the song no matter what, and you're still there recording a song I wrote when you could be here with me."

She wishes that she could rewind the clock to the time when the police officer was here and she could accept that ride to the Springs, back to William. She doesn't want to apologize again. She just wants to move past this. She's certain that they'll be together, so it would be easier to just skip the fight and get to the part where they're just together. She shakes her head, trying to clear all that unhelpful nonsense. "Listen, William, I'll get a ride down there. Like now. I'll be there in a couple of hours. I promise, okay? William?"

Back in the time before cell phones, when she got upset with someone, she would literally slam the phone back into its cradle. There was something satisfying about slamming the phone receiver down, and it also had an impact on the person being hung up on. Now, with the touch of a screen, the call can end, and many times, the person on the other end doesn't even notice. She speaks into the phone, but William is no longer there to answer. She holds it up, staring at the black screen, trying to understand what the hell just happened.

She wanders back into the sound booth and hands Zack his phone. He and the other guys are just hanging out. They've listened to the song a few times, and the energy coming off them is palpable. "Hey. The guys and I were just talking. If you want to record more, we're all down. I'm not even worried about charging you for it. This has been great."

The excitement in the room produces enough electricity to power the studio. She's certain this is the same euphoria she'd been feeling when she'd turned down the ride to William. A part of her longs to step back in the studio. After not playing music for so long, she suddenly has this itch to play, to play and never stop. The tips of her fingers long to press into the steel of the strings. But she shakes her head. "I would love that, Zack, but I've got to get back to the Springs. And I don't have a car."

Zack's face changes as the smile falls away. "I understand. Got that guy you've got to catch up with. Well, let me say this then: we're here anytime you want to come back. Maybe you could re-record your earlier stuff and release it as your own."

Jane smiles. "I hadn't considered that. Not a bad idea, Zack." She smiles at him, and it helps ease her mind.

"Hey, I've got a truck, and I wouldn't mind a drive to Colorado Springs." She turns to find Mark standing there. He's all smiles. "As long as you don't mind me picking the soundtrack."

She doesn't even have to think about it. "I wonder what the perfect soundtrack for a ride to Colorado Springs would be."

"I guess we'll find it!"

Chapter 51

Jane doesn't rush to get going. She listens to her song one more time, smiling the whole time it plays. She thanks each of the guys for their help and gives Zack a hug. "Thank you for your help with my...problem."

"You're welcome. Come back soon."

"I will."

Mark leads the way to his truck. The ride is uneventful aside from the conversation. Mark tells her stories of shows he got to play in Europe. He also talks about his favorite bands, a weird assortment of U2, Green Day, the 80s Christian band Stryper, and Garth Brooks. Now that Jane lives in Oklahoma, she finds it fascinating that Garth Brooks is actually from there.

Once they get to the Springs, Jane has Mark drop her off at the hospital. "Thank you, Mark. I hope to play with you again someday."

"If you're ever in Denver, let me know. I'll be there. With drums if you need them."

Once in the hospital, Jane feels the familiar butterflies fluttering around inside at the thought of seeing William. She steps into the gift shop and gets him a bag of candy. She's not sure what it is he likes, but everyone likes candy. She approaches the reception desk. "Can you tell me where I can find William Holiday?"

The lady behind the desk smiles and searches on her

computer. Jane glances at the TV; a news channel plays there, and she's surprised to see her face. It's a picture that's probably twenty years old, but she recognizes herself. It's one of the last headshots she had to sign for people. Benny probably still has boxes and boxes of them around his house. Clearly, the story of her return to the stage followed by her sudden disappearance has caused quite the stir in the music world. She wonders briefly what they're saying about her before the receptionist gets her attention.

"I'm so sorry, ma'am, but it looks like he checked out about an hour ago."

For Jane the hospital falls away, out of the world; her stomach flips thirty times in rapid succession, and she thinks she might vomit. "He's gone?" Her eyes flick to the ceiling, where she finds no answers.

"Is there something else I can help you with?"

Jane shakes her head and steps back away from the desk. She feels like she's floating as she makes her way to the waiting room. She sits and stares up at the TV. Her picture has been replaced with a picture of her ex-husband. Still in the world that seems to have lost gravity, Jane floats over to the TV and turns up the volume. "The singer's husband, who is accused of kidnapping her late last night, was arrested on those charges. They found him dead in his cell this morning. Police are questioning whether or not foul play may have been involved."

She drops back in the nearest chair. She stares at the TV, no longer hearing it as it cuts to a Denver police officer, not the same one she took a selfie with, and they ask him questions about the security of their jail. She holds a trembling hand over her mouth. A weight, one that she's carried for over ten years, slides free of her shoulders. She understands the Ancient Mariner now that her albatross has fallen into the sea. A tear slips free from her eye and rolls down her cheek. He's gone, she thinks, and she smiles.

Then she thinks of Roger. She reaches for her phone and remembers she doesn't have it. She hopes they were kind enough to call him so he doesn't have to find out by watching the news. She approaches the receptionist and asks to borrow the phone to call her son. After Roger answers, she explains that she's calling from the hospital phone.

"You heard, then?"

"I just saw it on the news. Are you all right?"

He sighs. "Sure. I'll be fine. I know you guys didn't get along, and he was more or less terrible to you, but he was my dad. I guess a part of me loved him." He lets the line go silent. Jane doesn't interrupt it, allowing him a moment to think. Finally, he says, "I didn't call earlier when I found out. I heard what he did to you, and I thought that you might be busy with the police or William. Also, I didn't think you would care."

The admonition breaks her heart, and she nearly sobs out of control. After arriving at the hospital and not finding William, here's her son saying she wouldn't care that he lost his dad. A few more tears, bitter and stinging, roll down her cheeks. "I'm sorry you thought that, but I'm calling you now, Roger, because I do care. I hope you know that now. I may not have loved Benny, but I love you. If you're in pain, I want to be here to comfort you."

He sighs again, and when he speaks, his voice is thick with tears. "I know. I guess I'm still trying to get used to you being back in my life. I've got a few years to process through at this point, you know?"

"Sure, I know."

"Listen, Mom, I've got some stuff to take care of for Dad, but once the funeral is all over, I'll come out to Oklahoma and stay again. I really enjoyed my time there with you."

She smiles. "I would like that."

She ends the call and stares up at the TV for another moment. She thinks about being home and realizes her car is five hours away in Santa Fe. Suddenly, her body reminds her that she hasn't really slept all night. She moves back to the chair and sits. Her whole body falls into the chair, and she sighs. She closes her eyes, and sleep finds her there where it's always been, waiting like a parent waiting for their child.

Time passes, but in a hospital waiting room, no one notices the person waiting, even if they're asleep. She rests and doesn't even know she's resting. Sometimes that's the best kind. But all good things come to an end. But so do bad things. Someone jostles her when they sit down, and she startles awake. She hears the person saying something that might be an apology. She waves a hand at them. She's trying to figure out her bearings, where she is, and how long she's been here. She stares up at the clock on the wall beside the TV. The fog that she has to swim through to even understand the most basic and mundane things is incredible. Apparently she'd been asleep for close to two hours.

She blinks, glancing around the room. She remembers sitting down in the hospital waiting room after speaking with Roger. That's it then; she's in the hospital. And now, she has to get to Santa Fe. She once more borrows the hospital phone to call for a taxi. Fortunately, they have those here. She needs a ride to get a rental car. She'd hoped to be riding back to Santa Fe with William, but she apparently really hurt him.

Getting a rental car is easy. She almost gets a convertible with the idea of driving back to New Mexico with the top down, but the fall is turning colder here in the mountains. She opts, instead, for a basic sedan.

Before leaving the rental place, she uses their phone to call the Miner's Delight. "Hey, Jack, this is Jane!"

"Jane! Holy hell, it's good to hear your voice!" Again, Jack has all the energy of a caffeinated chihuahua.

"Have you heard from William?"

The energy falls away from Jack. "I had hoped you were with him. He called several hours ago to get his gear. When he left your guitar behind, I knew something was up. I'm sorry as hell for what happened to you guys."

She nods, even though he can't see it, fighting off the sudden emotion that's swirling around her. "Can I come by and get my guitar then?"

"Sure." He huffs out a breath into the phone. "And for what it's worth, Jane, I've never seen William as happy as he was with you. That's got to be worth something."

"It does."

That quick stop by the Miner's Delight to get her guitar, and then she's in the car and heading south. Somewhere in the back of her mind, she wishes she actually was driving on I-35. What started as a needed vacation has turned into the weirdest trip of her life.

Chapter 52

The tires on the rental car gobble up the miles like a starved lion eating a zebra. It feels good to drive, but she's certain that by the end of this trip, she'll get tired of it. For now, she embraces it, enjoys it, and lets the road sing its song to her. She makes her way through Colorado toward New Mexico in a blur. Without her phone, she puts on the radio. Every time a news bulletin breaks in to say something about her or Benny, she turns to a new station. Unfortunately, the stations are harder to find in New Mexico, but the country stations don't say anything about her.

She makes a couple of stops along the way, for coffee, for a bathroom, and once, for a burger. She fills up the tank at one point, but mostly, she just drives. Now that she's on the road, she finds herself missing home, her little place that's all her own.

At long last, she arrives in Santa Fe. It's a relief even though she knows she still has ten hours to drive until she's home. Probably, she won't be doing that tonight.

She rolls up to the car rental place to return the car and then waits patiently with her guitar for another taxi to get there to pick her up. Not having a phone is worse than she could have predicted. She's able to give directions to Jonas's house and relaxes in the backseat. It's not a long drive, but it gives her enough time to figure out her next move.

She needs to talk to William, to apologize, and to try to make amends. She wasn't kidding when she said she loved him, but now that he's gone, she's consumed with thoughts of him. If only she'd been that way in the studio, maybe she would have made it back to Colorado Springs to sit with him in the hospital for a while. Then when he checked out, she would have insisted on driving to Santa Fe. She sighs as she gets out of the rideshare and grabs her guitar. She strolls up to Jonas' front door and knocks.

When the door opens, Jonas is all smiles. "Hello, Jane, how are you? Come in, please." He asks the question but doesn't give her the time to answer. She must not look great. She is exhausted and hasn't had the chance to reset herself in a couple of days.

"Hi, Jonas, I'm just here to get my stuff and my car. I've got a long drive ahead of me."

"Come in." He opens the door wider for her, clearly not accepting a no from her.

She proceeds over the threshold into the living room. He takes her guitar and sets it near the front door. "Obviously, I knew you'd be by here for your things. You missed William by about four hours. I'm not sure what happened. He wouldn't tell me a thing, so I hoped that when you came, maybe I could figure it out."

She sucks in a deep breath and puts her hand over her face. She hasn't said a word, but already she can feel the tears welling. The fact that she missed him by a few hours nearly breaks her heart all over again. "I messed up. I'll probably never make it up to him, but I'm going to try."

To her surprise, Jonas wraps his arms around her. For the second time in just a few hours, she's being hugged by someone that she hardly knows. It's a feeling she's forgotten all about, having not experienced many hugs in the last ten years. Mostly, she gets them from Martha. Her heart aches all the more when she thinks of her best friend that she hasn't spoken to in three days. She can't stop herself from crying into Jonas' shoulder. The tears and sobs rack her body, and Jonas holds her. He shows her kindness in this time of pain.

For a while, she doesn't think she'll be able to stop, now or ever. But soon the sobs subside, and she regains control of herself. "I'm sorry. Thank you." She nearly says the two phrases simultaneously.

"It's quite all right, really. I didn't mean to make you cry. I just don't know what happened between you two. I heard some of the things about you on the news, but I wasn't sure how much of that was real. Clearly, William has been through an ordeal. He still had a hospital bracelet on and didn't move as confidently as normal."

Jane nods, wiping at her face. "My ex-husband stabbed William and then took me off to Denver to record a song for him."

"Oh shit." Jonas holds a hand up over his mouth. Now it looks like he might cry, and Jane doesn't have it in her to comfort him.

"I messed up when I didn't come back the second that I could." She shakes her head. "And I may have stolen William's idea for a song to record."

Jonas pulls off his glasses and wipes at his face. "I can't believe William didn't say anything to me."

Jane rubs at her arm absentmindedly. "Maybe he just didn't want to talk about it. Or maybe he just wanted to get as far away from me as possible and knew I'd be here before long."

"I guess that could be it. Listen, why don't you come in, and I'll make some dinner for us? No, really. You aren't in any shape to drive back to Oklahoma tonight. Stay back in my guest house, and you can leave first thing in the morning. I'll be at work, so I won't get in your way."

Jane wants to protest. She's in the kind of mood where she doesn't feel like she deserves any kindness, but then the thought of the long highway makes her pause. "I'd like that. Thank you."

Jonas claps. "Get comfortable, and I'll start cooking."

Jane slips out to the guest house where she left her suitcase so that she can shower and change her clothes. The bed, a reminder of her first night with William, calls out to her when she goes in the small space, but she manages to ignore it. Her suitcase is where she left it, and she never thought she'd be so happy to see it.

The water reinvigorates her. She cries again, over the loss of William, the harrowing experience she had with Benny, and the fact that she recorded a new song. The shower water mixes with her tears and washes them down the drain.

When she returns to the house, her damp hair leaving wet patches on her shoulders, Jonas is just finishing his cooking. She stands nearby while he tells stories about how much he loves cooking for people and how he wishes more people would come over to enjoy it. She doesn't have the energy to add to the conversation but listens intently.

Jonas doesn't mess around with dinner, and she's thankful she chose to stay. The homemade tortillas that Jonas claims he's been perfecting for the last ten years are as close to heaven as she'll likely ever get.

"This was delicious." She leans back after the meal to allow room in her midsection for the food.

"I'm so glad you think so. Do you need another taco?"

She holds up her hands. "No, thank you. I'm fine after one."

Jonas stands and clears the plates away. With a full belly, she cannot keep back the weariness any longer. She fights off a yawn and stands.

"You look exhausted. Why don't you go on to bed?" Jonas pauses in his cleanup just long enough to say this.

"I could help."

"No need. I've got this. Please."

She smiles gratefully at him and picks up her guitar.

"You can leave that by the front door if you want."

She smiles. "But what if I'm tempted to search through the secrets of my soul, and I left this behind?"

Jonas laughs, but Jane doesn't. It's the words she said to William back in their hotel room that inspired the third verse. She has to finish that song. "Thank you, Jonas. Goodnight!" She darts out the back door to her backyard oasis.

Chapter 53

For a musician, something near to worship happens when they sit down to play their instrument. Whether it is running their fingers over the ivories or tucking the violin under their chin, each musician has a moment when they leave behind the woes of the world and focus solely on their music. For Jane, it happens when she unlatches the clasps on her guitar case. As she does this in the tiny house behind Jonas's place, she's amazed at the sense of peace that washes over her. She can't believe she went so long without touching her guitar. Her ex-husband won so much more from her, and she didn't even realize it at the time.

The first time she picked up a guitar, she was five. She'd held it the way other girls her age held their dolls. The guitar was a relic of her grandfather's. They'd gone to his house to clean it out after he died. Jane found the guitar and fell in love. Her dad tried to take it, thinking it could get them at least fifty bucks at an estate sale. But Jane couldn't let her father win that fight. And honestly, he didn't have much fight in him when it came to Jane.

Three weeks later, she had her first lesson, learning what a chord was and where to put her fingers. Practicing was hard, but every night, she went to bed with her fingertips hurting and joy in her heart. Eventually, she could string together a series of chords quickly enough that it didn't interrupt her strumming pattern.

By the time she was seven, she could play and sing. Her voice wasn't quite up to par yet, but her dad celebrated her anyway. He always asked her to play for anyone who came over, so Jane became an entertainer at a young age.

In her teen years, she discovered the joys of writing, as many young women do. She explored her deepest fears and the depths of the sadness she carried with her ever since her mom died. And in all of that, she found she could set those thoughts to music and create songs.

She would never consider songwriting anything less than wonderful. Though it could be difficult at times, it still held for her the healing and happiness she needed.

The first time she performed one of her original songs was at her eleventh-grade talent show. She gathered all of her bravery and signed up. The night before the performance, she sat in bed picturing all of her classmates laughing at her. She worked herself up to the point that she had to sprint to the bathroom to vomit. She had so much doubt for that first performance, but it went perfectly. She found the conflicting emotions to be one of the most stimulating experiences. Before the performance, she thought she would never eat again; after, her food somehow tasted better than it ever had before.

She never doubted herself again after that and worked tirelessly to play more in front of people.

Lovingly, she removes the old guitar from the case and drops the strap back in. She pulls the pick from the strings and gives them a strum. The sound of a tuned guitar ringing out through the room damn near sends chills down her spine. She places her fingers in the correct spots on the neck and strums out an open C chord.

"Right now," she sings.

Writing songs has never been easy for her. She's wrestled with what she wants to say in each song, trying to make the lyrics poetic and catchy at the same time. Other times, she's focused solely on the music, trying to get the precise movement of the chords and the rhythm of those chords. Some songs emerge out of her fully formed, while others are tortured over, a Herculean effort. The song she worked up in the studio that morning, for instance, came out nearly completed with the help of William's inspiration. This song, though—this one requires all of her attention.

She sings through the first few verses and the chorus a few times, as she already has many times before. She pauses only to pull the notepad from her bag so that she can cross out a couple of words and add a couple more, just to go back to what she'd already written the first time.

She plays through the chords again and hums along with them. She reads the words to remember what they mean, and then, without warning, she sings another new verse.

"Right now, I'm burning all the doubts inside my head." That feels right, like exactly what she wants to say. "And finally…"

The chord rings out in the small room while she considers. If she's burning away all the doubts, then, "And finally I'm who I want to be."

She pauses long enough to write the words down, not wanting to forget them. Another thing she's learned is that when writing a song, sometimes it's just as straightforward to lose the words as it is to find them. If she doesn't write them while she knows them, she may never know them again.

She sings those two lines again. Then, "Every day I make a change to something that can't stay the same."

She smiles, the words falling right out. The last line of the song comes to her without any thought. "With these sins I know I can't be free."

She lets the last chord ring out and stares off beyond the walls of the small house. In her mind she can see herself, clutching the phone in her hand, trying to explain to William why she stole his song and why she didn't come to him the second she could. Then she hurriedly writes down the last words she came up with and then plays through the whole song again. Not knowing how to end it, she sings, "Right now." And let the last chord ring out.

The chord reverberates, then dies. She stares down at her notepad, at the words she wrote. Sometimes, it can be difficult to know when a piece is finished, but not with this song. She knows every word works together and paints the picture she wants for the listener. Finally, she smiles.

She wishes she had a phone now so that she could record it, though she doesn't think she'll have any trouble remembering it now that it's over. This song has been consistently begging to be written for the last week. And now, it's finished.

She plays through the song two more times just to make sure she's got it down. Then she replaces the guitar. With the ritual done and her hair dry, she knows she can lie back and sleep. Tomorrow will be a day of driving with plenty of time to think of ways to get William back.

Chapter 54

She leaves two handwritten notes behind in the spare room behind Jonas's house. One of them she addresses to Jonas, thanking him for the hospitality and hope. The other she addresses to William in case he stops there before they're reunited. She hopes the words in the letter are enough to make William see how sorry she is.

Before she leaves Santa Fe, she's able to get a replacement phone with the same number. She had everything backed up to the cloud, so all of her pictures and contacts are saved. Once more being connected to the world feels wonderful.

Somehow in the interim of days, she'd forgotten how long and empty the road between New Mexico and home is. Still, the drive gives her time to work through her life. She avoids the radio, not wanting to hear any more stories about her wild kidnapping or the death of Benny. Instead, she plays music from different decades, singing along at times, but mostly, she thinks of William and what it will take to convince him to come back to her. With all other avenues explored, she grabs her phone and makes a call, the one she should have made two days ago.

"When I don't hear from you, I think that you've been kidnapped or something." Martha never answers the phone in a normal way whenever Jane calls. She just jumps into the conversation like she's been waiting for it to start. It's something that Jane has always found endearing. She also appreciates that her best friend answers her phone call even when she's at work.

"Hi, Martha, you haven't been watching the news, have you?" The sun down low on the horizon forces her to pull on her sunglasses.

"Why would I watch the news? Henry has been watching football all weekend, and now I get to watch *The Voice* tonight. Why? What's happened?"

Jane sighs. "Well, I was kidnapped."

Through Martha's exclamations, Jane explains all that happened to her over the past few days. As the words tumble out, the relief courses through her. Just like when she told Roger her whole story, she finds the act of talking about the events helps clear them from her mind. She manages to not cry while she speaks, though it is close a couple of times. Martha knows how to react to stories, knows the proper places to gasp and exclaim, and saves all of her questions for the end.

"Oh, goodness. And you're coming home?" Martha asks at the end. Jane didn't hesitate to include the part about losing William. She needs her friend's insight on how to handle this.

"I'm on my way now." She can't help but smile when she says it. She's excited to be home, even if that means she goes back to being a regular person in a regular town. In her rearview, if she sits up a little in the seat, she can see the guitar case in the backseat. She wants to play the song again.

"You come see me when you get here. We can make popcorn and watch a movie. I'll send Henry out to do something else."

"Oh, but Martha, you had plans for what to watch

tonight. Are you sure?"

"Of course I'm sure. I can save it for later, and I'll be able to fast-forward through all of the commercials and boring parts."

"I appreciate you more than you know."

"I know you do. What I don't know is how you're able to function at the moment. You make it here safe, and we'll figure out how to make things right with William."

They chat for a while longer, Martha easing every single part of Jane's mind as she rolls on. The sun moves along in the sky, first in front of her, then above her, and finally behind her. She left early enough that it isn't too late when she rolls back across the state lines. After catching up with Martha for the last five hours, she finally ends the phone call.

She stops in a town that consists of a gas station and not much more. She fills the tank and stretches her back. One of the best parts of driving long distances is getting out and stretching. After that, she goes on down the road.

With an endless highway, she finds it easy to get lost in her thoughts, something that she does over and over. Her thoughts mostly consist of William, but they also come back to music. She wonders if she can rig up her computer to record that new song or if she knows anyone in Crescent who could help her out. Probably that guy, Tom, who owns the Treasure store down the street. He seems to always know how to do everything. She wants to sing again, to play her guitar, but she's not sure if she wants to be on the road like this, driving from show to show. Maybe she can just write songs.

With her thoughts chasing each other, she finally pulls into town, down her street, and into her driveway.

She's home, and she's exhausted. She grabs her guitar and her bag and heads into her house.

It's weird to think that the last time she was here, Benny was alive, getting dragged away by the cops. The experiences of the last few days have transformed her into a different woman. She's older now and currently sadder. She sends Roger a text to let him know she's home. He doesn't respond. She puts her clothes away and finally gets her guitar out. She strums it, letting the sound resonate through her like she, herself, is the guitar.

She puts it back and stands. She's supposed to go to Martha's house, maybe eat some food, and drink some gin, but she keeps thinking about work. She hasn't been in the bookshop in so long, and she somehow feels like that is where this whole thing started.

She picks up her phone and calls Sylvia. "I wondered when I'd be hearing from you." Sylvia has adopted Martha's way of answering the phone when she calls.

"Well, I'm back in town. Thought I'd call."

"Yes, that needed to happen. Meet me down at the shop. I'll answer some of your questions."

Jane starts to reply, but the line is dead. She's tired, wants to just go to bed, but knows there's something at the bookshop. She shoots Martha a text to let her know where she's going. Martha responds with a series of emojis that make Jane smile. Martha only recently learned to use emojis, and the result is many messages with fewer words and sometimes indecipherable meanings.

She pulls her shoes back on and climbs into the car. She hasn't gotten enough sleep this weekend, but more than that, her life has been haywire. She's not sure how

Sylvia could possibly have anything to do with it, but maybe she'll get some answers at Paper Pages.

She certainly isn't the first person heading to Paper Pages to find answers, but hers probably won't come from books.

Chapter 55

The bells tinkle, and the smells of books and other worlds bombard Jane the second she walks through the door. The store is so different after the sun goes down. Somehow the things that make it special during the day are brought to a new life when it's dark. Maybe it's because there are no customers and the rules can be broken, like moving the shelves to set up chairs for book club.

Sylvia sits in one of the comfy armchairs by the front window and pats the other one. She offers no other welcome. Jane walks to the chair, her steps soft and timid. This reminds her of being called to the principal's office as a kid.

"And did you have a nice vacation?" Sylvia asks, taking a sip from her mug of tea. Jane hadn't even noticed the mug until now.

"Well, the first part was nice. Then it sort of went off the rails, you know?"

"Actually, I do. I saw the news stories, and I must say, Jane, I am sorry about the way things happened." Sylvia laughs a little and takes a sip of tea. "I'd hoped to get you going, but I didn't expect to get you moving in that sort of way."

Jane doesn't respond to this strange statement but watches her boss drink her tea. Finally, Sylvia sets the mug aside. She lifts a small cookie and takes a bite of it.

Jane isn't sure where she got the cookie. She glances up at the case where they keep the food, but as she suspected, it's empty.

"I've always liked you, Jane. From the first day you came into my shop, I've enjoyed our conversations and your love for books. Naturally the latter is the most important attribute one must have to work here, but I also prefer my employees to be liked. And clearly, you are liked.

"In those early days, you'd been running from something. I didn't venture to ask what, but rather decided that I could provide you with some comfort and a safe place to hide.

"But years go by, don't they? We weave our lives together with the threads that we have. And while you had only a single thread when you landed here, you managed to find more. Martha, the bookshop, and me. Just a few examples. And then you created a life. It seemed like you were no longer running from something, but it also didn't look like you were running toward anything."

She places a hand on Jane's knee, a momentary brush that Jane finds both odd and comforting. "I know, dear, it really isn't my place to judge, but I couldn't help it, you know? I'm just running a bookshop over here, trying to carve out a little place. But I also have some extracurricular activities, aside from attending all of the local softball games, of course."

Here she pauses and gazes at Jane for a moment. Sylvia's hair, always a little wild, is tamed down tonight. Jane wonders if she always spends her day off from the bookshop correcting her unwieldy hair. She shakes her head to stop herself from laughing.

"Are you not going to ask?" Sylvia arches one eyebrow and smiles. "Fine, then. I know that you've noticed some strange things in the bookshop. Seemingly endless space on the shelves, or people visiting from everywhere. Or how about magical mugs of tea?"

Sylvia lifts the mug to her lips, and Jane is stunned to see it's full. "How did…?" She doesn't finish the question, but her eyes widen. Part of her wants to crawl backward out of the chair she's sitting in.

Sylvia laughs and replaces the now-empty mug. Jane blinks. Maybe the mug actually was empty?

"Jane, your eyes don't deceive you. I am a witch. Not that I love that term. I guess what I'll say then is I use magic. I know, it doesn't seem totally possible, right? Well, it is. And there's no more fitting place to share this information with you than in a building filled to the brim with books about magic."

Jane's breath is coming to her chest too quickly, and she's suddenly forgotten how to regulate that breathing. What does she normally do? Also, are there hidden cameras in here for a TV show, or has she literally crossed into a fantasy novel? Life seemed to be going pretty normally.

Not knowing what to say, she remains silent, hoping that this weird story will resolve itself without her input. She's starting to believe her boss is actually crazy. She might have to intervene on her behalf.

"So, back to you then." Sylvia takes another sip of tea from the once-more full mug. "You were stuck, dear. I don't like to see people I like stuck in a rut of their own making. I didn't know much of your history. You've always been so quiet on that front, but I did know that you were single and had nothing real tying you down to this place.

"And that's when I decided to help."

Jane's not sure where this is going. Is it possible for someone to have become so wrapped up in the books they're selling that they actually think they're a part of it?

"What I did," Sylvia continues, "is cast a spell around you. See, I thought maybe I could help move things along."

"You cast a spell on me?" She finally chooses this moment to speak, but her voice creaks like an unused door.

"Well, that's not really what it was, but that's what all the books call it, so I thought you might be more familiar with that terminology."

Jane shakes her head. "This can't be real, right? You can't actually do magic."

"I know. I suppose this mug of tea just appeared here in my hand because the universe willed it to appear. Or the shelves hold more books than they should. Or people come from all over the country to see this tiny bookshop in this tiny town."

Jane gazes around the room. "It is a really cute bookshop."

"I know, dear, but people have *heard* of it, you know?"

Jane nods. She remembers the conversation she had with Martha about the bookshop and all the oddities about it. Still, she can't quite believe this.

Sylvia waves a hand in her direction, clearly dismissing her disbelief. "Doesn't matter. What does matter is that when that traveling musician came through the store, I knew the spell had worked. My plan was simply to get things going for you. But then, things kept going.

"When your son came into the store, I knew the spell had gone too far. To be fair, I didn't know about your son or your ex-husband. I just knew you were running from something, not that the things you were running from would come chasing you."

Sylvia pauses and wipes a hand across her face. Jane simply cannot believe what she's hearing. The audacity of this woman deciding to take Jane's situation into her hands. She's so frustrated, but at the same time, she's still struggling to believe any of this. But when she thinks about it, all of it makes sense.

"What I mean is, I set in motion things that upset your life. I didn't mean to, really I didn't. But don't you remember that one time I accidentally ordered a case of *The Beekeeper's Bullet* when I only meant to order one? Sometimes, I make mistakes." She shrugs and laughs, but Jane doesn't join her. "I did try to reverse the spell after your son came, but I'm afraid it was too late at that point."

"You mean to say that my ex-husband finding me and turning my life inside out for a few days is your fault?"

"Well, yes."

"He's dead now, you know?"

"I am sorry. But I don't doubt he would have died regardless of my interference."

Jane stands and runs a hand through her hair. She paces a few steps and stops. "You can't compare this to ordering too many books. This isn't something you can just send back to the store."

"I know that, dear. There is the possibility that your

son and ex would have come and found you regardless. But I do believe I helped that traveling musician find you. Listen, I understand why you're upset."

"Do you? I didn't ask for you to do any of this." Her voice is too loud for the small store.

Sylvia breaks eye contact and looks down at the floor. For a second, Jane's sure she's going to cry, and a sinister part of her wants to see those tears. "People do not normally ask for things to happen to them, whether good or bad. We become complacent." Sylvia looks back up, eyes entirely dry. "You see, when we can simply live our lives without any kind of interference, we think we're happy. If something comes along to disrupt that, whether good or bad, we are disappointed. You would have been far worse off if your ex-husband had found you and you hadn't had Santa Fe to run off to. You're stronger now, dear."

Jane sits down, her hair falling down over her face as she contemplates this. "So you're saying that some bad things happened to me, but I would have missed out on the good things without those bad things?"

Sylvia shrugs. "I'm saying the bad things would have happened anyway, but the good things may not have."

Jane nods. Again, she thinks of William and what she's missing right now. "Do you have any magic that can bring William back to me?" She can't keep the emotion out of her voice. Her eyes sting with fresh tears, but she fights them. She doesn't want to cry right now.

"You don't need my magic." Sylvia stands, taking her mug to the kitchen. "You have your own magic that he cannot ignore for long. Don't worry, dear, he'll come back. Would you mind locking up for me?"

Jane watches her walk away. She's starting to wonder if this conversation actually happened or not. The part of her that still enjoys novels set in fictional places wants to believe, but the part of her that occasionally reads nonfiction knows this isn't how the world normally works. *But why can't Sylvia be my fairy godmother?*

"Oh," Sylvia says from the chair next to Jane, "please don't tell anyone what I told you today. Magic still seems to be on the outskirts of what people want to believe."

Jane watches in silence as her boss once again gets up with her mug and walks away. She shakes her head, and slowly, she leaves the bookshop, locking the door behind her. There's some Police song or CCR song that would fit this moment perfectly if she wanted to make a soundtrack for this bookshop.

Chapter 56

Days pass. Jane's calls and texts to William go unanswered. She doesn't share Sylvia's secret with Martha, as she was sworn to secrecy by her boss, but she does hint to Martha that they were on the right track. Sylvia's points sit heavy with Jane for a few days. She goes back to work, but it takes some time to forgive Sylvia for her interference. Overall, she spends far too much time thinking about William and analyzing the Tennyson quote about loving and losing. Is it better to have experienced William and lost him? At times, her broken heart makes her think that maybe it isn't.

One night, her phone rings while she's enjoying a book and the quiet night. The fall weather has turned colder, something that is guaranteed to happen in Oklahoma sooner than is ever necessary. She looks at the number, and it isn't one she recognizes. She almost dismisses it, but at the last second, she answers.

"Jane! You are so missed up here in Denver!"

In the background, she thinks she can hear some music. She smiles at the sound of his voice and racks her brain trying to remember his name. It is one of those short, four-letter names, but for just a second, it doesn't come to her.

"I sure miss Denver. Well, at least the recording studio." She chuckles.

"Right on! I wanted to let you know that your song

is ready. I didn't have an email for you, but I remembered you gave me your phone number. I know a guy up in Minnesota who does great work on mastering. I sent it to him. I'll cover the price of the mastering as long as you come back to record your next song here."

"It's already been mastered? That's great news!" She almost calls him Eric, but that doesn't sound right.

"Yeah, and it sounds so good. Bert, Travis, and Mark are here listening to it right now."

She smiles. "Zack," she says and knows for certain that's his name. "I have that email address for you."

"Go on then!"

Jane rattles it off and closes her eyes as she says it. She needs this. She wants to hear the song she wrote so that something good will have come out of that whole vacation she took. Then she remembers what she was like before William, how afraid she was to play music again, and how her resentment toward Benny kept her from experiencing things like this. She realizes in that moment that while Sylvia had done something without her permission, Jane probably never would have given it. And without Sylvia's interference, she maybe wouldn't have ever picked up a guitar again.

"So when will you come back?" Zack asks. "You have more songs?"

"I do. At least one. But I could be persuaded to write more."

He laughs. "All right then, do it!"

After a few more pleasantries, they end the call, and Jane opens her email. The song is there waiting for her. She doesn't want to listen to it alone. She calls Martha. "Would you like to hear a song?"

Martha comes right over. She sits on Jane's couch

in the living room and listens as Jane opens the file from her email. She plugs the laptop into a stereo system in her living room. She has a top-notch stereo despite no longer making her own music up until now. The song starts, and the music bangs away. Jane finds herself singing along with the song and smiling while she does. Martha sits wide-eyed listening. At the end of it, they sit in the silence of the living room for a few minutes, not speaking, but letting the song resonate through the room.

"That's you." Martha's first words are not quite what Jane expected. "And that's who you were before."

Jane nods. "What did you think?"

"Oh, Jane, I love it. I'm just trying to make the Jane I know match up with the Clara singing person. You know, I've never known you as a singer."

"I know. Do you really like it?"

"I do. What part did you borrow from William?"

Jane bites her lip and tells her.

"One line is all he's upset about? You fleshed out the rest of the song and probably wrote something he couldn't have."

"Maybe."

"Can we listen to it again?"

They listen to it four more times. By the end, Martha is singing along, not just with the chorus but with the whole song. They're laughing and dancing around the living room. Jane is once more whisked away to her teenage years, when singing and dancing around the living room would have been normal behavior.

"Maybe that's the answer. Maybe he just needs a song."

Jane stops dancing to look Martha in the eye. "A song?"

"Sure, why not? You borrowed an idea from him. Maybe you need to send him your own idea."

Jane hadn't thought of that. But now that the idea is out there, she knows exactly what song she would give William. "That's a brilliant idea, Martha. I'll just need someone to help me record it."

"Well, don't look at me. You probably need some younger person to help you out."

Jane nods. "Roger said he would be coming to town soon. Maybe he could do it?"

With the plan made, Jane's heart lightens, and the two turn back to dancing. Maybe everything could work out.

Chapter 57

Roger comes to her house two days later. She's excited to see him, but he looks a little rough. She gets him set up in her spare bedroom, and they sit down in the living room to talk.

"I guess Dad was into some bad stuff, stuff I didn't know about." Roger runs a hand over his face, staring down at the ground. He has that haunted look of someone who hasn't slept well in a while.

She lays a hand on his shoulder. "I gathered that when he went to such desperate measures to get me to record a song."

Roger's smile is bitter and crooked. "Well, the guys still want their money. They've contacted me. It seems Dad's death may not have been an accident after all."

She leans forward, her eyes wide. "Have they threatened you?"

Roger shakes his head. "I'm not sure where I'm going to get the money, though. I'll have to sell his house and a few other assets to be able to make it work."

"How much did he owe them?"

He lets out a bark of bitter laughter. "Nearly seven hundred thousand."

She cannot stop the gasp that bursts out of her mouth. "That much? Well, you've got my catalog, right?"

He nods. "I do, but that doesn't bring in a lot of

money. Not anymore."

"Maybe after I put out a new song. Hell, I'll even go play a few shows if that'll help."

His mouth pops open. "Would you really?"

"Sure, I could do that for you. That's not a big deal at all. But could you do something for me?"

"Sure." His face lights up, so that he doesn't look as tired. He's almost bouncing. "What do you need?"

"I need to record a song. Do you know how to do that?"

"Of course. I grew up with a musical mom. Until she left."

She can tell that he means it as a joke, so she doesn't let it bother her. "Would you help me?"

It has to be just perfect. Roger sets up a microphone and plugs it in to her computer. She's recorded a few things here and there, but not on her computer. That was back when it was a four-track recorder. That certainly made demos a whole lot easier. Making them on the computer is more complicated, as there is a bit of a learning curve, but it is possible to finish recording and have a song that sounds nearly complete. That's why so many home studios exist now.

She plugs in her guitar and tunes it. She keeps thinking about William, about the hope that this gives her. Maybe sending him a song will bring him back. Maybe it won't. But the one thing she understands for sure is she won't know unless she tries.

Roger mans the computer and tests all the inputs. "I think we've got a good level here," he says. "Want to run through it one time to make sure?"

She does. She stands in her living room, blankets draped up against the wall, creating a sound barrier. She closes her eyes as she plays the song she worked on for so long, the one that brought her out of her retirement and inspired her to bring her guitar from its case. She strums, her fingers knowing their places, moving to the right notes on the fretboard.

Before she's quite ready, the song is over. She finishes and opens her eyes. Roger is staring at her. "Mom, that was beautiful."

She smiles. "You think so?"

"I do. I don't know that we need to do anything, but let's go ahead and record another vocal track to make sure we've got some options."

The next couple of hours go something like that. She plays the song a few more times on her guitar, adding a few more tracks to give the song more depth. She even picks through the chords one time to add another musical layer to it. It sounds as good as they can possibly make it, and just like that, Jane has two new songs she can be proud of.

"Thank you, Roger." She gives him a hug, and her son feels right in her arms.

"Thanks for letting me be a part of it. You think William will like this one?"

She steps back and faces her son. "I hope so."

They sit down to dinner later at Jane's small table. While they eat, Jane fills Roger in on what happened with William and her hopes for this song. "So maybe he'll take me back, right?"

Roger laughs. "I hope so. If you could get him to at least talk to you, maybe you won't even need to give him the song."

"Maybe the song will convince him to talk to me."

"Maybe."

And with all the maybes in the world laid out before them, Roger and Jane enjoy a quiet evening.

Chapter 58

The most important thing Jane does during the next few days is put the song Roger recorded for her onto a thumb drive. She prints off the lyrics and chord chart and puts them in a padded envelope. She also creates a contract that she signs, giving him the rights to the song. She's going to release the song she recorded in Denver, so she hopes a song for a song will fix things. She has to release it to help make money for Roger. But she does make sure William is credited as a co-writer on the song. She doesn't have an actual address for him, so she sends it to Jonas. He's been sweet enough to stay in contact with her and pass along any messages for him that she has. So far, nothing has worked to convince William to come back to her, but Jane tries not to dwell on that.

She could have emailed the song to him, but this way, she can ensure that Jonas will play his part and play it for William the next time he's in Santa Fe.

She doesn't sit idly by waiting on time to pass. Roger, along with a lawyer, works to get her catalogue changed from Clara Rigdon to Jane Davis. It takes some time, but little by little, the streaming services begin to reflect the change. She even conducts an interview with the Associated Press to point out the change and to put out the information about her new song. Roger reports a surge in streams and even a few sales. They even discuss what it would take to get the original songs remastered for vinyl.

She finally releases the new song, and it gets thousands of plays on the first day. Roger is all smiles about this, as it means he'll be able to pay off his father's debts after all. Jane smiles too, and already, she's thinking of new lyrics and new chord progressions. Not playing a guitar put a stopper in her songwriting instead of ending it completely. Now that the stopper is removed, the songs are ready to explode out of her.

She manages to play a couple of concerts at some of the casinos around Oklahoma. It seems like stars from the nineties, whom most people remember with that burning nostalgia, play at the casinos. She's lucky that Oklahoma has so many.

The turnout is beyond expectations, and when she plays that new song, most of the crowd sings along. Maybe she's still got it.

With the sale of his dad's assets and the increased revenue from the catalogue, Roger is able to pay off the creditors or the mafia, whatever it was. The less Jane knows about her ex-husband's affairs, the better. And Roger decides to relocate to Oklahoma, so she's once more near her son.

A month after she dropped the letter to Jonas in the mail, not that she's counting, she's working in the bookshop. She's completely forgiven Sylvia for her interference. Her life has turned out to be so much better since then, so it's difficult to stay upset. Clearly Sylvia had her best interests at heart when she placed the spell on Jane.

Most days the shop is bustling with people who hope to speak with Jane about her music, and they even buy books. At least that part has worked in Sylvia's favor.

Sylvia keeps a small record player up on a shelf in the front of the store. Today is surprisingly quiet; even Bowl Cut has failed to come in, so Jane pops a record on while she works around the store. She's singing along with Janis Joplin as she straightens the shelves. She steps back into the office to grab the next box of books. It's heavier than she thought, and she has to pause to remove a few from it to be able to move it. While she's working, she thinks she hears the record player stop. She pauses to listen. The music definitely stopped.

She picks up the box and steps out into the bookshop. She hears the scratch of the needle landing in the groove of a new record. Someone else is in the store. She pauses, straining to hear anything. She hadn't heard the bells over the door, but then she'd been in the office and had music blaring, so it would have been difficult to hear. She takes a couple of tentative steps in the direction of the door. Then the record starts.

She hasn't listened to the Velvet Underground since she got back to Oklahoma, but she still remembers the opening chords to that song. She drops the box of books she's holding; it lands with a boom on the floor. Her heart races faster than her feet can carry her as she zooms to the front of the store. A man is standing in front of the record player wearing tight black jeans and a gray dress shirt, untucked. But it's the fedora that gives him away.

"William?" she says in a breathless voice that barely carries over the music.

He turns to her, his gray eyes electrifying her soul. "Sweet Jane?"

She runs to him, and his arms wrap around her. They embrace like two clouds combining on a warm summer day. "You're here."

"Had to come. Someone wrote me a song."

She pulls back to look at his face, his beautiful face. "You got it?"

He sighs. "I didn't want it, not after I kept hearing my song on the radio. But when I stopped at Jonas's, he made me listen to it. I'm not sure what spell you put on Jonas, but he's a tiger when it comes to Jane Davis."

Jane laughs. "He's been a big help to me."

"And me, as it turns out." William gives her a light kiss on the cheek as if he's testing the waters for temperature. "I was an ass, Jane, and I'm sorry. No, listen. I forced you to be Clara on stage that night, and had I not done that, your ex wouldn't have found us. I can be mad about the song, but what I stole from you is far worse. I planned on coming last week, but I had some prior obligations."

"You're here now, but ass or not, you could have called."

He laughs, a sound better than breathing. "I could have, but I would have missed this reaction from you."

He pulls a sheet of paper out of his pocket. It's the contract she'd written up. "Listen, I'm not signing this. You put me down as a writer on your song, and that has gotten me in so many doors I couldn't have opened before. Besides, the song sounds better when you sing it. I tried and just couldn't get it to work."

She starts to protest, but he tears the paper into strips. "I love you, Jane Davis, and if you can forgive me, I'd like to keep on loving you."

She kisses him then, good and long. "I love you, too, William."

"Go on and take the rest of the day off, Jane. I think you'll need it." Sylvia's voice startles them both.

William jerks away from Jane. "I didn't know she was here."

Jane laughs and kisses him again. "I didn't either."

They leave the bookshop with the Velvet Underground playing through their systems. It's a pretty good song to end on, Jane thinks, and takes William back to her place.

A word about the author...

Nicholas Lyon is a father, husband, teacher, woodturner, musician, and writer. He discovered his love for writing during a Creative Writing class in college. Since then, he's completed five novels and multiple short stories and won several awards in the OWFI Writing Contest, including best published novel for The Baptist Bootlegger. Currently, he teaches high school English in Crescent, OK, volunteers as a graphic designer at Life.Church. He lives in Oklahoma with his wife and two boys. He buys all of his books at Paper Pages bookstore. Check out his blog for weekly stories at writernicklyon.wordpress.com

Thank you for purchasing
this publication of The Wild Rose Press, Inc.

For questions or more information
contact us at
info@thewildrosepress.com.

The Wild Rose Press, Inc.
www.thewildrosepress.com